THE DUKE'S RAPIER

The Duke's Guard Series,
Book Ten

C.H. Admirand

ARE YOU SIGNED UP FOR DRAGONBLADE'S BLOG?

You'll get the latest news and information on exclusive giveaways, exclusive excerpts, coming releases, sales, free books, cover reveals and more.

Check out our complete list of authors, too!

No spam, no junk. That's a promise!

Sign Up Here

www.dragonbladepublishing.com

Dearest Reader;

Thank you for your support of a small press. At Dragonblade Publishing, we strive to bring you the highest quality Historical Romance from some of the best authors in the business. Without your support, there is no 'us', so we sincerely hope you adore these stories and find some new favorite authors along the way.

Happy Reading!

CEO, Dragonblade Publishing

Additional Dragonblade books by Author C.H. Admirand

The Ladies of the Keep Series
Liberating the Lady of Loughmoe (Book 1)
Bargaining with the Lady of Merewood (Book 2)
Rescuing the Lady of Sedgeworth (Book 3)

The Duke's Guard Series
The Duke's Sword (Book 1)
The Duke's Protector (Book 2)
The Duke's Shield (Book 3)
The Duke's Dragoon (Book 4)
The Duke's Hammer (Book 5)
The Duke's Defender (Book 6)
The Duke's Saber (Book 7)
The Duke's Enforcer (Book 8)
The Duke's Mercenary (Book 9)
The Duke's Rapier (Book 10)

The Lords of Vice Series
Mending the Duke's Pride (Book 1)
Avoiding the Earl's Lust (Book 2)
Tempering the Viscount's Envy (Book 3)
Redirecting the Baron's Greed (Book 4)
His Vow to Keep (Novella)
The Merry Wife of Wyndmere (Novella)

The Lyon's Den Series
Rescued by the Lyon
Captivated by the Lyon
The Lyon's Saving Grace

Historical Cookbook
Dragonblade's Historical Recipe Cookbook:
Recipes from some of your favorite Historical Romance Authors

Dedication

One enchanted evening...

You were in the lighting booth and looked down across the crowded auditorium and saw me escorting attendees to their seats...

Later that evening...

After the show, I was looking for my brother, my ride home, and saw you across the crowded hallway...and our hearts recognized one another...

DJ ~ My first, my only, my forever love...

Acknowledgements

A special thank you to my wonderful editor Arran McNicol! Thank you for keeping me focused on the story and writing tighter. Have you heard the news? Webster's Dictionary will be adding my picture under the definition of "verbosity,"—wait, no, that's not right... Hmmm...I know! It's going to be under the definition of "run-on sentence"!"

Book ten is finished! With six more men in the Duke's Guard to write about, I'm even more in love with these handsome-as-sin Irishmen than I was when they introduced themselves to Jared Malcolm Lippincott, the Duke of Wyndmere—and me—on the pages of **Mending the Duke's Pride**! It is not going to be easy to say goodbye to them. I have a feeling they'll pop up in my next series: **Wyndmere's Warriors**…along with Killian O'Ghill, who tolerates his sainted O'Malley cousins. Somehow Killian managed to sneak into Thomas and Caro's story in the first few pages! That was not my idea…

Thank you for joining me on this wild ride, and the biggest series I have ever written. Your encouragement and support—in reading, commenting, stopping by events and takeovers—means so much more than you can imagine. I am so grateful for each and every one of you.

C.H.

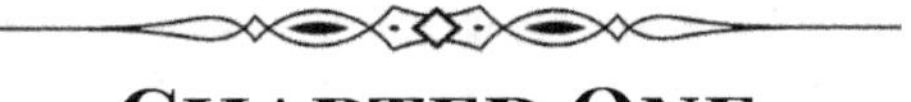

CHAPTER ONE

THOMAS O'MALLEY WAITED while his cousin Ryan Garahan read the missive he'd received from his brother Darby. The youngest Garahan brother was recovering from a serious injury, and the entire guard had been on tenterhooks waiting for good news. After a few moments, the wait became uncomfortable.

A realist, Thomas knew dreams were best left to children, hopes to lasses just out of the schoolroom, and that prayers often went answered. "Sure and yer ma is a firm believer that bad news arrives ahead of the good, like me own."

His cousin's shoulders were rigid with tension. "Three weeks, and Darby's eyesight has not changed. How could one blow have such an effect? I've been punched in the eye too many times to count. When the worst of the swelling had gone, me vision always improved."

O'Malley was careful not to add to Garahan's worry. "'Tis the same for meself. Did yer brother say his sight worsened?"

Garahan sighed. "Nay. Did ye ever wonder how the lot of us avoided serious injury during our time fighting to claim our county's bare-knuckle championship title?"

"Skill, I'm thinking. Why?"

"Our older brothers held the titles before us," Garahan said. "We had to fight harder than they did, the competition was fierce."

"Aye, but not one of us were willing to let the titles our brothers fought for and won go to just anyone." O'Malley grinned. "Unless it was one of us—their stronger, smarter younger brothers."

Garahan nodded. "Did ye ever think that when it was our turn to cross the Irish Sea to seek employment that we'd end up serving His Grace?"

"Nay. I figured we'd be spread out across the city of London. 'Tis big enough."

"Why do ye think His Grace wanted Coventry to find us and hire us?"

O'Malley thought about it for a moment. "I'm thinking 'twas Uncle Patrick's doing. I've no doubt he has been gathering and enlisting his own band of bare-knuckle guardian angels in Heaven. Can ye just picture them, after going a few rounds, finding a few bottles of *poitín* and trading tales of glory?"

Garahan frowned. "Are ye telling me there's bogs in Heaven?"

"And why not?" O'Malley asked. "'Tis the best place to hide Ireland's illegal brew. It may be all the encouragement those walking that thin line between right and wrong here on earth need...if they knew they'd be sipping Ireland's *uisce na beatha* in Heaven."

"Water of life me *arse*," Garahan grumbled. "I'll have to settle for me flask of the Irish, since ye can't find *poitín* in England. But ye won't find me wasting me time praying for something that won't happen."

O'Malley's frown was fierce as he remembered the gut-wrenching worry when his eldest brother was seriously injured protecting the duke and his family in London. "We all prayed Sean would not lose his arm." He met the intensity in Garahan's gaze. "Me brother did not heal without heavenly influence."

"What of two gifted surgeons, our cousin Emmett the healer, and the lass who married yer thickheaded brother?" Garahan asked.

"Sure and they helped, but prayer tipped the scales in Sean's favor."

"Are ye telling me that I need to pray harder?" Garahan asked.

"Aye," O'Malley said. "Every prayer whispered from the heart adds weight. Do not discount them, and don't forget that me ma may have married an O'Malley, but she was born a Garahan. She may be a distant cousin to yer da, but if I know Ma, she'll be spreading the word to family and friends to keep Darby in their prayers, as will yers."

When Garahan remained silent, O'Malley laid a hand on his cousin's shoulder. "If ye add the prayers of the rest of yer family, which includes the lot of us in the duke's guard, surely God Himself cannot help but hear and heal and restore yer pain-in-the-*arse* brother Darby's vision."

Garahan's snort of laughter was a relief. O'Malley had achieved what he'd intended to by distracting his cousin from the worry of Darby adjusting to life with half his vision. He waited a beat before adding what needed to be said: "I've heard more than one lass mention a black eyepatch adds intrigue and a bit of danger to a man's appearance. Though why a lass would be attracted to danger is beyond the likes of me."

"The lasses who've married into our families are living, breathing proof the element of danger attracted them," Garahan said.

O'Malley agreed. "Beautiful proof."

Garahan jabbed him in the ribs with his elbow and shoved him with a shoulder. "That's for staring at me wife yesterday. 'Tis past time ye found yer own woman."

O'Malley chuckled. "Ye might try putting a sack over her head. 'Tis the only way to keep us from staring at Prudence."

Garahan's expression darkened, and O'Malley recognized the look. He understood it wasn't only jealousy. His cousin needed to purge the twisted mass of temper and worry swirling inside of him. Luckily for Garahan, O'Malley had the cure. "Well now, I'd be happy to go a few rounds with ye."

Garahan's face lost all expression as he pivoted, balanced his weight on the balls of his feet, and struck the first blow.

O'Malley had been expecting the uppercut. He took it as his due for inciting his cousin to throw the first punch. He responded with a quick jab to his cousin's smiling face. Garahan's split lip had O'Malley grinning. "That's first blood, me boy-o!"

In answer, Garahan hit low and inside, close enough to O'Malley's *bollocks* to have him sweeping a foot under Ryan's leg, knocking him off balance. Garahan quickly recovered and rallied with a right cross. O'Malley evaded the blow and growled, "What the *feck* is wrong with ye? I'm after helping ye blow off steam— and ye thank me trying to cripple me ability to procreate?"

Garahan just stood there. No expression. No smart-*arsed* comeback.

O'Malley's blood chilled in his veins. He knew then that his cousin hadn't told him everything. He lowered his guard and stepped back. "What aren't ye telling me, Ryan?"

The pained expression lasted a heartbeat before his cousin set his jaw and shrugged.

"If ye don't tell me, how in the bloody hell can ye expect me to understand and try to help?"

"Ye can't help. No one can. 'Tisn't up to the likes of us to wonder why Ma's youngest will have to live the rest of his life with the use of only one eye!"

O'Malley understood the depths of his cousin's worry. "Why didn't ye tell me, or at least tell Flaherty?"

Garahan didn't answer.

O'Malley *needed* answers. "How long have ye known?" The stubborn *eedjit* shrugged again, prompting O'Malley to remind him, "Captain Coventry has learned to use the rest of his senses to balance for the loss of his vision—and his eye! Every one of us has seen him fight. The captain is fierce in hand-to-hand combat, and the very devil with a blade. I would know. I'm the family expert and dubbed the duke's rapier."

His cousin blew out a breath and glared at O'Malley. "Ye may be the expert with *thin* blades," he countered, "but I'm the duke's *saber*."

O'Malley had prodded his cousin's pride to see how deeply Garahan's worry was. The fact that Garahan would use the thickness of his blade against his cousin's told O'Malley that Garahan's worry went all the way to the bone. O'Malley taunted him, "Ye want to cross blades with me?"

Before Garahan could respond, a familiar deep voice rumbled from off to their left. "I knew the Irish were a bloodthirsty lot, but you O'Malleys, Garahans, and Flahertys must be a rare breed."

O'Malley faced the baron and said, "'Tis why we were hired to protect His Grace. We're not just bloodthirsty, we know the importance of constantly testing our strength and skill against one another. Keeping our skills honed and sharp in order to protect and defend His Grace's family." With constant practice, the duke's guard had become a force to be reckoned with.

Garahan, God love the *eedjit*, squelched his temper instantly and told the baron, "'Tis our pleasure to be guarding yer family, especially those twin scamps ye have been fostering while waiting for the squire's trial and his wife's."

"They are a handful," O'Malley agreed. "A fond reminder of when we were their age."

Summerfield sighed. "As they're related to you, Garahan, it shouldn't be a surprise that they are always getting into mischief."

O'Malley grinned. "Ye're forgetting one thing, yer lordship."

"What would that be?" Summerfield asked.

"The squire's twins are blood kin to Prudence, but Garahan only through marriage."

The baron raked a hand through his hair. "True, it is a relief."

"Why would that be?" Garahan asked.

Summerfield chuckled. "It isn't in their blood to be as thick-headed as you and O'Malley."

"Don't forget Flaherty," Garahan replied. "His head is thicker than most."

"Are either of you going to tell me what's happened that has the two of you growling like a pair of territorial wolfhounds?" the baron asked.

O'Malley had to ask, "What makes ye think anything's going on?"

"You men have adhered to my request not to get involved in a bare-knuckle contest—"

Garahan interrupted, "Practice, yer lordship."

"I have seen your *practice* sessions, Garahan. This was not practice, leaving me to ask, what has you ignoring my edict?"

O'Malley didn't want the baron to think they would go against their word. "Ryan needed a well-placed reminder. He received news from Darby that has him rattled. I was encouraging him to share the rest of what the missive contained."

"With threats of crossing blades with him?" the baron asked.

O'Malley knew he needed to explain fully. "As with all blows traded, it escalated when I used Coventry as an example of a brave, fierce warrior relying on the sight in one eye. I could not mention Coventry's skill in a fight without mentioning his skill with a blade."

"And I felt compelled to remind O'Malley that he may have earned the nickname of the duke's rapier, but I'm the duke's saber." Garahan turned and smirked at his cousin. "Everyone knows a saber is the thicker blade, and therefore deadlier."

"Neither blade is as thick as yer head," O'Malley grumbled.

"Enough!" The baron's voice brooked no argument. "I need to speak with you, O'Malley, before you leave to patrol the area between here and the village."

O'Malley and Garahan's attention instantly riveted on the baron. "Is there something ye need me to be on me guard for while on patrol?" O'Malley asked.

"Vicar Chessy sent word that his niece wasn't on the mail coach as expected."

O'Malley's gut clenched at the news. The baron had mentioned the lass's predicament to them in passing. Until now, Summerfield had not asked them to include Miss Gillingham with those they already protected. "Where was she last seen?"

"At an inn a few hours' ride from here. The missive the vicar received is from the keeper of the inn where they changed horses yesterday."

"Did the vicar give any indication as to what happened?"

"Only what the innkeeper advised in his message, and I quote: Miss Caroline Gillingham arrived as expected, but did not depart on the mail coach for the final leg of her journey." Summerfield added, "Miss Gillingham was last seen walking toward the shops near the inn."

"Alone?" Garahan asked.

O'Malley locked gazes with his cousin before asking, "There's more that ye aren't telling us. Isn't there, yer lordship?"

The baron inclined his head. "One of the female passengers approached the innkeeper, expressing her concern. Apparently, Miss Gillingham had confessed that she did not have the fare to continue on to Summerfield-on-Eden, but had a plan for how to get the coin."

Garahan's frown was fierce. "The vicar has to be beside himself with worry after what his daughter, me wife, and the blacksmith's daughter experienced when they were abducted a few weeks ago."

Summerfield reminded them, "No one was unduly harmed."

"Thanks to me wife, O'Ghill, and meself," Garahan added.

"Aye," O'Malley agreed. "Me cousin-in-law is a brave lass." He turned to the baron and asked, "Can ye tell us anything about Miss Gillingham's background, yer lordship?"

"Vicar Chessy's widowed sister passed away a fortnight ago. He has been in constant communication with his niece, but given his circumstances with what happened to his daughter, the vicar was not able to leave to collect his niece and bring her to the vicarage. He feels responsible and fears something untoward has happened to her."

The baron fell silent then, and O'Malley sensed his lordship was reliving the sequence of events that culminated with the baroness being struck on the back of the head and the squire's twin sons coming to live with them. To distract him, he said, "The vicar has had his hands full keeping a close eye on his daughter and the blacksmith's daughter. 'Tis common to have a delayed reaction to trauma."

"Prudence, having shared in that experience, seems to have helped the lass's recovery," Garahan reminded him.

O'Malley asked, "Do ye need me to go to the posting inn and make discreet inquiries?"

"Inquiries, me *arse*," Garahan grumbled. "Find the lass!" When the baron cleared his throat, Garahan ducked his head. "Begging yer pardon, yer lordship, for speaking out of turn."

"As it happens, Garahan," Summerfield said, "that is precisely what the vicar has asked, and I have agreed to."

O'Malley nodded. "I'll need as many details as ye have, yer lordship."

A QUARTER OF an hour later, O'Malley had a firm grip on his temper. Garahan had received yet another missive—this time from his cousin Killian. Whenever O'Ghill showed up, *shite* happened.

Somehow, O'Ghill had ended up at the same inn the vicar's niece had last been seen. Moreover, he had somehow gotten involved. Along with sending a description of Miss Caroline Gillingham, the irritating O'Ghill assured Garahan that the lass was unharmed and waiting for one of the duke's guard to come and fetch her, as O'Ghill had other business that prevented him from delivering her.

Hah! O'Malley ground his teeth together until his jaw ached. O'Ghill always acted on his own and never listened to reason. Damned if the bugger didn't always come out of whatever trouble he was in smelling like a *fecking* rose.

O'Malley urged his horse to a gallop as he rode hard toward the last place the vicar's niece had been seen...the inn. His gut had never been wrong, and he trusted it now. The lass was in trouble, and O'Ghill was somehow tangled up in it.

CHAPTER TWO

CAROLINE ADJUSTED HER spectacles. The familiar movement reminded her that she had control over her actions. It calmed her when she was flustered, or in this case...afraid. She absolutely refused to give in to tears—it would fog her lenses. To not be able to see would give the pawnbroker the advantage. She needed to retain the upper hand to bargain with the odious man.

The smug, lustful look on the man's face, while he continued to help the customer before her, worried her.

If her mother's health had not been so dire, she would not be in this situation. Caroline had exhausted their meager funds searching out any new tonic recommended by not one, but three apothecaries. She had hoped at least one of them would have the miracle her mum needed. Her faith faltered when none of the tonics or remedies seemed to help. Mum's health faded as their coin dwindled. Her death had not been unexpected, but gutted Caroline just the same.

And she had had her fill of men who looked at her as an object.

In the last few years, Caroline had suffered loss such as she had never thought to endure. Three years ago, her older brother, and his best friend, the man she'd promised to wait for, perished in the Peninsular War. Her father succumbed to illness the previous year, and a fortnight ago, she'd lost her mum. Sheltered all of her life, Caroline had not expected the turn of events that led to her to this run-down, crowded shop near the inn. What other choice did she have but to pawn the only things of value she had left? Tangible reminders of her parents: Mum's locket and Papa's pocket watch. She had three shillings in her reticule, not enough to pay the fare for the final leg of her journey to Summerfield-on-Eden.

Caroline had spent all but her last three shillings just to reach the inn—one stop shy of her destination. Providence was on her side when she chanced to overhear a conversation between two of the passengers. The men had been discussing a reputable pawnshop near the inn. Though she had never considered selling either the locket or the watch, she knew they held value and would be able to pawn them in exchange for coin. Confident in her ability to exact a trade, she'd said goodbye to the woman she had befriended on the trip and set off for the shop. Thankfully, it was not far from the inn.

The overweight, unwashed man blew out a foul-smelling breath, bringing her promptly back to the present and his crowded, dust-filled shop. The speculative look in the rotund man's narrowed eyes had her sensing that he would not be purchasing her treasures for their full worth. Hoping to sway the man, she blurted out, "I had both appraised recently."

The pawnbroker stared at her. Her skin crawled in reaction to the intensity and unholy gleam in his eyes. She had high hopes that the man would hand over the coin she needed. Did the last tangible evidence of her parents' lives only have value to her? He continued to study her. Closely. *Much too closely.* His gaze swept from the top of her head to the tips of her half boots and back again, settling on her bosom.

With her red hair, freckles, and spectacles, Caroline knew she did not have much to recommend her. Going without food when necessary to procure what her mum needed had not enhanced her looks. Her complexion had paled to the point where her freckles stood out all the more. Her last hope of salvation had been the widower Mr. Humbolt. At first she had been surprised when he presented himself on their doorstep ingratiating himself with Mum. He claimed to have spoken to her father before Papa passed, and hinted they had come to an arrangement. He was seeking a suitable wife. But when her mother required care around the clock, Caroline had no time for visits. The widower seemed to lose interest, no longer sending notes inquiring as to her mother's health. She had not seen or heard from him until three days ago, when he called to offer his condolences. He never once mentioned their supposed understanding, nor did she ask how she fared.

Caroline hunched her shoulders for a moment, remembering his harsh words and the impolite suggestions he had made as to how she would be able to make a living, now that she had had to sell her parents' home—and its contents—in order to pay the enormous debt she owed the apothecaries. His true nature had surfaced. Whether or not he had been on the cusp of offering for her hand, she thanked the Lord she had seen past his feigned regard for her. Otherwise, she would never have known he had designs on her parents' home and its contents, with an eye to how much coin it would bring when he sold it…after they married. *"You're naught but extra baggage… How could a farsighted, redheaded woman be anything but?"*

"Are you addled in the head?" the shopkeeper demanded. "I asked you a question!"

His first question rendered her momentarily speechless. He laid the locket and watch on the counter in front of him, then leaned over the counter to leer at her. Her stomach churned.

"I…er…beg your pardon. It was not intentional."

The shopkeeper studied her for a moment, as if considering his words carefully. "Why don't we adjourn to my office in the back, where we can discuss what else you have to offer…privately?"

The lust in the man's eyes had thoughts of success, and receiving the coin she so desperately needed, fading. She would not go anywhere with him, let alone the back of his shop! The pawnbroker would be the undoing of her, and not her salvation.

Caroline grabbed for the locket and watch, but wasn't fast enough. The man's sweat-slickened palm landed on top of her hand. Revulsion coiled with fear as she tugged against his hold.

"Not so fast. If I am to pay for this battered watch and locket with the broken chain, I will have to inspect them—and you— more thoroughly without interruption."

With a strength born of desperation, she yanked her hand free, spun around, and ran out of the shop. Behind her, the pawnbroker shouted, "Stop, thief!"

Icy fear chilled her to the bone. Determination had her dashing through the darkening streets, retracing her steps to the coaching inn where she'd arrived earlier.

A glance over her shoulder cost her far more than she bargained for. She barreled into a solid wall of muscle. Lifting her gaze, Caroline stared into the dark eyes of a stranger. The very large and—judging from his hold as he steadied her—very strong stranger wore an open expression of surprise.

Relief filled her. There was no malice nor lust in his gaze. "Are ye a thief, lass?" he asked.

Caroline banked her fear and replied, "Nay. He wanted more than my mum's locket and my father's pocket watch…which he kept." A solitary tear trickled across her cheek, but she brushed it away and held back the rest. Something about the dark-eyed man's posture, and the way he held her wrists firmly, but not bruising her, had her praying she was not about to make the second biggest mistake of her life in the span of a few short hours.

The man nodded and released her. She reached into her reticule and produced three shillings. "This is all the coin I have left. The coin I would have gained trading my parents' things would have paid my fare to Summerfield-on-Eden. My uncle's expecting me."

As the pawnbroker waddled toward them, the stranger lowered his voice. "Save yer shillings, lass." He waited for her to return them to her reticule. "As it happens, I have a cousin staying there. If I trust that ye have not told me a tale that will land me in the gaol beside ye, I'll deliver ye to yer uncle. What is his name?"

"Vicar Chessy."

The astonished expression on his face lasted less than a moment, but she noticed it just the same.

"Well now, I happen to be acquainted with yer uncle and have met yer cousin Miss Melanie Chessy. Ye have me word of honor that I'll deliver ye to the safety of yer uncle's arms. But ye have to trust me and do exactly as I say."

Caroline's heart nearly stopped when she heard the pawnbroker calling for the Watch. She made a snap decision. "Y-yes. I trust you."

He laid his hand on her shoulder. The warmth was a comfort as the watchman and the pawnbroker approached. "Name's O'Ghill. Me cousin is no thief!" He frowned at the pawnbroker. "I'll have yer apology and explanation now as to yer baseless accusations against her."

For a moment the shopkeeper was silent, then he blurted out, "She stole coin from me! Check her reticule."

Caroline was petrified. Between the crooked pawnbroker and the frightening frown on the watchman's face, neither looked as if they believed her. She stole a glance at her rescuer—O'Ghill. Finding her voice, Caroline said, "The three shillings in my reticule are mine."

O'Ghill spoke up. "I saw the coin in me cousin's reticule earlier. 'Tis no question she did not take them from this man." His sigh was exaggerated as he locked gazes with the watchman. "Me cousin has a stubborn streak." He frowned at her. "I expressly told ye to wait for me at the inn."

The pawnbroker pointed a dirty finger at O'Ghill and told the watchman, "He's lying."

Caroline had a sinking feeling. Despite O'Ghill's promise of help, she was going to pay for a crime she did not commit. After resigning herself to whatever happened next, she was not prepared for O'Ghill's chuckle.

"I assure ye, I am not lying, nor have I ever had a need to." He turned, ignoring the pawnbroker, and told the watchman, "Me cousin has been sheltered by me aunt and uncle all her life. They appointed me guardian last year, when me uncle became quite ill. He never recovered."

His gaze met Caroline's, and she silently prayed the watchman would be inclined to believe her savior over the pawnbroker.

"Me aunt passed away recently. As ye can plainly see, me task as her guardian is not an easy one. Although I hate to say it, me cousin should not be left to her own devices." He raised his gaze skyward before meeting the watchman's eyes. "Nor should she have gone off on her own after being strictly told not to go anywhere without me escort… Especially after dusk!"

"I'm sorry, cousin," she apologized. "I did not want to be a burden to you. You have done so much for me, and I was anxious to find a way to pay for my own fare."

O'Ghill shook his head. "That red head of yers is going to be a trial to yer betrothed. I confess I'm looking forward to meeting him." He smiled at the watchman. "We'll be staying at Summerfield Chase, as guests of the baron and baroness."

The watchman's eyes widened. "Baron, you say?"

"Aye. Baron Summerfield is a good and trusted friend."

The watchman nodded to Caroline. "I beg your pardon, miss. There is obviously a misunderstanding." Facing O'Ghill, he said, "I do not envy you the task of keeping your cousin out of trouble. I have a younger sister who was nearly the death of me before she wed last year."

O'Ghill chuckled. "Ye understand, then. The both of us have had to be stout of heart, and arm, in the guardianship of our loved ones."

"I would not wish the task on any man," the watchman said. "Though I would do it all again, because I would never neglect to do my duty to protect my sister. I have no doubt you feel the same about your cousin."

O'Ghill seemed pleased by the watchman's words. "Ye have given me hope that I'll be able to keep her out of trouble until we arrive at our destination. We've a good distance to cover tomorrow if we are to arrive before the baron sends out one of the duke's guard to find us."

The pawnbroker's eyes widened and glassed over. "Duke?"

"Aye, did me cousin fail to mention our connection to the Duke of Wyndmere through his brother-in-law Baron Summerfield?"

Caroline felt faint at the story that fell from O'Ghill's glib tongue. Was it all a tale, or did he truly know the baron and the duke? She bit the inside of her cheek to keep from asking.

The watchman poked the pawnbroker in the shoulder. "Apologize and be on your way."

The man blinked, but nodded and begged Caroline's, and her "cousin's," pardon before waddling back the way he'd come.

The watchman shook his head. "He's not a bad sort, just doesn't believe anyone is honest."

"Most likely because *he* isn't," O'Ghill muttered. Louder he said, "Thank ye for aiding in me cousin's rescue."

The watchman inclined his head. "Best keep a tight rein on her until you reach the baron's home. A newly married woman, and two younger women, were abducted recently...at the inn near the village there."

O'Ghill's eyes narrowed, and Caroline wondered if he knew something about it. "What did ye hear?"

"I thought it was idle gossip at first, as nothing like that has occurred around here before. It happened a few weeks ago. Apparently, the woman's husband and another were able to track the women down before anyone was unduly harmed."

Caroline sensed that O'Ghill knew more than he admitted to when he said, "The husband and his companion must know how to handle themselves in extreme circumstances."

"I imagine so, though I haven't heard any of the particulars," the watchman replied. Nodding to O'Ghill, he said, "I'm happy to have been of assistance to you and your cousin."

"Thank ye." O'Ghill held out his hand to the man, who shook it.

Caroline's thoughts were scattered, but not to the point where she did not notice that she was being ushered toward the inn. It seemed like hours had passed since she had come to the decision to seek out the pawnbroker and not to wait for the mail coach—which she did not have the coin to pay for. Her stomach felt empty and her throat parched. In her haste to seek out the pawnshop, she had not joined the other passengers for a light meal. Now that she was not going to be apprehended for a fictious crime, she sincerely regretted not stopping for a least a cup of tea to fortify her before striking out on her own. She felt more drained by the moment.

Thankfully, O'Ghill had interfered in time to save her from a disastrous situation. Was there a grain of truth to his tale? Did he know Baron Summerfield and the Duke of Wyndmere? His voice held a note of veracity and authority, but there was only one person that she knew who could confirm or deny what she had been told—her uncle, Vicar Bertram Chessy.

She prayed that she could trust her rescuer as she was led into the noise-filled common room at the inn. Caroline shivered, instantly grateful for the warmth. She was chilled to the bone. Exhausted, she sat quietly, waiting for the tea O'Ghill ordered to arrive. What would the man's reaction be if she did not ask any questions, but merely called his bluff?

"Yer eyes give away yer thoughts, lass."

"It's Caroline…Gillingham."

One of the serving girls arrived with a teapot, but before she could pour their tea, O'Ghill thanked her and said, "Me cousin Miss Gillingham is going to do the honors."

Caroline leaned toward him, pitched her voice so only he could hear, and rasped, "What do you intend to do now?"

"Wait for ye to pour our tea. I apologize, Miss Gillingham, should I have asked if ye were hungry, too?"

She would bide her time and pry the truth from the man before she went anywhere with him. Lifting the pot, she poured his cup, then filled her own. While he sipped his tea, she added cream to hers and stirred. "Do you expect me to believe that you know my uncle?"

"Why wouldn't ye? Have I given ye reason not to trust me?"

She narrowed her gaze, staring at him over the rim of her cup while carefully considering her reply. He had not only come to her rescue, but treated her like a lady. Something Humbolt had not done. O'Ghill seemed to believe her responses when he questioned her. Moreover, he'd asked her to trust him, and she agreed. *Botheration!* "You have not."

His dark eyes gleamed, as if he were satisfied that would be the end of the topic.

"However, while I do believe you know my uncle," Caroline continued, "given his position of importance as shepherd over his flock in Summerfield-on-Eden, I do question whether or not you are acquainted with the baron or the duke."

He set his cup on its saucer and held her gaze for long moments. O'Ghill did not try to hide his irritation when he said, "Me cousins are members of the Duke of Wyndmere's private guard stationed at Summerfield Chase. I passed through the village recently and made meself useful, at which time I was introduced to the baron and baroness."

Caroline noted that he did not mention *how* he'd made himself useful. Wanting to ask, but not willing to interrupt him, she had to bite the inside of her cheek to keep from doing so. Instead, she nodded, hoping he would go into detail, especially regarding his connection to such lofty personages.

"The watchman is correct. There were three women abducted from the village—Prudence, me cousin Ryan Garahan's wife; yer cousin, Miss Melanie Chessy; and Miss Olivia Coleman, the blacksmith's daughter."

Tears filled her eyes at the thought of her younger cousin and the others involved in such a frightening situation. The distress tangled with anger in his dark brown eyes had her believing him. "My uncle never mentioned it." Her voice wavered as she told him, "Then again, Uncle Bertram has always been protective of my mum and me. Moreso after my father passed. He may not have wanted us to worry. His letters always mentioned my aunt and cousin were in good health, though he never went into any detail as to what was happening at the vicarage, not even to share news of his congregation or the goings-on in the village." She paused and looked him in the eye. "Now then, as to your connection to the duke—"

O'Ghill interrupted, "Where did ye plan to stay tonight, if yer plans to gain coin went awry?"

He *would* ask her that. "I was confident that I would succeed."

O'Ghill muttered something she could not quite hear, then said, "A lass traveling alone needs to have her wits about her at all times, and even then she could still run into trouble. Did ye not think of that before ye hatched yer plan?"

Caroline lifted her chin and glared at the man who was rapidly becoming quite irritating. "I was confident."

He scrubbed a hand over his face, placed his hands on either side of his teacup, and leaned toward her. "What would ye have done had I not been there to poke me nose into yer business?" He did not wait for her to reply. "Ye're just like Brigid, Siobhan, and Aisling!"

Of course the handsome man would have a bevy of females chasing after him. "Friends of yours?"

"Hah! Me sister and our cousins. They think they can handle any situation that comes their way. Stubborn females."

She had heard enough. While grateful to O'Ghill for rescuing her, she did not wish to hear a lecture. Nor did she plan to sit and listen to him harangue her. Blotting her mouth with her napkin, she folded it neatly, placed it beside her teacup, and rose to her feet. "Thank for your timely intervention, and the tea, Mr.

O'Ghill."

He was seated one moment and standing in front of her the next. "Where do ye think ye're going?"

"I beg your pardon?"

"And so ye should, Miss Gillingham. I told ye I'd take ye to yer uncle, and although I can see it's going to be a trial if ye continue to ignore me advice, I always keep me word."

"While I am grateful to you for coming to my rescue, I assure you it is not necessary for you to escort me. I shall find other means to reach my destination."

"Oh aye, with three shillings to yer name? Sure and ye would too, headed in the opposite direction from the vicarage, bound and gagged on the back of a horse." He slipped his hand beneath her elbow and steered her toward the innkeeper's wife, who was speaking to two of the serving girls. She smiled at O'Ghill. "Thank ye for yer assistance earlier, Mrs. Black. I'd like to introduce ye to me cousin, Miss Caroline Gillingham. Caroline, Mrs. Black was kind enough to reserve a room for ye for the night, while I made arrangements for the last leg of our journey to Summerfield-on-Eden."

The innkeeper's wife beamed. "Such a lovely little village. It has been years since I have been there. I'm not able to leave our inn for more than an afternoon at a time. You are fortunate your cousin arrived earlier than expected and was available to arrange for accommodations, Miss Gillingham. He procured our last two private rooms."

"Er...yes," Caroline said. "So fortunate. Thank you, Mrs. Black. What time will the mail coach be arriving?"

"I've made other arrangements," O'Ghill informed her. He smiled at Mrs. Black. "Me horse enjoyed keeping pace with the mail coach, as he enjoys a good run." Turning to Caroline, he said, "I have no doubt that our uncle would feel the need to lecture me if I allowed ye to arrive exhausted from traveling in such close quarters as those one expects on the mail coach."

"Such a thoughtful man," Mrs. Black said.

Caroline's stomach tied itself into knots. "Yes…quite. What would those arrangement be, cousin? You haven't had a chance to mention them yet."

Without missing a beat, he smiled and answered, "I have hired a beautiful gelding for ye to ride. I know how much ye have missed being able to ride on a daily basis."

How could he possibly know that? She hadn't mentioned it. Then Caroline remembered a brief conversation with the woman sitting beside her as they'd approached the inn. They discussed their shared love of horses. While Caroline went in search of the pawnbroker, the others from the coach had gone in search of tea and biscuits. Her former companion must have mentioned their pleasant conversation and been overheard.

She blinked, then smiled at O'Ghill. "You are too good to me. Uncle Bertram will be so happy that you were able to escort me."

"Ye know I do not mind," he told her.

"I'll have hot water brought up," Mrs. Black told them. "Here are the keys to your rooms. I am sure you would like to rest until it is time for the evening meal, Miss Gillingham. Supper will be served in an hour."

Caroline could not help but notice how quickly O'Ghill grasped both keys. She held her tongue. She had plenty to say to the man, but it would wait until they were in the hallway outside of her room, when she planned to demand he hand over her key.

Mrs. Black called to one of the serving girls, who followed behind them with the promised hot water. In her room, Caroline had no choice but to nod and agree with the kind young woman as she set the pitcher on the washstand and said to let her know if they needed anything else.

After the servant left, O'Ghill asked, "Do ye intend to follow Mrs. Black's advice?"

She frowned in answer.

His sigh reminded her of her father's when he had been exasperated with her. "That is what I thought. That leaves ye two choices if ye do not plan to rest. Ye may have a quarter of an hour to freshen up and accompany me to the stables, or I can lock ye in ye room."

Incensed, she demanded, "What kind of a choice is that?"

"The only one I'll be giving ye. 'Twasn't me plan to rescue ye before I completed me business, Miss Gillingham. Now that I'm responsible for ye, I'll expect ye to cooperate. 'Tis the least ye can do, since I have guaranteed yer safety to the vicarage."

Her mouth opened and closed without a sound emerging. Though it pained her to agree, he was correct. It *was* the least she could do. Caroline prayed for patience. "Thank you again for your timely assistance, accommodations inside the inn, and a horse to ride tomorrow. I shall prevail upon my uncle to repay you."

"Not necessary. He's a good man, who has been kind to me cousin-in-law, Prudence, and Lady Phoebe."

He had mentioned his cousin's wife's name earlier, but not the lady. "Who is Lady Phoebe?"

"Baron Summerfield's wife, sister to the Duke of Wyndmere and his brother Earl Lippincott."

He spoke with ease. His open expression told her she really had no call to disbelieve him, except for the fantastical notion that this stranger had such high connections within the *ton* as a duke, an earl, and a baron.

"Do ye wish to remain in yer room?"

"Locked in? No thank you, Mr. O'Ghill."

"Fine then, why don't ye wash up? I shall return shortly." He waited for her to close the door.

She placed her ear to it to listen for the sounds of his footsteps retreating. After listening a few minutes, she opened the door and retraced her steps to the staircase, startled when a hand gripped her elbow.

"Going somewhere?"

"Mr. O'Ghill!"

"With that red head of yers, I knew ye were going to be a trial to me." He escorted her back to her room, opened the door, and waited for her to enter.

She did so, then turned to him. "Do forgive me, but—"

O'Ghill shut the door in her face and locked it from the out-side.

CHAPTER THREE

THE HOSTLER APPROACHED as O'Ghill stroked his horse's neck. He nodded to the man. "I promised this lad an extra cup of oats earlier, but had business to attend to."

The man smiled. "I'll see that he gets it. How long will you be staying?"

"Me cousin and I will be leaving in the morning." O'Ghill walked over to the horse he'd hired for Miss Gillingham. "Thank ye for recommending the gelding for her. I'll see that we come down early enough to introduce her."

"Excellent notion. I have to say that although most of our horses for hire have an even temperament, every once in a while, there are people the animals take an immediate dislike to."

O'Ghill stroked the gelding's neck. "I'm impressed that there are no visible marks on any of yer horses' hindquarters."

The hostler narrowed his gaze at O'Ghill. "We do a brisk business and have a reputation for only accepting horses that have not been abused."

"I meant no disrespect," O'Ghill said. When the other man gave a curt nod, he continued, "I'm expecting another of me cousins to arrive late tonight. O'Malley's his name. About me height and build, but with light hair and green eyes. Fierce frown and will be irritated, though trying to hide it."

The hostler chuckled at the last part of the description. "Have you spoken to the innkeeper or his wife?"

"I have," O'Ghill replied. "O'Malley will no doubt be inspecting yer stalls and horses before he turns his mount over to ye for a good rubdown."

"I cannot fault any man for taking care of his horse."

"Or for spoiling him," O'Ghill said.

The hostler smiled. "Will he be staying the night?"

"Aye," O'Ghill answered. "He'll be bunking with me." He had a feeling his cousin would be more than irritated, but could not put his finger on the why of it. Anything that had to do with O'Ghill seemed to irritate his holier-than-thou O'Malley cousin.

He'd have to ask his ma—she'd know the family history and if there was bad blood between the O'Ghills and the O'Malleys somewhere in the past. It could be Ryan's da who had the falling-out with his cousin Eileen Garahan O'Malley.

He shook his head. Now was not the time to think of family arguments. "I have an appointment, but will return and be waiting for me cousin in the common room."

"Do you want me to send someone to tell you when he arrives?"

O'Ghill chuckled. "No need—O'Malley will make his presence known, whether we like it or not."

With that, he thanked the hostler and left the inn yard, confident that his plans were all in place, despite the wrinkle to them when he had to rescue the vicar's niece. Caroline Gillingham was attractive, but his heart had already been captured. Trouble was, the lass who'd done the catching was six and ten. Miss Chessy, the vicar's daughter, was a slip of a lass who should not be able to sneak into his thoughts as often as she did. He intended to keep his distance for at least another year or two.

Making his way through the village to the location where he was to meet his contact, O'Ghill noticed the street lamps had not been lighted near this section of shops. Four shops to the left of him were well lit, as were the five shops to the right.

The hair on the back of his neck stood on end before he spun around in time to dodge the blow from behind. The heavy staff hit him in the shoulder instead of his skull. O'Ghill reacted with a swift jab to the man's face, followed by an uppercut. His attacker's eyes widened a moment before they rolled up in his head.

O'Ghill did not have time for this. His contact would be expecting him momentarily. Ignoring the unconscious man at his feet, he slipped into the alley between the shops and walked toward the man hidden in the shadows.

"You're late." His contact struck a match, and for a moment his pockmarked face was illuminated.

"Had to take care of an obstruction in me path," O'Ghill replied.

The man paused with the stub of a cigar halfway to his lips. "Obstruction?"

"Aye. If ye thought to have one of yer lackeys lying in wait for me, 'tisn't me fault that he was easy to take down." O'Ghill hedged his bets, anticipating that another man had crept up behind him. He kicked backward. The satisfying groan told him he'd hit his mark. "Now then, if ye don't want me to cripple the rest of yer men, ye'd best tell them to back off."

His contact swore ripely, then said, "To your posts, men."

The shuffling of feet had O'Ghill counting… Just two. Good to know how many would be waiting to exchange blows when he retraced his steps.

He stepped into the faint light from the window above them. "I came prepared to do business, but seeing's how ye decided to attack me and steal the coin I brought with me, ye just lowered yer fee by half."

"You aren't in a position to make demands."

"Well now, there's where ye'd be wrong." O'Ghill took aim. He threw his blade, which skimmed past the other man's ear, nicking it before sinking into the doorframe behind him.

Hand to his bleeding ear, the man sputtered, spilling the information O'Ghill had been prepared to pay for. "Lord

Anderson is free. Mrs. Barstow, and the squire and Mrs. Honeycutt, will go to trial in a fortnight."

O'Ghill digested this information. "Anderson was to be charged with kidnapping and attempted murder. He must have influential connections at a high level within the *ton*."

"The highest."

O'Ghill knew without asking that it was Prinny. He made the split-second decision not to hold back any of the coin promised for the information. His contact had told him what he needed to know, and with the prince regent involved, O'Ghill would do well to pay the man in full. Well used to being attacked, no matter where on this godforsaken land he stood, he braced for it, handing over the small leather bag of coins before turning to walk away.

"O'Ghill?"

He paused but did not turn around. "Aye?"

"Watch your back."

"No need to warn me. I know yer men'll be waiting for me."

The man with the pockmarked face corrected him, "Not my men...Anderson's."

O'Ghill glanced over, met the other man's gaze, and nodded. "Thank ye." As he strode out of the alley to make his way back to the inn, he wondered how soon O'Malley would arrive. He would have to convince his cousin to move quickly. Given what he had just learned, they could not wait until morning. They had to leave tonight. Having worked with O'Malley a few months ago, he knew the man would need to send an urgent missive to Baron Summerfield, His Grace, and their London contacts.

The duke's contact on Bow Street and his London-man-of-affairs would alert their men, and contacts on all levels of society, while the duke would alert his family and the individual arms of the duke's guard—spread out from London to Sussex, Cornwall, and the Borderlands—to be prepared for imminent attack.

O'Ghill intended to stand with his cousins and prepare for the onslaught before he continued on his rambling. Anderson had kidnapped three women, with the intention of violating his cousin Ryan's wife. God only knew what Anderson had planned for the two innocent lasses. O'Ghill still had trouble believing that the bloody bugger had stabbed Ryan in the back and lived to tell of it. Anderson could have killed Garahan—yet one more reason O'Ghill would stand beside his cousins. He was sick to death of a one-sided justice system where the poor and downtrodden were always convicted, while the rich and well-connected members of Society often received a warning or a slap on the wrist.

Resolved to put up with one of the sainted O'Malleys for the next few hours until they reached Summerfield-on-Eden, he returned to the inn. He needed to speak to Mrs. Black about their change in plans. For a moment he thought about knocking on Miss Gillingham's door, to let her know they would be leaving tonight. He chuckled. The surprise in her eyes when he shut and locked the door had been comical. She'd have something to say, mayhap at a volume that would attract attention. He decided to leave the pleasure of unlocking Miss Gillingham's door—and more than likely having to listen to an argument—for O'Malley.

He was smiling when he spied the innkeeper's wife and made his way over to speak with her. O'Ghill planned to be unavailable when the fireworks erupted upstairs. He couldn't think of a nicer welcome for the sainted Thomas O'Malley.

O'MALLEY RODE LIKE the devil was nipping at his heels. His mind raced with questions he would not have the answers to until he met the most irritating of his cousins—Killian O'Ghill. Then he could unravel how in the bloody hell O'Ghill had gotten involved, and why he was escorting the young woman O'Malley was supposed to be searching for.

What had happened to the lass to prevent her from getting on that coach? All O'Ghill had said in his message was that he'd rescued the vicar's niece from a pawnbroker and the Watch. Knowing O'Ghill, the black sheep of the clan related to O'Malley's ma, he could be stretching the truth, or bending it to suit his own needs.

O'Malley signaled to his mount to slow the pace as they drew closer to the inn where Miss Gillingham would be waiting for him.

The hostler approached and nodded to O'Malley, who had dismounted and was stroking his horse's neck, praising him for his strength and speed. "I promised this lad an extra cup of oats."

The hostler smiled. "I'll see that he gets it. How long will you be staying?"

"I'll be staying the night with me cousin." He nodded to his mount and told the hostler, "I haven't traveled far, but me horse would appreciate a good rubdown."

"I have just the young man to see to the task while you introduce yerself to Mr. and Mrs. Black—they own and run the inn."

"Thank ye." From the itch between his shoulder blades, O'Malley knew the man watched him walk away. He could have told the hostler who his cousin was, but did not feel the need to. O'Ghill had a habit of speaking out of turn, and O'Malley did not need their situation to be fodder for discussion over any of the guests' evening pots of tea.

He entered the inn and was pleased the innkeeper and his wife were both in the common room. He introduced himself. "Name's O'Malley."

"Welcome, Mr. O'Malley. Mr. O'Ghill is expecting you."

"Thank ye, Mr. Black. I have no doubt he is. I'm after speaking to our cousin Miss Caroline Gillingham as well. Where would I be finding her?"

The couple exchanged a glance and gave him the room numbers for his cousin and Miss Gillingham, advising that she had already retired for the night.

He nodded. "Thank ye." Mumbling to himself as he ascended the stairs, he wondered what in the bloody hell to say to the lass that would not frighten her. O'Malley hadn't had the time to request a letter of introduction from the vicar, or one explaining the situation. Mayhap just a quick conversation about the vicar and his family, and the baron and his, might be all that she needed as proof of who he was.

So as not to disturb the other guests, he knocked quietly on his cousin's door. No response. *Of course.* Knocking harder, he said in a firm, even tone, "Open up, O'Ghill."

He heard movement in the room next door, where Miss Gillingham was staying. "Even if O'Ghill was inside," she said, "he only answers if he wants to."

That certainly sounded like O'Ghill. "Miss Gillingham?"

"Who is it?"

Her voice sounded wary, hesitant. *Good.* The lass was sensible enough not to open her door to strangers. "Me name's O'Malley. I'm here to fetch ye to yer uncle."

"What makes you think I have an uncle?"

He didn't have time for long-winded explanations. "Vicar Chessy is worried sick about ye." That should convince the lass to open her door.

"How do you know the vicar?"

The cagey lass had yet to admit the vicar was her uncle. O'Malley heartily approved. "He and Baron Summerfield insisted I come after ye when ye did not arrive on the mail coach as anticipated."

There was a long pause—with the door still closed—before she asked, "How do you know Mr. O'Ghill?"

O'Malley scrubbed a hand over his face. "'Tis me great misfortune to be related." He was listening carefully for the sound of the key turning in the lock, but instead, he heard her soft laughter.

"I'm pleased to meet you, Mr. O'Malley."

"Would ye mind opening the door? I need to speak to ye without a door between us."

"I... Er... I would like to comply, however, your cousin

locked me in."

O'Malley's frustration shot straight to boiling. "He what?"

Silence behind her door. Had he frightened the lass?

"Forgive me, Miss Gillingham—I should not be shocked, as it does sound like something me cousin would do. I'll ask the innkeeper for the spare key to yer room." He put his hand to the door when she did not respond. "Lass?"

"Very well," Miss Gillingham responded. "When you unlock the door, it is with the understanding that you will not enter my room, and will allow me to precede you to the common room. There will be plenty of witnesses there. You, however, will remain right here and count to fifty before joining me."

He dropped his hand to his side and swallowed a chuckle. Well used to forthright women, he was more than pleased with the lass's gumption. "Well now, lass, that sounds intelligent and is agreeable to me. I'll be right back." He paused for a moment, then asked, "Begging yer pardon for asking, Miss Gillingham, but the innkeeper's wife said ye had retired. Do ye need time to dress?"

She sighed. "No. I have been waiting for Mr. O'Ghill to return and unlock the door."

"Fine, then. Ye'll be presentable when I open the door—no doubt the innkeeper and his wife will be counting the minutes to see how long it takes ye to appear downstairs after I let ye out."

"Whatever for?"

Her softly asked question had him adding *innocent* to *intelligent*. "Ah, lass, if ye don't know, I'm not the one to be explaining it to ye. Though if ye ask the innkeeper's wife, I'm certain she'll be happy to tell ye."

"Why would she?"

"Do ye intend to spend the next hour asking questions, when I could be fetching the key and unlocking yer door?"

"Forgive me, Mr. O'Malley. When I am unsettled, I tend to ask questions."

"I'll be right back with the key… Better yet, I'll return with the key and Mrs. Black."

"Thank you, Mr. O'Malley."

As he reached the bottom of the staircase, the innkeeper was waiting for him. "What can I do for you, Mr. O'Malley?"

"I need the key to Miss Gillingham's room."

The man narrowed his eyes. "Our inn has a rule about visitors, especially the rooms of our female guests, even if she is your cousin."

Thinking quickly, O'Malley replied, "Apparently there was a mishap. Me cousin changed her mind and was coming down for a pot of tea and a bite to eat. She explained that she was in the hallway with her key in the door, locking it, when she realized she'd forgotten her reticule. She rushed into her room and stumbled, knocking into the door, which closed and locked her in."

The innkeeper's wife joined her husband and placed her hand on his arm. "Poor woman. She must be desperate for a meal and that pot of tea by now. It has been a few hours since she went upstairs."

"If the key was in the lock—" the innkeeper began.

O'Malley interrupted him, "It wasn't just now. Must have fallen to the floor and someone picked it up."

"One moment, Mr. O'Malley," Mrs. Black said. "I'll get the spare key and accompany you upstairs."

"I'd be grateful. Thank ye."

A few moments later, the innkeeper's wife had the key in the lock and opened the door. Miss Gillingham rushed out, tripped, and nearly plowed into Mrs. Black. O'Malley reached out, grabbed hold of her arm, and steadied her. "Easy, lass."

She tipped her head up and stared at him. Wide eyes the color of morning mist, magnified by her spectacles, locked on his. Her expression, a mix of wonder and attraction, went to his head like three fingers of the Irish on an empty gut. Her red head and sprinkling of freckles across the bridge of her nose, dotting her cheeks, charmed him. He briefly wondered if her freckles had been painted by a wood sprite or flower faery. The lass reminded him of home.

When the innkeeper's wife cleared her throat, he dropped his hand. "Ye'll need to mind yer step."

"Thank you so much for bringing the key. You see, I was afraid—"

"That someone ye did not know would find the key and open the door while ye were sleeping. Understandable. I've explained to Mrs. Black how ye locked yerself in yer room by accident."

"I have done that myself more than once changing the bed linens," Mrs. Black admitted. She linked arms with Miss Gillingham and proceeded toward the stairs. "Mr. O'Malley mentioned you were hungry. You missed the evening meal, but there is plenty of stew left over. Would you like a bowl?"

"Yes, thank you," the lass answered. "I *am* hungry."

"I'll bring you a bowl, too, Mr. O'Malley."

"Thank ye," O'Malley said. "And the pot of tea?"

"Of course," the innkeeper's wife replied. "I will be happy to bring that to you, along with cream and sugar. Would either of you like something sweet to go with the tea? I baked tarts earlier."

O'Malley noted the hint of moisture pooling in the lass's eyes. Before the first tear could fall and splash on her spectacles, he chuckled. "Ye sound like me ma. Always offering something sweet with tea. Thank ye for yer kindness, Mrs. Black."

The older woman's face flushed a soft rose, reminding him of his ma even more. "Think nothing of it. Would you be comfortable in the taproom, or would you prefer a private room?"

"Taproom, please," Miss Gillingham answered before O'Malley had the opportunity.

He was preoccupied wondering why a beauty like Miss Gillingham was not married. Mayhap she was a widow. There were many due to the Peninsular War. For once, his gut and his head were in agreement. Both needed to know the answer. He would be asking the lass later.

They were soon settled on the far side of the taproom near the fireplace. The entrancing lass thanked him when he pulled out her chair. "Ye're welcome. If ye get too warm with yer back to the fire, let me know and we'll switch places."

"This feels lovely. I did not realize how chilled I was. It has been a long…and eventful day."

"Up with the sun to catch the mail coach, no doubt. I've ridden in one a time or two when me brother and I arrived. Packed us in so tightly, the hostler at the first stop needed a bar to pry us out."

Her smile reached her eyes, and he found himself getting lost in their changeable gray depths.

"I wondered when ye'd get here," a familiar voice rumbled from behind him.

The lass shot to her feet and poked O'Ghill in the chest. "How could you?"

Without missing a beat, his cousin grabbed her finger and wrapped his arm around her, escorting her back to her seat. "I was not certain until the last minute that our cousin would be joining us," he glibly replied.

"You—"

"I did not mean to be gone so long, Caroline." From the way he interrupted her, it was obvious O'Ghill did not want the lass to have a chance to speak. O'Malley's suspicion was confirmed when his cousin said, "Did ye forget that I had a meeting to attend?"

O'Malley did not like the fact that his cousin and the lass were on a first-name basis. He shoved that emotion aside and told O'Ghill, "Our cousin locked herself in her room and has been waiting for someone to realize it."

O'Ghill turned and held O'Malley's tension-filled look for a moment, then asked, "How did it happen?"

Shapely, dark brows drew together above eyes darkening to the hue of winter storm clouds. "I'll tell you—"

"Here you are," the innkeeper's wife, followed by a serving

girl carrying a tray, approached the table. "Oh, Mr. O'Ghill. We did not expect you back so soon. Will you be joining Mr. O'Malley and Miss Gillingham for a meal?"

"Aye, thank ye for asking, Mrs. Black. Me cousins and I have much to catch up on."

The serving girl placed the meals on the table as the innkeeper's wife instructed her, "Bring one more order of stew."

The girl nodded and hurried off.

"It must be wonderful to come from a large family," Mrs. Black remarked.

"Aye," O'Ghill replied.

"At times," O'Malley added.

Mrs. Black shook her head. "Without family, where would we be?"

"Alone," Miss Gillingham murmured.

O'Malley heard and turned to her. "We miss them too, lass."

Attuned to the conversation going on at their table, the innkeeper's wife glanced over her shoulder and motioned for the girl to bring O'Ghill's meal.

He looked up as he was served and smiled at the young woman. "Thank ye, lass."

Mrs. Black told them to enjoy their meal and shooed the serving girl toward the kitchen.

After the women left, O'Ghill leaned close to O'Malley. "We need to leave right after we eat."

"Best tell me why," O'Malley said.

O'Ghill's sharp glance swept the room. "Not here."

O'Malley could tell from his cousin's expression that whatever the news was, it was bad. "Do ye need to send someone to fetch yer things?"

O'Ghill shook his head. "Already have what I need, though Caroline will need to collect her belongings."

"Do you need help packing your things, Miss Gillingham?"

"No thank you, Mr. O'Malley. I—"

O'Ghill reached for her hand and patted the back of it, interrupting her. "With the news our cousin has brought from home, I am certain we can impose on Mrs. Black, or one of the servants, to do so." He nodded to her bowl and asked, "How is your stew?"

"Is that your way of changing the subject?" she asked O'Ghill, who smiled and dug into his meal.

"Have you spoken to the hostler yet?" O'Malley asked.

"Aye," O'Ghill replied.

"After everything that's happened—since the abduction," O'Malley said, "we'll not be leaving ye alone, lass. I'll speak to the innkeeper or his wife. If I have to invoke me employer's name to get their attention, I will."

O'Ghill frowned and shook his head.

Caroline spoke up. "You used your connection to the baron and the duke—is there a reason why your cousin cannot?"

O'Malley's eyes narrowed. Glaring at his cousin, he asked, "And just who did ye mention it to?"

Caroline glanced about her, leaned close to O'Malley, and said, "He told the Watch and the pawnbroker."

O'Malley touched a hand to his heart, and the embroidered emblems of his status. "Well now, that'll come in handy, as I'm head of the duke's guard at Summerfield Chase."

Caroline's gaze met his. The emotions swirling in the depths of her smoke-gray eyes—hesitation, hope, and wonder—had his gut clenching as his instant attraction to the lass deepened. But he had no time to listen to his heart. He was on a mission: find the lass and bring her home. Although it irked that O'Ghill had somehow managed to arrive before him, and in time to rescue the lass. He did not have the time to delve too deeply into the reasons why. The end result was the same: the lass was unharmed, and O'Malley would deliver her safely to her uncle.

"Why would it help matters that the watchman and the shopkeeper know of Mr. O'Ghill's connection to Baron Summerfield and the Duke of Wyndmere?" she asked.

For her safety, O'Malley had no intention of telling her. "We'll meet ye at the stables as soon as we finish eating."

"Was even half of what you just said to Mrs. Black the truth?" Miss Gillingham asked O'Ghill.

From her tone it was clear to O'Malley that this was a woman who would not bow under pressure. He bit back on the urge to smile. She had grit and was as lovely as a morning in May. When she snorted in disbelief, he realized his cousin must have answered her.

"Knowing me cousin, probably not," O'Malley said. O'Ghill glared at him, and O'Malley glared back. "Ye'd best have a good reason for it."

The temper in O'Ghill's eyes fizzled out. "I have."

O'Malley nodded, finished his meal, and blotted his mouth with his linen napkin. While he waited for the lass and his cousin to finish eating, he made a quick study of those gathered in the common room. Satisfied everyone seemed as they appeared—travelers who'd stopped for a meal or the night—he turned back to his cousin and the lass. They had finished eating.

Before O'Ghill had the opportunity, O'Malley stood and held the back of the lass's chair, then helped her to her feet. "I was planning to hire a carriage in the morning, but circumstances have changed. I hope ye know how to ride, Miss Gillingham."

His cousin answered before she could. "She does. Let's go."

CHAPTER FOUR

CAROLINE WAS NOT certain what unspoken messages the cousins had been communicating to one another with a look, but she was tired of being treated as if she were incapable of handling her own affairs. Now that her brother and parents were gone, she was fully in charge of her own life, and had been since her mother had passed. She did not plan to relinquish the reins to her life, even if it were to hand them over to her aunt and uncle in exchange for a roof over her head.

Listening to O'Malley ask the innkeeper's wife to escort her to her room and help her pack was more than enough. "I am quite sure that I can manage on my own, *cousin*." She rolled her eyes, shook her head, and confided to Mrs. Black, "While I appreciate that my cousins are determined to see that I reach Uncle Bertram in one piece, they are a bit high-handed at times."

The older woman smiled. "Let your cousins have their way. Do you know how fortunate you are to have their protection? A lass alone in the world could easily fall prey to innumerable predators. The possibilities of what could happen are end-less...and not to be discounted."

Caroline glanced at O'Malley, but his expression was closed. She had no idea what he was thinking. Before she could refute Mrs. Black's warning, he said, "As head of the Duke of Wyndmere's guard at Summerfield Chase, I have firsthand knowledge of what could happen."

The innkeeper walked over to join their conversation. "How long have you worked for the duke?"

"A few years now," O'Malley answered. "Originally me brothers, cousins, and I were stationed at His Grace's London town house, but after he married and settled at his country estate, the sixteen of us were divided into groups stationed at his other residences."

Caroline could not help but wonder if O'Malley always gave such detailed information when questioned about his position within the duke's guard. Was it for her sake?

"So you've been to London," Mr. Black said. "We heard rumors of a madman holding the duke's sister at knifepoint a few years ago. Was there any truth to it?"

O'Malley's eyes hinted at emotions that were being suppressed. "'Tisn't a rumor. Our duty to protect the duke and his family have had us calling upon our combined skills with bare-knuckle fighting and all manner of weaponry."

The stocky innkeeper nodded. "I keep a blunderbuss behind the desk, a pistol in our private quarters, and carry a knife in my boot."

O'Malley smiled. "Yer wife is a treasure. Ye're wise to protect her at all costs. 'Tis why the lot of us have been rotating between the duke's properties every four months until recently."

"Was it because of the kidnapping attempts on his twins?" Mrs. Black asked.

O'Malley's face darkened, and Caroline sensed he had firsthand knowledge of the attempt. "Ye heard about that, too?" When the couple nodded, he said, "I'm sure ye'll understand that I'm not at liberty to discuss what happened. I will tell ye that, aside from Summerfield Chase, I have been stationed at Wyndmere Hall in the Lake District, Lippincott Manor in Sussex, Penwith Tower in Cornwall, and Chattsworth Manor in Sussex, and am familiar with all of the surrounding land."

Caroline did not expect to be so impressed by O'Malley, nor

did she anticipate being so distracted by his presence. But she could not deny that the pull she had felt the moment he opened the door to her room, his green eyes boring into hers, was growing stronger the longer she was in his presence. He was at least a head and a half—nay, two heads—taller than her. She had always been close in height to her brother's friends.

While Mr. O'Malley answered a few more of the innkeeper's questions, she watched his facial expressions. His strong features added to the appeal of his ruggedly handsome face. When he turned and met her gaze, his brilliant green eyes held her captive. She could not quite catch her breath until he turned back to answer another question.

She had no idea why she felt the instant pull toward O'Malley, or why she hadn't had a similar reaction to O'Ghill. They were both broad, though O'Malley had a few inches on his cousin. Mayhap it was his light hair and those bright emerald eyes.

Caroline needed to stop thinking of the man and concentrate on her need to arrive in Summerfield-on-Eden—and speak to Melanie to see for herself that her cousin was unharmed.

Finally, she was able to get control of her wayward thoughts, but not before taking a moment to admire the breadth of O'Malley's chest and the width of his shoulders. But it was not just his physical appearance and obvious strength that had her enthralled—it was the way he treated those he came in contact with. His honesty and integrity were part and parcel of the man himself. Papa would have highly approved of O'Malley.

"I'll be leaving ye in good hands while ye gather yer things, cousin," he told her. "I need to have a word with O'Ghill and the hostler, and check on our horses."

The innkeeper said, "My wife and I will watch over Miss Gillingham for you before you come to collect her."

"I'm in yer debt," O'Malley rumbled. "Thank ye."

A few moments later she was staring at the Irishman's broad back, wondering just what he and O'Ghill had to discuss that they did not want her to hear.

"Let us see to our task, Miss Gillingham," Mrs. Black urged when Caroline had not immediately followed her. "You do not want to keep Mr. O'Malley or Mr. O'Ghill waiting, do you?"

Caroline wanted to say yes, but did not want to seem ungrateful for all that the two men had done for her. "No, of course not."

She followed the innkeeper's wife up the stairs, all the while wondering how soon the men would be ready to leave.

❯❯❯❯❮❮❮❮

O'MALLEY LISTENED AS O'Ghill relayed the information from his contact. He could not believe what he'd heard. "Bleeding bastard! Ye're telling me Anderson will never have to pay for kidnapping me cousin's wife and the others?"

"'Tis exactly what I'm telling ye." O'Ghill sounded irritated. "Though I do wonder how Prudence will take the news about her mother and aunt being held at Newgate until their trial."

O'Malley's frustration roiled beneath the surface. "Those two women should have to pay for their part in the plan they hatched and what they would have allowed to happen...if Anderson managed to do what he had intended and force himself on Garahan's wife!"

"What about the attempted murder of Lady Phoebe?" O'Malley asked.

"Her aunt and uncle will have to answer for those charges," O'Ghill answered. "'Tisn't up to the likes of us to pass judgment."

"If her aunt and uncle are found guilty, they could hang," O'Malley remarked. "I cannot feel sorry for either of them. Lady Phoebe could have lost her babe."

"But she didn't," O'Ghill reminded him.

"She could have suffered a loss of memory, or been killed!" O'Malley said. "What kind of a world do we live in when members of the *ton* can kidnap someone and not face the consequences? Time and again those that we've captured, after they've attacked the duke and his family, or libeled them publicly by spreading falsehoods, have gotten off with but a warning."

"Ye should not be surprised, Thomas. 'Tis the same back home in Ireland," O'Ghill quietly reminded him.

"Da and Uncle Patrick should have never been tossed into prison for a crime they didn't commit. There was no bloody proof!"

"Aye," O'Ghill agreed. "None of us will ever forget what happened to Uncle Patrick."

O'Malley nodded. "I've an errand to see to and should be back shortly. I left the lass in the care of the innkeeper and his wife. They will not let her out of their sight." He stared hard at his cousin, warning him, "Do not even think of leaving without me."

O'Ghill narrowed his gaze at O'Malley. A moment passed before his eyes widened and understanding of what his cousin intended dawned. He grunted and jabbed O'Malley in the shoulder. "Bloody hell, Thomas! Ye cannot take out yer frustration on the pawnbroker. He didn't harm her, he just—" He clamped his mouth shut.

"I don't have time to ask what happened now. Do not leave without me."

"God help me," O'Ghill mumbled, "the sainted O'Malley has spoken. I heard ye the first time." When O'Malley continued to hold his gaze, he sighed. "Ye have me word on Uncle Patrick's soul."

O'Malley grunted in answer. He knew O'Ghill could be trusted, but that didn't mean his cousin did not irritate the *shite* out of him.

Following the direction the hostler had given him, O'Malley found the shop, and the owner. He locked gazes with the man as he crossed the threshold. "I understand ye have a locket and pocket watch in yer possession that ye didn't pay for. I'll take them now."

The rotund man's eyes narrowed. From the time it took for the shopkeeper to respond, O'Malley knew the man was preparing to lie and reach for whatever weapon he stashed beneath the counter.

"You're mistaken," the man replied. "But I do have a selection of necklaces and watches that you are welcome to look at."

O'Malley held on to his temper, knowing it would not help the situation if he let it loose. "O'Ghill advised that I should bring the Watch when I came to retrieve our cousin's locket and pocket watch." He looked over his shoulder at the doorway and then back. "The watchman will be here in a moment."

The pawnbroker's face paled as sweat beaded on his brow. "Now that you mention it, I...uh, do recall a young woman who came into my shop earlier. She was—"

O'Malley growled, leaned across the counter, and grabbed the man by the throat. "Did ye touch her?" Incensed at the very idea that they gray-eyed lass had suffered the man's touch, O'Malley fought the need to squeeze on his larynx.

The shopkeeper held up his hands. "Nay. I didn't touch her."

"No one would ever find yer body if ye had." O'Malley let go of the man with enough force to have the shopkeeper smacking the back of his head against the wall behind the counter. Holding out his hand, O'Malley said, "I'm waiting."

Frantic to comply, the pawnbroker reached into his waistcoat pocket, pulled out a locket and pocket watch, and dropped them into O'Malley's outstretched hand.

Without a word, O'Malley spun on his heel and left, retracing his steps to the inn. His head was at war with his gut, which told him to go back and beat the ever-living *shite* out of the pawnbroker. His head reminded him that the duke would not tolerate such actions taken by any of the men in his guard.

Grinding his teeth, he increased his stride, arrived at the inn yard, and made a beeline for the stables. He found O'Ghill speaking with the stablemaster and said, "I'm ready to leave. I'll fetch the lass and be right back."

O'Ghill didn't bother to ask if he had retrieved the lass's belongings. He would know without asking. "I'll have the horses brought around."

O'Malley entered the inn and, as hoped, found the lass waiting. The size of the satchel at her feet wasn't what he'd expected. Was that all she had brought with her? What of the rest of her belongings…her worldly goods?

"I see ye're ready to leave. O'Ghill's taking care of the horses." He turned to the innkeeper's wife. "I cannot thank ye enough for watching out for our cousin, Mrs. Black. Please extend me thanks, and O'Ghill's, to yer husband as well."

"You are welcome, and I'd be happy to tell him. Safe journey."

With his hand to the small of the lass's back, O'Malley guided her outside to the waiting trio of horses, and his irritating cousin, who stood there with a knowing grin on his face. *Bugger it.* O'Malley realized that he had yet to remove his hand from the small of Miss Gillingham's back. He dropped his hand, took her bag, and pushed it at his cousin, then nodded to the lass. "Let me help ye mount yer horse."

CHAPTER FIVE

CAROLINE TRIED TO control her reaction to O'Malley's touch, but the heat from his hand seared through her gown, and chemise, to her flesh. She shivered.

"Are ye cold, lass?"

The rumble of his deep voice filled her with an ache she had never felt before. Speech was beyond her. She shook her head.

He lowered his hand and frowned at her. "Do ye not have a heavy cloak or coat ye can wear?"

Bereft at the loss of his touch, she struggled to find her voice. "I… That is, you see… No."

Embarrassed by her circumstances, heartbroken that she'd had to leave her mother's locket and her father's watch behind with the crooked pawnbroker, she turned her attention to the gelding she was to ride. Stroking the tips of her fingers between the horse's eyes down to his velvety-soft muzzle, she whispered, "You are a beautiful horse. Thank you for letting me ride you to the vicarage."

The horse blew out a warm breath in her face as if he understood and agreed, prompting her to confess, "It's been an awfully long time since I have had the opportunity to ride." Tears welled in her eyes as she remembered how hard it had been to part with their horse. He had been the first to go when they had to economize.

She wished things had been different, that the tonics had given her mother a much-needed boost of energy. The hardest day of Caroline's life had been the day her mother was buried beside her father and brother, a few gravestones away from the young man she had promised to wait for. She had made plans for their future that included getting to know more than why David's quiet presence and gentle kiss soothed her. They would become accustomed to one another's likes and dislikes as they laid the foundation of their future together, when he returned and the banns were read.

Wishes were the stuff of fairy tales, and she could no more wave a magic wand or concoct a spell that would bring her family back than she could attract a man like O'Malley with her freckles and spectacles.

"Caroline, we need to leave." O'Ghill's voice and steady gaze drew her out of her reverie.

"I'm ready."

Without asking, O'Malley put his hands around her waist and lifted her onto the sidesaddle. "Are ye certain ye'll be able to handle yer horse, and the sidesaddle, once he's moving at a fast trot?"

It took Caroline a moment for the heat, and the imprint his hands left behind on her waist, to fade. Her reaction to his touch was unsettling. David had kissed her, but that was only after he asked her to wait for him. She never suspected he had feelings for her until the day he and Neil left to join their regiment. It was odd to realize that David had never even touched her hand…just that brief, featherlight brushing of his lips to hers.

"Lass?" The concern-laced frustration in O'Malley's tone urged her to answer.

"It has been a while since I have ridden, but I am quite experienced. You do not have to worry about me."

O'Ghill mumbled beneath his breath, but she ignored him, still angry with him and unable to believe he had locked her in her room.

"What was that?" O'Malley asked.

"The moon is on the rise," O'Ghill said. "We'll have enough light, provided we stick to the road."

The men mounted, and O'Malley told his cousin, "Take the lead—I'll bring up the rear."

Caroline protested, "I thought we would ride side by side."

"'Tisn't a social ride in Hyde Park, lass," O'Malley reminded her. "We'll ride single file with ye in the middle so Killian and I can protect ye."

Though she wanted to argue the point, she inclined her head and waited for O'Ghill to lead the way.

It wasn't full dark until they had been riding for an hour. The chill in the air descended and had her shivering again. It took all of her concentration as she struggled to control her body's reaction to the damp night air. She did not want to be a bother, and dearly hoped O'Malley had not noticed from his position riding behind her.

As soon as the thought entered her mind, O'Malley called out to his cousin, "Slow it up, O'Ghill." He maneuvered his horse alongside hers, slipped off his frockcoat, and wrapped it around her shoulders. "Slip yer arms in the sleeves, lass."

When she did as he bade her, she started to push the sleeves up. He cautioned, "Let the sleeves be—they'll keep yer hands warm." His voice deepened as he said, "Tuck it around ye, now. Otherwise ye'll catch a chill and the good vicar will be taking a strip off me hide."

"My uncle would never do that," she murmured. "He's mild-mannered."

O'Malley snorted. "Ye weren't there to witness his reaction when he learned his daughter had been abducted with the blacksmith's daughter and Lady Phoebe."

His coat settled around her, wrapping her in his warmth and unique scent—a mix of sun-warmed cedar, soap, and a hint of horse. *Bliss.*

He shifted the shoulders of his coat, settling the garment

more securely around her. For a heartbeat, she felt the intensity of his gaze. Turning to meet it, she watched an emotion no man had ever had in his eyes when looking at her. *Desire.*

She shivered as he brushed his knuckles along the line of her jaw. Illuminated by the light of the moon, his features appeared more rugged...fierce. It must be his sense of duty, and concern for what may lie ahead before they reached the vicarage, and not anything to do with her.

"Thank you, Mr. O'Malley."

"Just O'Malley, lass." He resumed his position bringing up the rear.

The rode together in relative silence until the miles started to blur. Exhaustion caught up with her and began to weigh her down. Her eyes grew heavy, and she struggled to keep them open. Every once in a while, O'Malley's deep voice would call her name. Not willing to admit she was struggling to stay awake, she answered she was fine.

"Lass?"

She blinked and straightened in the saddle, surprised that she was leaning precariously to one side. Try as she might, exhaustion muddled her brain and she could not remember if she had roused when he called to her. He said her name again, in a low, rumbling tone that felt like a hug. She desperately needed one. Smiling to herself, she closed her eyes as she murmured, "Mmm... Fine."

O'GHILL FLANKED THE lass on the left, while O'Malley rode on the right. "She hasn't even noticed that we've been riding beside her for the last half-hour."

Now was not the time to stop, even if he wanted to. The inn they'd left behind was now further away than their destination. There was no other choice, they had to keep riding until they reached the village of Summerfield-on-Eden.

"From all that ye've mentioned from yer meeting," O'Malley said, "and the look on the crooked pawnbroker's face when I retrieved her belongings, we have to push on."

"Did I mention me contact warned me to watch me back?" O'Ghill asked.

"Nay. I thought ye paid the man."

"Ye know I did," O'Ghill grumbled.

O'Malley chuckled. "I've heard tales of ye not paying the full amount for information a time or two—'twas no wonder he was warning ye."

"I was tempted, but the information he relayed was too important," O'Ghill said. "I paid the full amount, and my contact wasn't warning me about his men, but Anderson's."

"That bloody *fecking* bugger!" O'Malley bit out. "We'll need to get word to Coventry and King, now that we know Anderson won't have to pay for what he's done."

O'Ghill frowned. "Ye're thinking the bastard will come after Garahan or Prudence." It wasn't a question.

"I wish I could tell ye otherwise, but I've a noxious feeling inside. 'Tis exactly what I was just thinking. Then there's her ladyship's safety, too. We have to be on guard and cannot let her out of our sight. Though the squire and his wife are not as well liked as either perceives themselves to be, there are those loyal to them because of their former position of influence in the village, before his lordship and Lady Phoebe moved into Summerfield Chase."

"No doubt they will use them to exact revenge in some form or another," O'Ghill said.

O'Malley's gut roiled. "If not for their loss of standing in the village, definitely because the very person they struck out at has temporary custody of their sons."

The lass tilted to the side again, and O'Ghill swore. "The next time, she'll land on her head! Caroline can ride with ye. I'll lead her horse."

O'Malley had not wanted to suggest that she ride with him because his cousin could be perverse at times, especially if O'Ghill sensed O'Malley was attracted to the lass. He didn't wait, scooping her off her horse and onto his lap. He settled her within the circle of his arms and tucked her head beneath his chin. A sense of peace he'd never felt before radiated from where her cheek rested against his heart. "Nearly there, lass."

She sighed and snuggled closer. Emotions bombarded him until he felt as if he were strung out on the rack, and the dungeon master was cranking the wheel, stretching his limbs to the breaking point. It was torture, but he managed to rein in the feelings rioting inside of him.

Confident that he'd won the war to control his desire, he allowed himself to accept the knowledge that she fit perfectly... And, God help him, he wanted more. He allowed himself one boon, and bent his head until it brushed the top of hers. Drawing in a deep breath, he was assailed by the intoxicating scent of the lass...lavender and lemon. A strand of hair brushed against his chin. 'Twas soft as silk. He reveled in the fact that even her hair carried her scent. O'Malley had never been so enthralled by a woman's scent before. It called to him, pulled at him, drawing him toward the intoxicating woman in his arms.

O'Malley did not want to admit—even to himself—that the attraction he felt the first time their eyes met had not waned, just the opposite. It had steadily grown the longer he was in her company. The woman's quick wit, temper, and acceptance of her situation added to her appeal. The lass had not complained once since he'd arrived. Faith, but his parents would love the lass.

Love? Couldn't be...'twas too fast. He loved his family—even his irritating cousin O'Ghill. But never had he felt the inexorable pull toward a woman before. It was strong. Inevitable.

O'Malley's gut clenched, and he caught himself before admitting, even silently, that he was falling fast for the redheaded lass. Instinctively, he knew that once he let his heart hold sway over his head, there would be no turning back. At the moment, he could still control his feelings, though what he felt for her had reached the point where it could not be ignored. Thomas would have to be vigilant to ensure she did not distract him from his duties. *Nothing* would compromise his vow to the duke.

The moon slid behind a cloud, and the men were forced to slow their pace until it reappeared, shining its light on the road ahead of them.

An hour later, they entered the village. Though it was late, a light shone from a window on the second floor of the vicarage, and another downstairs in the parlor. "The vicar's waiting," O'Ghill said.

The front door burst open, and the vicar rushed toward them, his eyes wide with worry at the sight of his niece in O'Malley's arms. "What happened to the carriage? Was there an accident? Was anyone else injured?"

"Plans changed, necessitating the need to hire a horse for yer niece," O'Malley answered.

"Is she ill?"

"Nay," O'Malley replied. "Exhausted. She's been asleep for the last hour."

"We'll fill ye in after we get her inside," O'Ghill said.

"Forgive me." The vicar finally noticed O'Ghill was leading a horse with a sidesaddle. "I'm grateful for whatever reason brought you to the same inn as my niece, O'Ghill. This is the second time you have aided my family. I can never thank you enough."

O'Ghill shrugged off the compliment. "I'm glad I was there to intervene."

"Thank you, O'Malley." The vicar wrung his hands before dropping them to his sides. "My wife has had the water warming for the last hour in case Caro wanted a cup of tea."

"Caro? I suppose 'Caroline' is a bit of a mouthful." O'Malley smoothly dismounted without jostling the lass in his arms.

The vicar's eyes widened at the ease with which O'Malley moved, but did not comment on it. If he had, O'Malley would have told the man the number of times he'd carried more than one of his cousins on horseback, dismounting with them tossed over his shoulder, when there was no other option. In comparison, the lass was light as a feather. From the worried look in the vicar's eyes, he decided 'twas best saved for a later conversation.

Vicar Chessy finally answered his question. "It is. We've called her Caro since she was a little thing." He cleared his throat and shook his head. "You are obviously used to dismounting with your arms full."

"Aye." O'Malley kept his answer short. Simple.

The vicar held the door open. "Please carry her inside. My wife and daughter have been keeping me company, trying to help me remain calm waiting to either hear from you or see the whites of your eyes."

O'Malley stood glued to the spot. The vicar's worry was palpable. "Yer niece was not injured, nor did we have to rescue her from being abducted. Ye can rest easy."

The tension in the vicar did seem to ease.

Mrs. Chessy appeared in the doorway and, at the sight before her, placed a hand to her breast. "O'Malley! Thank goodness you are here! Bring Caro in before she catches a chill. Bertram, don't just stand there—invite O'Ghill in, too."

"We're coming," the vicar answered.

The sound of his cousin mumbling to himself had O'Malley wondering if something was wrong. A glance over his shoulder showed O'Ghill staring at the building, shifting from foot to foot. "Problem?"

"Nay. I was thinking of rousing the blacksmith to see if he can stable the gelding until morning. One of us will have to return the animal to the inn tomorrow."

"We'll bring the horse with us to Summerfield Chase," O'Malley suggested. "Ye aren't leaving when ye've only just arrived, are ye?"

O'Ghill shook his head. "I could use a few hours' sleep and a full belly before I leave."

"Let me get the lass settled first."

O'Ghill agreed. "I'll see to the horses."

The vicar paused on the threshold and said, "Please make use of our barn. You can leave the gelding here for the night. We have an empty stall, and our old horse would enjoy the company."

O'Malley met his cousin's direct look and sensed that whatever the problem was, it was no small thing. He'd ask when they were alone. "I'll be out to help ye with the horses in a minute."

"After you and O'Ghill tell us what happened," the vicar said.

"We'll tell ye," O'Malley answered. "But I'll be helping me cousin first. He was the one who found yer niece, rescued her from an untenable situation, and guarded her until I arrived."

"I can handle taking care of the horses," O'Ghill grumbled. "Ye can fill the vicar in on what happened when ye arrived."

O'Malley sighed. When O'Ghill got something stuck in his head, he was a pain in the *arse*. There was no point arguing with the stubborn *eedjit*.

He ducked his head to enter the parlor. The lass stirred in his arms as he gently laid her on the settee. Her thick, dark lashes fluttered, and she slowly opened her eyes. She frowned. "Did I fall asleep?"

O'Malley smiled at the perturbed look on her face. "Ye could say that, lass."

"Caro!" Mrs. Chessy leaned down and hugged her niece before resuming her protective stance next to the settee. "We were so worried about you. What happened?"

The vicar's relief was clear as he stared at his niece. "I am so happy to see you, Caro. We were worried sick when you were not on the mail coach yesterday."

"About that, Uncle Bertram—there was a slight problem."

O'Malley cleared his throat, and the lass turned to face him, her expression pleading with him to let her tell what happened.

"My mouth is so dry," Caroline said. "May I have some water?"

Mrs. Chessy hurried to the kitchen. "The tea should be ready in a few moments. I'll check on that and bring you a cup of water, dear."

The vicar frowned at his wife's back. "It will take a bit of time for Josephine to regain her calm."

"Here you go, Caro." Mrs. Chessy handed Caroline a cup. "Drink up."

A few minutes later, Melanie Chessy entered the parlor carrying a small tray. "Tea's ready." She paused when she noticed O'Malley standing beside her cousin. "Hello, O'Malley. Thank you for bringing my favorite cousin safely home."

The front door opened and Melanie glanced up, bobbling the tray when the door closed. O'Malley reached for the tray, steadying it in time to avert disaster. "Have a care, lass. Ye don't want to burn yerself or yer cousin." He hid his grin. Melanie was staring at the black sheep of the Garahan clan—Killian O'Ghill.

O'Malley noted her unease as Melanie bit her lip and quietly thanked him, setting the tray on the small table by the settee. Brushing her hands against her gown, she finally looked at O'Ghill. "I didn't think we would see you for some time. I'm so happy you're back."

O'Malley noted the lass sounded a bit breathless. From the stunned look on O'Ghill's face, he knew his cousin was uncomfortable. His head kept turning between Melanie and her father. O'Malley saw that his cousin was trying *not* to let his gaze stay on Melanie for more than a moment or two. "I was just about to join ye in the barn and help with the horses," he said.

"Already gave the three of them a good rubdown," O'Ghill told him. "I came in to ask ye, vicar, if I could give the horses a handful or two of oats. They would welcome the treat, as we've still to reach Summerfield Chase."

"Of course," the vicar replied. "Whatever they need."

O'Ghill murmured his thanks and hurried out the door. O'Malley knew then his cousin was trying to avoid the vicar's pretty daughter. Given the lass's age, 'twas a good idea. "I'm right behind ye, Killian. The vicar needs to hear what happened before we leave."

"No need. I've got everything in hand."

"We don't want to keep the baron waiting," O'Malley said. "I'll help ye."

He didn't wait for his cousin to argue. He closed the door behind him and nudged O'Ghill with his shoulder to get him moving. Noting the stiffness in his shoulders, O'Malley recalled Garahan telling himself and Flaherty that, during the rescue, O'Ghill had had to catch the lass when she swooned, and had been distracted afterward. Testing his theory that O'Ghill was not immune to the vicar's daughter, he said, "Miss Chessy has the loveliest green eyes."

"They're blue," O'Ghill corrected him, then swore beneath his breath. "Not another word, or I'll shut yer gob for ye."

O'Malley wisely let his cousin think that would be the end of it. There was more than an appreciation for a lovely lass here. If he gauged his cousin's actions and feelings correctly when O'Ghill had left the first time a month ago, the man's head had been turned by the lovely lass…but she was too young for him. O'Malley would have to think carefully before broaching the subject with his hardheaded cousin.

Between the two of them, they made short work of taking care of their mounts and returned to the vicarage. The front door opened as they approached the house.

"There you are," the vicar said. "Would either of you like a sip of brandy while you tell me what happened?"

O'Ghill shared a look with O'Malley and said, "If ye wouldn't mind stepping outside for a moment, I think we should speak of it privately."

At the vicar's look of concern, O'Malley added, "'Tisn't what ye think. Yer niece is not without her pride. I'm after saving what is left of it…after she tried to bargain with that pawnbroker—"

The vicar's shock was palpable. "What in the world was my niece doing at a pawnbroker's?"

"Apparently Miss Gillingham left a bit out of her letters to ye, especially regarding her circumstances," O'Malley replied.

The vicar scrubbed a hand over his face and followed the men to the barn. "She should have had more than enough coin from the sale of their home. What of the contents of their home? Did she arrange for shipping yet?"

O'Malley told his cousin, "Ye take it from here, as ye were the one who was there when she ran out of the pawnshop."

O'Ghill briefly explained how she'd run into him when fleeing from the pawnshop, and had been accused of theft as the Watch strode toward them. "She mentioned her uncle the vicar and yer village, and I knew then I needed to send word to me cousin. I had no idea of her circumstances, that she was overdue, or that ye were expecting her and would be worried."

The vicar's eyes widened, but he held his tongue. The hair on the back of O'Malley's neck stood on end just from thinking of the pawnbroker's claims… *His lies!* He wished he had gone with his gut instinct and squeezed the man's throat till he turned purple and confessed. *The bloody liar!*

"And you are certain she was unharmed by that blackguard?"

The vicar's words echoed O'Malley's thoughts, surprising him. He had not realized that he, too, needed to hear O'Ghill's confirmation that the lass had not been manhandled by the shopkeeper. At least the pawnbroker had not lied about that.

O'Malley listened to his cousin assure the vicar that she had been rattled, but not harmed. He also noted O'Ghill failed to mention he'd locked the lass in her room at the inn. In all fairness, it was to protect her while he went off to meet with his contact. Neither of them mentioned what O'Ghill had learned. They had to report the information to the baron first.

"Yer turn, O'Malley. Tell the vicar what happened when ye went back to the shop to retrieve Caroline's things."

The vicar stiffened. "What things?"

O'Malley reached into his pocket and pulled out a golden chain and locket. "'Twas her ma's."

The older man was visibly moved as he reached for his sister's locket. O'Malley then handed the vicar the pocket watch.

"My brother-in-law's," Vicar Chessy rasped. His gaze met O'Malley's and then O'Ghill's. "Why do I have this feeling this is all she has left of them?"

"'Tis why I didn't want her to overhear our conversation," O'Malley said. "We need to leave the lass the smidge of pride that had her refusing to ask ye for the coin she needed for the last leg of her journey."

The vicar cleared his throat. "She would rather give up what she treasured than ask for coin from me?"

"Aye. I'm thinking ye'll understand when ye speak to the lass," O'Malley said. "She'll be needing these. When ye give her the locket and watch, there's no need to say anything when ye do."

The vicar's hands closed over the objects. "I had expected Mr. Humbolt to declare himself if anything happened to my sister. Caro mentioned him more than once, and I thought there was an understanding between them...though she had never said as much."

O'Malley ground his back teeth at the thought of a man having a claim on the redheaded lass. His hands curled into fists, ready to pummel whoever this Humbolt was for backing away from someone as vibrant as the lass. His actions may have forced Caroline into a situation beyond her control, one fraught with danger, given her lack of coin or protector.

Keeping his expression neutral, he asked the question that seared through him. "Were they betrothed?"

"Not to my knowledge."

At the vicar's words, the anger bubbling inside of O'Malley quieted, settling until all he felt was mild irritation. He relaxed his hands. "Please send word if ye have need of either of us, vicar." With a nod to his cousin, he added, "O'Ghill should be around for a few more days."

The vicar offered his hand to O'Ghill, then O'Malley. "Thank you, men. I don't know what I would have done if anything had happened to Caro. She's been through so much in such a short period of time." He straightened and vowed, "We are her family now, and we will happily make room for her in our lives."

"She's lucky to have ye," O'Malley said.

"That she is," O'Ghill agreed.

The men said their goodbyes and retreated to the barn to collect their horses. As agreed, the gelding O'Ghill hired from the inn would spend the night keeping the vicar's horse company, and they would speak to the baron about who would return the animal.

They set off for Summerfield Chase and rode in companionable silence until they approached the stables. "Garahan'll be surprised to see ye."

"No doubt he'll put me to work without a full night's sleep," O'Ghill muttered.

Garahan and Flaherty were waiting for them. "Tell us what happened, O'Ghill," Garahan demanded. "And do not leave anything out!"

"Has the baron retired yet?" O'Ghill asked.

"Nay," Garahan answered. "He is waiting for O'Malley's report."

"Let's tell this once," O'Malley suggested.

The men trooped toward the back entrance to the house, only to discover they would not have to go in search of the baron—he was walking toward them.

"O'Ghill, if you're here, there must be a tale to tell. Join me in my study, men."

CHAPTER SIX

CAROLINE RELAXED IN the company of her aunt and cousin. She had always enjoyed whenever her family had visited the vicarage. With Uncle Bertram's last transfer to Summerfield-on-Eden, and the distance from her home, the time in between visits had grown longer with each passing year. The news of her brother's death was the catalyst that continued to take the lives of those she loved. Was there a curse? Was she, too, destined to die within the year?

Shaking that grim thought from her brainbox, she concentrated on the moment and being with the family she had missed dearly.

"Now that your uncle is out of hearing," her aunt said, "is there anything you need to speak of?"

Caroline set her teacup on its saucer and placed it on the cherry table next to the settee. "I am fine, Aunt Josephine. Before you feel the need to remonstrate me about my lack of confiding in you or Uncle about Mum's health, at the time I thought it was prudent for me not to speak of our situation. I couldn't take the chance that word would get back to her of my concern, and just how desperate her health had become."

"Very well," her aunt replied. "Though how you couldn't see a way to confide in us is something I will never understand."

Grief filled Caroline as she thought of how frail her mother had become in the last few months. Instead of answering her aunt, she said, "It gave Mum pleasure to read your letters. I did not want her to know that we were struggling because she would have insisted that I stop visiting the three apothecaries that had become her lifeline. I was afraid that I would lose her if that happened. Regaining her health was of the utmost importance to me. Strain between your family and what was left of mine could be dealt with later, if it came to that."

She twisted her fingers in her lap, wondering if she had done the wrong thing entirely. Then she remembered the light in her mother's eyes whenever she returned with a new bottle of tonic to try. "It gave her such hope every time I brought home the latest herbal or tonic. She would smile, and for a brief moment, I could forget how deep the ache of losing Neil, David, and Papa was. I am sorry if you are displeased with my decision, but I would never take away those last few weeks Mum and I had together. She fought until she breathed her last. She had a smile on her face, and I knew..." Her voice broke, and she had to stifle the sob constricting her throat to continue. "I knew Papa and Neil greeted her with open arms, surrounding her with their love and beautiful feathered angels' wings."

Her aunt reached for Caroline's left hand, as Melanie reached for her right. Unable to hold back her tears, she let them come. Her aunt handed her a soft white linen handkerchief to mop up her tears.

"Brave Caro," her aunt said. "I ache for your loss, and wish we did not live so far apart. I did not question you because I doubted your judgment. I asked because of *our* need to help, which, all things considered, has no bearing on the situation."

"I prayed for wisdom," Caroline whispered. "The only answer that came to me was to keep trying. The herbals and tonics did not harm Mum, though they did not improve her health."

"Did you ask for the return of the coin you paid in good faith?"

Caroline drew in a breath and willed herself to stop crying. "It did not occur to me until after we buried her between Papa and Neil."

Her aunt put an arm around Caroline. "You shouldered such a huge burden, Caro. Agatha and Nelson must have thanked the Lord daily for your support when the news of Neil's ultimate sacrifice for king and country arrived. It had to be just as devastating to you to lose your older brother and David. Agatha mentioned that he had asked Nelson for permission to court you."

Caroline nodded. She felt so lost, knowing neither her brother, nor the man she'd pledged to wait for, would ever return.

"Forgive me, Caro. It is so easy for one to make suggestions," her aunt said, "especially when one is not standing in the thick of things, facing such important decisions regarding a loved one's health and well-being."

"There is nothing to forgive. You and Uncle Bertram have always opened your home and arms to my family. Did you know that Mum always called you the sister of her heart?"

Her aunt's eyes filled at the endearment. "I am so sorry that Bertram was unable to go to you after receiving Agatha's note with the news of dear Nelson's sudden illness, so soon after the news about Neil."

Caroline removed her spectacles to wipe the lenses. She knew her aunt needed to hear everything, in order to properly grieve for Caroline's parents. She dug for the wherewithal to continue. "We both understood. Your letters uplifted us and gave us the courage to keep going."

"When you wrote a month ago, telling of Agatha's health being tenuous"—Aunt Josephine shifted her gaze to her daughter and then met Caroline's eyes once more—"we were in the midst of trying to find Melanie."

Caroline stared at her cousin. "Can you speak of what happened?"

Melanie placed her teacup on the table next to Caroline's. "Olivia and I were speaking with Prudence—she's married to

Garahan, one of the duke's guard at Summerfield Chase—and were planning to take tea with her at the inn in the village, when a carriage pulled into the innyard. When we heard what sounded like a young woman crying for help, we all rushed to do so."

The tension in the room was palpable. Caroline nodded. "You and Olivia have never lacked courage. I would have been surprised if you did *not* attempt to give aid."

Her cousin nodded. "Prudence was right behind us. But things are not always what they seem," Melanie rasped. "Voices can be disguised to lead one to false conclusions."

"The young woman was not in need of your help?" Caroline asked.

Melanie shifted on the cream wing-backed chair. Instinctively Caroline knew there was more to the story.

"What aren't you telling me, Melanie?"

Her cousin hesitated, then said, "We were grabbed and gagged the moment we entered the coach."

Caroline's eyes widened. "What about Garahan's wife?"

"The men got hold of her and pulled her into the carriage with us a moment before the reprobate, disguised as a lord, returned and ordered his coachman to drive."

"With the three of you captive inside his carriage?"

Melanie nodded, her eyes giving away the fact that the incident was still quite fresh in her mind.

"What of the kidnapper?" Caroline asked. "Who was he impersonating?"

"He was not disguised as a lord," Aunt Josephine reminded her daughter. "Even though Lord Anderson is a member of the *ton*, he is a reprobate, a rogue, and a rounder!"

Caroline studied her cousin, looking for any sign that she was injured in the kidnapping. Finding none, she asked, "Did he hurt either of you?"

To her shock, Melanie slowly smiled. "A few bruises, but they were soon forgotten when Olivia kicked one of his henchmen when he…"

When her voice trailed off, Caroline stood and walked over to where Melanie sat staring into space. "Whatever reason your friend had for kicking the man, if he were here right now, I'd kick him, too."

Melanie giggled. "Cornelius let us practice kicking him the last time he was here and those boys were picking on us. Remember, Caro?" As soon as the words left her mouth, her expression changed from joy to grief.

Their eyes met and Caroline knew Melanie had not spoken of Neil to make her sad. The memory of her brother had the opposite effect. Her lips lifted into a small smile. "Neil was the best of brothers. I was so lucky to have him looking after me. Don't you remember me telling you that the last thing he did before leaving to join his regiment was to show me more than one way to stop a miscreant from attacking or attempting to abduct me?"

"I do, and that there is more than one place to kick and elbow our attackers. You showed Olivia and me those moves," Melanie said, with a quick glance at her mother.

Caroline knew her aunt would not have approved, but her brother had insisted that she teach their cousin, who of course was never without Olivia. So Caroline ended up showing the both of them.

Turning to her aunt, Caroline said, "It must have accomplished what Neil hoped if Olivia was able to keep her head and kick her abductor. My brother only wanted Melanie and me to be safe."

"Cornelius was so much like your father," Aunt Josephine said. "Both men possessed a spine of steel, a core of honor, and a heart of gold."

Caroline's heart warmed at her aunt's compliment. "Uncle Bertram is so much like Papa and Neil in that regard." She paused and waited a moment to find the words to help her aunt know that she understood what had not been said. "Uncle would have wanted to chase after the kidnappers, but did not because he had to protect you, and could not leave his congregation—and the village—without its spiritual leader."

"We would never want you to think that we did not want to rush to Agatha's side. By the time Melanie had been safely returned, we were packing our bags, making ready to leave...then your letter with the news of Agatha's passing arrived."

Struggling not to break down and cry for the second time in the last half an hour, Caroline gathered her composure and swallowed her tears. "From what Mr. O'Ghill tells me, he and his cousin were able to rescue Melanie, Olivia, and Mrs. Garahan without incident."

Melanie frowned. "Is that what Mr. O'Ghill told you?"

Surprised by her cousin's expression, Caroline agreed.

"By the by, Mr. Garahan, who prefers to be called Garahan, was stabbed in the back and had to be sewn back together." Hand to her breast, Melanie confessed, "I swooned at the vivid description of the injury."

It was Caroline's turn to frown. "Who in their right mind would have described such in front of a lady?"

"At the time, O'Ghill and Garahan were arguing about the whiskey Prudence added to our teapot. Then Garahan was explaining why he wasn't the one responsible for our slightly inebriated state because of his injury. I cannot repeat the description or what he said, or I'll likely swoon again."

"Ah." Caroline nodded. "Mayhap I will have to take into account that Mr.—that is, Garahan was in pain at the time and upset by the fact that you and Olivia, who are too young to be swilling whiskey, had done just that."

Melanie squared her shoulders and huffed. "We were not 'swilling whiskey.' Prudence added a few drops to the teapots."

"Teapots?" Caroline asked.

"Yes. We were still quite anxious, as you can imagine, having been abducted and then hearing that Garahan had been severely injured by the lord who kidnapped us. One pot of tea was not enough to fortify us."

Caroline glanced at her aunt, who was staring at the ceiling while her lips moved. She fought back the urge to smile, and told her cousin, "I believe your mum is counting again. Best not discuss the additive to your tea."

"Olivia and I have so much to tell you, Caro," Melanie said.

Caroline knew from the pained expression on her aunt's face that her cousin and her friend would be retelling their abduction in great detail as soon as the three of them were together. Out of earshot of her uncle and aunt.

"I'm looking forward to it." The front door closed, and Caroline straightened in her seat. Expecting to see O'Malley and O'Ghill, she was surprised at the disappointment arrowing through her when only her uncle walked into the parlor.

"The men had to report in to his lordship."

His words should not have come as a shock to her. Of course O'Malley had to go. He was head of the duke's guard at Summerfield Chase. But she had hoped to be able to bid him goodbye, and thank him and O'Ghill one more time before they left. Who knew when or if she would see the handsome, green-eyed Irishman again?

"Why don't you and Melanie head up to bed?" her aunt suggested. "We can catch up in the morning. After breakfast, we will need to set the vicarage to rights before the two of you seek out Olivia." She paused, then slowly smiled. "That is, if Olivia does not appear on our doorstep *before* breakfast."

Melanie rose and picked up the tea tray. "Caro doesn't look in the least bit sleepy after our tea. Why don't she and I straighten the kitchen, while you and Papa head upstairs?"

"If you are certain, Caro."

Caroline nodded and was hugged as if she had not seen her aunt and uncle in a decade instead of the few short years it had been. "Goodnight Aunt, Uncle. Thank you for taking me in when I had nowhere to go."

"You are family, Caro," her uncle replied.

"And always welcome here…indefinitely," her aunt added. "Still—"

Aunt Josephine shook her head. "Family protects family. You are our much-loved niece, and a welcome addition to our family. We anticipate the joy you will bring to the Chessy side of the family." One last hug and she and the vicar climbed the stairs.

Caroline's tears blurred her vision for a moment before Melanie tugged on her hand. "Olivia has set her cap for Dillon Flaherty!"

Caroline blinked and followed her cousin into the kitchen. "I don't remember you mentioning anyone by that name in your letters. Did he move here recently?"

Melanie's soft laughter caught Caroline's full attention. Her cousin only laughed like that when she had a juicy tidbit of gossip to share. "He's one of the duke's guard at Summerfield Chase."

"Has he called on Mr. Coleman to make his attentions known?"

Melanie snorted. "Hardly. When he's on patrol in the village, he has never even glanced in Olivia's direction."

"Why would she be interested in him, then?"

Melanie rolled her eyes in exasperation. "He's nearly as tall as O'Malley and O'Ghill, who are both a bit taller than Garahan. The duke's guard are all built like mythical heroes of old. Broad through the chest and shoulders, handsome men, and not a one has ever expressed an interest in the women of Summerfield-on-Eden. Well, that is until Prudence arrived to take up the position of nanny to her twin cousins."

"Don't you mean the women of marriageable age?" Caroline asked.

Melanie clapped a hand to her mouth before another loud snort of laughter could escape. "Just because Olivia and I are not as old as you, Caro—and may I remind you that you are only four years older—doesn't mean we cannot appreciate a handsome man when we see one."

Caroline was not certain how she felt about being reminded

she was old enough to be married with two babes by now. And she may very well have been if her circumstances had not changed so drastically.

At her silence, Melanie exclaimed, "Botheration, Caro! You must know that I did not mean it as a slight."

"I do know that, Melanie. Had my father recovered from his sudden illness, we expected Mr. Humbolt to offer for my hand."

Melanie threw her arms around Caroline and squeezed her. "Congratulations! When can we expect Mr. Humbolt to appear to whisk you away to his castle in the clouds?"

Caroline shook her head. "I cannot believe you are still holding tight to your belief in fairytale romance!"

They made quick work of straightening the kitchen and surveyed the room to ensure everything had been put away before heading upstairs.

"He won't be coming," Caroline finally confided. "Nor will he be asking for my hand."

Melanie paused halfway up the stairs. "Whyever not?"

"I have nothing of value to offer. I had to sell it…all of it. Our home, the furniture, our dishes—everything of value—to pay our debts."

Her cousin's grip was surprisingly strong as she hurried up the stairs. For the second time that night, Caroline let herself be pulled along. Melanie opened the door to her bedroom and quickly closed it behind them, motioning Caroline over to the wardrobe.

Caroline was swept back in time to when they were young, and knew instantly what her cousin was about. "Do you and Olivia still use your wardrobe to hide in when you share your secrets and do not wish to be overheard?"

"Of course we do! The walls are quite thick and muffle our voices. Hurry up and sit down so I can close the door." When Caroline complied, Melanie said, "Now then, Caro, tell me everything. And I mean *everything*."

CHAPTER SEVEN

O'MALLEY TOSSED AND turned for the few hours he was able to be in bed. The image of the red-haired lass with the spectacles kept him company through the sleepless night. Her thick-lashed, wide gray eyes and feisty nature had him wondering if there would be a suitor following after her to Summerfield-on-Eden. Humbolt, was it? And just how did the lass feel about the man? Had she loved him? If the man loved her, he would never have abandoned her in her time of need. O'Malley would never have, and nor would his brothers or cousins!

One question had him wrestling with his conscience off and on, disturbing what little sleep he had: should he have brought the lass to the baron's home, where she would be well protected? Knowing how worried her uncle was, and considering the probability that she would balk, he had ignored the urge to head directly to Summerfield Chase, and delivered her to the vicarage as promised.

O'Malley had been awake for a few hours by the time it was his turn to man the post on the roof, but it was not an uncommon occurrence. He had gone with little to no sleep many times before. The most stressful were the times the duke or his family had been under attack. The other instances were not concerning—when he was in the middle of an investigation, meeting contacts on the docks or in the stews during the midnight hour.

He had been stationed at Wyndmere Hall after the duke married, until he was tasked with the assignment of escorting Lady Phoebe, and the duchess's mother Lady Farnsworth, to London. Guarding the duke and earl's younger sister had taken every bit of his patience and cunning. When Lady Phoebe married Marcus, Baron Summerfield, O'Malley had been assigned as head of the duke's guard at the baron's home. He enjoyed living in the Borderlands, and it had been relatively quiet...until two recent events: Garahan's wife and two lasses from the village being abducted, and the squire, or his wife, clubbing Lady Phoebe on the back of her head. The baroness was seriously injured, requiring round-the-clock protection. The men were constantly rotating their positions and patrols more frequently now, catching an hour or more of sleep when they could.

He wondered if the circumstances surrounding Miss Gillingham's ill-advised stop at the pawnshop would have trouble coming to their door. He patrolled the rooftop, scanning the wooded area surrounding the estate. It may seem like one of the easier posts to man, compared to the patrols on horseback. However, it required a sharp eye. There were numerous places attackers could hide and capture their unsuspecting victims. A sharpshooter needed a steady hand when wielding their weapon of choice. His was the Kentucky long rifle.

As the sun's rays shone through the trees, O'Malley remembered the first time he'd fired one. It had been a gift their cousins living in America brought with them on their last visit home, a year or so before the O'Malleys, Garahans, and Flahertys left to find employment in London. The Kentucky long barrel fired a .50-caliber lead ball and had a barrel length that varied between forty and forty-six inches. What had impressed him, his brothers, and their cousins was the ease loading the smaller lead ball, and its accuracy at a range of up to four hundred yards. They all preferred it to the British Baker rifle.

O'Malley smiled, recalling the reply his cousin Patrick had received after writing to their cousins, telling them of their new positions as the Duke of Wyndmere's private guard. Patrick had mentioned how useful the rifles were during an attack on the duke and his family at Wyndmere Hall. Patrick, being Patrick, explained in detail. Their cousins' reply had been to ship four more of the rifles with the caveat that they send details of the skirmishes fought, and the number of men the guard had wounded—or, preferably, killed. Time had not tainted the warrior blood running through the O'Malley, Garahan, and Flaherty clans, though it had been tempered with a reserve their ancestors had not had.

The Irish were a fierce, fighting people. Time had not changed that. Those that had gone before them had instilled the same pride and loyalty their ancestors had had. Those inherent skills had enabled the men of the duke's guard to react quickly and decisively, which had saved the day more than once since they had been employed by the Duke of Wyndmere.

O'Malley had not admitted it to anyone, least of all Garahan or Flaherty, but he still woke up in a cold sweat from the reoccurring nightmare of the time Lady Phoebe slipped out of Lady Farnsworth's town house on his watch, intent on rescuing the man she loved. His heart still shuddered at the memory of following Lady Phoebe and discovering her armed with a handful of ribbon-wrapped hatpins and a brass paperweight, instead of the ransom demanded in exchange for the release of Marcus. Alerted by one of the footmen, O'Malley had followed her to the docks. Had the duke or the earl caught wind of her leaving without O'Malley hot on her heels…they would have skinned him alive.

The lass, Miss Gillingham, reminded O'Malley of Lady Phoebe. Neither one had listened to him. Thank God O'Ghill hadn't been in London at the time Lady Phoebe had slipped out of the town house, or else he'd have locked *her* in her bedchamber…and that would have not ended well for him.

A movement to the south near a copse of fir trees caught O'Malley's eye. He lifted the rifle, aimed it at the trees, and waited patiently. A fawn pranced out of the grouping of trees and lifted its nose toward the warmth of the sun, scenting his freedom. A doe followed closely behind her young, nudging the little one on the hindquarters to get him moving back to the protection of the trees.

"Protective, just like Ma," O'Malley murmured. He lowered his rifle, slipped it over his shoulder, and proceeded to check the four corners of the rooftop. He could see in all directions for at least a mile, though not as deeply into the heavily wooded areas.

His mother had reminded him in her most recent letter that it was still her job to worry about him and his brothers. He didn't mind her telling him what to do from a distance and smiled every time he answered her letters, enclosing the money he'd set aside from his wages to help maintain their family's farm. His brothers and cousins all did the same. 'Twas the only reason they had left home—looking for a way to earn enough coin for their families to hold on to land that had been in their families for generations. Blood, sweat, and tears had never been enough to hold on to it. 'Twas coin that made the difference.

O'Malley was surprised to see O'Ghill climbing up the ladder to the roof, near the end of his shift. "Nice view ye have up here." O'Malley grunted, and his cousin grinned and held out his flask. "Have a nip of the Irish—ye'll feel better for it."

"Later. I need to be alert."

"When has a sip or two of whiskey ever made ye slow-witted?"

O'Malley chuckled. "'Tis best not to speak of it until I am in between shifts and grabbing a bite to eat."

O'Ghill shrugged. "Don't say I didn't offer to share me flask with ye. By the by, his lordship wants to speak to ye."

"Why didn't ye say so right off?"

He shrugged. "Ye looked as if ye could use a drink."

O'Malley sighed. "Did his lordship ask ye to take over me post? Otherwise, I cannot leave until me relief arrives."

"Not exactly."

"Well then, I'd best wait until—"

A short, sharp whistle sounded—the signal every man in the guard knew and used to warn of danger or an emergency. O'Malley tightened his grip on his rifle, then sprinted for the ladder, climbed halfway down, and jumped the last few feet to the ground. O'Ghill was hot on his heels. Running full out, they rounded the corner of the house and skidded to a halt. Garahan and Flaherty were waiting for them.

"What's wrong?" O'Malley demanded.

"His lordship received a missive from Bow Street," Garahan answered. "King advised that Anderson has left the sanctuary of Prinny's household and was observed leaving his home by carriage, headed for North Road."

He did not need to elaborate on the situation. The general consensus among the duke's guard was that Anderson would seek revenge against Garahan and O'Ghill for the social embarrassment he'd suffered being questioned for a crime that would soil his reputation. O'Malley's temper erupted with the thought that the bloody bugger would never have to pay for his crimes.

O'Malley and O'Ghill agreed with Garahan when he told them what he feared most: Anderson would come after Prudence. Garahan suspected Anderson was still livid that she had married Garahan and slipped through his fingers before he could fulfill his part of the bargain, collecting the rest of the coin Prudence's mother and aunt had promised the bleeding bugger.

"We'd best not keep his lordship waiting." O'Malley didn't bother to wait for the men—he knew they would be right behind him.

The group entered through the back door, making their way along the hallway and series of rooms before reaching the kitchen and the door to the main part of the house. Each man wore an expression of determination as he strode down the marbled hallway to the baron's study.

The door was open, but O'Malley knocked on it anyway. Summerfield looked up from the bit of foolscap he held in his hands. "Good. You're all here. O'Ghill, I will need your help, too."

"Ye have it, yer lordship," O'Ghill replied.

"Excellent." Summerfield turned to his men and told them, "King has had men shadowing Anderson since he was questioned, expecting the lord to be released."

"'Tis what we feared as well," O'Malley said. "Do ye want me to speak to the footmen we recruited a month ago?" He did not need to explain their duties to them. The footmen temporarily assigned as guards had been performing them since Lady Phoebe was injured. The baroness was three months along with their first babe, complicating her recovery. Summerfield had asked their physician to extend his order that her ladyship remain in bed as a precaution to ensure she would not miscarry their babe. Dr. Higgins had readily agreed.

"No need. I have already spoken to Timmons," the baron replied. "He is speaking to the footmen now. The extra men guarding her ladyship are essential, as her medical confinement will be up in a few days." He met O'Malley's direct gaze and added, "Given my wife's propensity to jump before carefully considering the ramifications, I don't need to remind you that she will be poking her nose into the situation."

O'Malley's lips twitched. "Nay, yer lordship."

"Prudence, and our young wards, will be spending their time with my wife. It will be easier to protect them if they are all in one place." The baron slowly smiled. "Besides, those scamps make her laugh. They adore Lady Phoebe and feel as protective of her as they do Prudence."

Summerfield's smile faded. The bleak expression on his face was telling. He was preparing for attack. O'Malley did not disagree with him. He was pleased that the baron had the foresight to plan for the worst. They would be prepared.

"Have ye sent word to His Grace and the earl?" Garahan asked.

"Just now," the baron said. "I can think of three of our tenant farmers who are excellent shots. Timmons sent one of the footmen to summon them here."

"What about Miss Chessy?" O'Ghill asked.

Flaherty, who had been silent up until now, asked, "And the blacksmith's daughter?"

"They'll be targets as well," Garahan said, "seeing's how they were abducted along with me wife."

"I'll have Timmons—"

O'Malley interrupted the baron. "Begging yer pardon, yer lordship, but the vicar and the blacksmith may be more willing to listen if ye send one of us."

Summerfield nodded. "Excellent point, O'Malley. O'Ghill, the young women trust you, as you and Garahan were the ones to rescue them. Speak to their fathers, see if they will agree to allowing me to shelter their daughters here."

Flaherty cleared his throat. When all eyes turned to him, he said, "Don't be forgetting Mrs. Chessy and her niece Miss Gillingham. They should not remain behind. Anderson has no conscience, nor respect for women. He may retaliate and try to get his hands on both of them if he cannot find Melanie and Olivia."

The baron raked a hand through his hair. "Of course—see that they come along, too. We need to spread the word while there is still time to ensure that everyone in the village and our tenant farmers know of this volatile situation and take precautions."

"Aye, yer lordship," O'Malley answered for the group.

"Uncle Baron!" a youthful voice called from behind them.

"Uncle Baron!" a second voice echoed.

The men turned as Squire Honeycutt's twin sons raced toward Summerfield but rocked to a stop in the doorway to the study. "Can we... *May* we come in?" one asked.

"Aye, boys." Summerfield waved them in.

"We heard the *bast*—er, blackguard who tried to steal our cousin is coming to try again," Percy blurted out.

"And we want to help stop him!" Phineas said.

When the baron did not answer right away, Percy looked at his brother, and when he nodded, Percy added, "Phineas and me have a plan."

"Do ye now?" O'Malley asked.

"Lady Phoebe and I are so proud of how well you have adapted to living here at Summerfield Chase," Summerfield said. "You are a huge help in the stables with our horses."

"Don't forget how hard the lads have been working training with wooden swords and rope climbing," Flaherty reminded the baron.

"All the while continuing their studies with Prudence," Garahan added.

"Our cousin is a wonderful teacher, and not squeamish at all," Phineas said.

"She digs up worms to bait our hooks, and helps us collect tadpoles and salamanders," Percy added.

Garahan chuckled. "Me wife is a rare woman who enjoys being out of doors almost as much as the two of ye."

The baron knelt beside the twins and asked, "What plan did you have in mind, boys?"

Their chests puffed up with pride as they rushed to tell the baron their plan. "Phineas and I will stick with Prudence all day, every day," Percy informed him. "Until Garahan and the others take care of that *bugg*—er, blackguard."

Phineas nodded and said, "We were going to split up, and I was going to stick beside Lady Phoebe, but she's been awful sick in the mornings and only seems to get better after you bring her a cup of tea and one of Mrs. Green's scones."

The baron slowly smiled. "Noticed that, did you?"

"We both did," Percy said.

"And we noticed that her eyes turn a really deep blue," Phineas added. "She smiles whenever you walk in the room."

"Uh huh," Percy said. "Garahan said it's 'cause she's partial to you."

"That means she likes you," Phineas told the baron. "A whole lot."

Summerfield pulled the boys into a hard hug before releasing them to stand. "Our lives are richer having you boys living with us. We're partial to you, too."

The twins grinned. "So, do you like our plan?" Percy asked.

Summerfield glanced at his guard. "What do you think, men?"

"'Tis sound," Flaherty replied.

"A good idea," O'Ghill said.

"Well thought out," O'Malley added.

"Ye thought with yer heads and then yer hearts, lads," Garahan said. "Me cousins and I could not have thought up a better plan for guarding me wife."

"You are right about mine, too," the baron said. "Phoebe does perk up when I bring her a bite or two of scone and pot of tea. Knowing the two of you are guarding Prudence is a huge relief. I will be able to guard Phoebe without worrying about Prudence."

"We knew you'd see reason, Uncle Baron," Percy said.

"We won't let you, or the duke's guard, down," Phineas promised.

Summerfield laid a hand on each boy's shoulder. "I never thought you would. Now then, isn't it time for your midmorning visit to the stables to pass out the carrots and apples?"

"It is!" Phineas grabbed his brother's hand and tugged him into the hallway. "Come on, Percy! Bye, Uncle Baron! Bye, Garahan," Phineas called out over his shoulder.

"Bye, Flaherty. Bye, O'Malley!" Percy said.

Both boys paused and yelled, "Bye, Killian!"

Watching the twins race off, Garahan turned to the baron. "Ye've saved those two from a life of unhappiness, allowing them to live here while their parents are in the gaol. Prudence and I are grateful to ye."

Summerfield frowned. "Neither Phoebe nor I could stand the thought of where those two would end up, since your mother-in-law has been detained as well. Phoebe said she wanted to speak to me about their future—there is a chance they could end up orphans. We will not let that happen. No matter what, they are family now."

The men readily agreed, and O'Malley said, "We'll see to it we teach them how to protect and defend the women who look after them."

"From yer wife to the scullery maids," Flaherty added.

"The women in the village," O'Ghill said.

"And the tenant farmers' wives and daughters," Garahan reminded them.

The baron grinned. "That ought to keep those two rapscallions busy for the next few years."

"By then yer babe will be ready for the lessons Percy and Phineas have learned," O'Malley said.

"And they will no doubt be ready to pass on their knowledge," Summerfield replied. "Well done, men." With a nod to O'Ghill, he said, "Report back to me when you return from speaking to Vicar Chessy and Coleman."

"Aye, yer lordship."

Turning back to his guard, Summerfield said, "We may need to increase the number of footmen moving to guard duty."

"Aye," O'Malley agreed.

"Four ought to be enough," Flaherty said.

Garahan shook his head. "I'm thinking six or eight."

The baron looked up at the sound of his name being called. "Mrs. Green must have my wife's tea and scones ready." With a nod to O'Malley, he said, "You know where to find me."

"Aye, yer lordship."

TWO HOURS LATER, O'Malley was guarding the perimeter when O'Ghill returned with a black look on his face. "I have a message for the baron."

CHAPTER EIGHT

CAROLINE WATCHED HER cousin staring in the direction O'Ghill had ridden. It was obvious Melanie had feelings for him. Watching the way her cousin's shoulders slumped, and her eyes filled, Caroline sensed it was more than a passing fancy. She reached for another sheet to hang on the clothesline, securing her end with the clothes peg. "Grab the other end, will you, Melanie?" When her cousin did not answer right away, Caroline smoothed the sheet along the line and pegged the middle and then the end where her cousin stood still staring at the empty road.

It had not escaped Caroline's notice how her cousin reacted a short while ago, when O'Ghill had arrived. They had been in the kitchen at the time when he and her uncle entered her uncle's study. Melanie had hovered near the closed door, listening to the slightly raised voices on the other side.

She had not been able to attend to their task long enough to be helpful since O'Ghill left. Caroline did not feel right complaining, even if it would be easier to hang the freshly laundered sheets on the line with two people. When she had to ask Melanie to grab the other end of the sheet a second time, finally she complied, prompting Caroline to ask, "How long have you been in love with O'Ghill?"

Melanie sighed, then surprised Caroline by answering the

question. "Since the first time I saw him. When he rode toward the blacksmith's shop, so tall in the saddle—shoulders so broad, one would think he could handle anything." She closed her eyes for a moment. "Olivia and I had just delivered her father's noon meal when we saw him ride up and dismount. We were both momentarily speechless, captivated. For a brief time, I thought I would have to knock Olivia on her backside to keep her from trying to snag the dark-haired, dark-eyed god's attention when I wanted it all to myself. Thankfully, a week or so later, Olivia finally saw Flaherty."

"Who is he?" Caroline asked. The name sounded familiar.

"Really, cousin, I told you last night who he was. He's stationed at Summerfield Chase."

"I'm sorry, Melanie. I do recall now. Flaherty is one of the duke's guard."

"Yes, along with O'Malley and Garahan. They are all so handsome, tall, and broad, with a certain air about them, a mix of confidence and intrigue—and so handsome."

Caroline laughed. "You said handsome twice."

"Did I? Well, they are twice as handsome as any other man I have ever seen."

Melanie was not wrong, Caroline thought. She remembered having a similar feeling when she ran into O'Ghill. The way he handled her situation had called for arrogance, and he had more than his share of it. While O'Malley did have a bit of that trait as well, she did not find it to be overwhelming...especially when he was holding her in his arms. "If Flaherty is anything like O'Ghill and O'Malley, he is arrogant, too."

Melanie narrowed her eyes. "You say that like it's a bad thing, Caro."

"In my experience, arrogance is not always an attractive quality in a man." Caroline used to think it was an essential in the man she would one day marry. A few of her brother's friends who had managed to catch her attention, then spoiled it with their stiff-necked opinions, changed her mind about that. The exception was David. She had been drawn to his quiet manner, missed him, and mourned the chance they'd never had to court and fall in love. "Have you ever had a difference of opinion with O'Ghill?"

"Why would I want to do that, when he is never wrong? Besides, he is so handsome and brave and strong…and when he swept me into his arms, I thought I'd die."

Caroline shook her head. "I hardly think being picked up by O'Ghill would have such a dire effect on anyone, even you, Melanie."

Her cousin stiffened, and Caroline sensed Melanie was about to go into a long-winded explanation of how wonderful O'Ghill was, reminding Caroline of the last time she had visited before her father became ill. Though at the time, Melanie had stars in her eyes describing one of the tenant farmers' sons.

Hanging up another sheet, Caroline asked, "What ever happened to that tall, gangly, light-haired boy you were mooning after the last time I was here?"

Melanie dissolved into fit of giggles. "Lyman Stanbridge? I cannot believe you remember that. I thought he was so handsome, but he ignored my every attempt to speak with him. Lyman is still arrogant and has no reason to be."

"He was, what, two years older than you?"

"One," Melanie answered. "He's still gangly, and I daresay, I do not think he will ever grow into his feet."

"Really, cousin," Caroline admonished her. "He isn't a dog. He's a boy."

Melanie tugged her end of the sheet with enough force to loosen the clothes pegs Caroline had fastened. They refastened them together. "That is the whole problem. Lyman *is* still a boy at eighteen. O'Ghill…is a man."

"And too old for you, Melanie," Caroline warned.

"He cannot be that much older than me," her cousin protested. "Besides, I do believe I would do well marrying an older, experienced man."

Caroline bit the inside of her cheek to keep from giving her cousin any more advice. Melanie had never been one to accept it graciously. In truth, she would be more apt to ignore it. The four years between them may as well have been twice that for all the good it did when Caroline tried to give her cousin the benefit of her experience. To be honest, she had not had any experience with regard to relationships, other than promising to wait for her solemn soldier.

A dark thought filled her. There had been one other...*Humbolt*.

Though her brother's friends had been willing to attempt to charm her, they all seemed to be cut from the same cloth of arrogance. They purchased their colors, and spoke of the glory and medals they would receive when they returned after fighting in the Peninsular War. David Bantry hadn't thought of glory or medals, only of his duty to king and country. She remembered the day he had come to say goodbye. He had always been more reserved than the rest of her brother's friends. When he spoke, he meant every word.

As if it were yesterday, she recalled the way he held her hand to his heart and brushed a lock of hair from her forehead. He had touched the rim of her spectacles and traced the curve of her cheek and said, "I have committed every freckle on your face, your soft gray eyes, and your flame-bright hair to my memory. So I can pull them out and visit with you while we are apart." He asked if she would wait for him. When she said yes, his lips brushed hers. Softly, tenderly.

There was no point in thinking of what might have been. Their future had been taken from them. Mr. Humbolt, a solemn man seventeen years Caroline's senior, had been the only other to show interest.

Shoving the memory of him from her mind, she asked Melanie, "Do you have any idea how old O'Ghill is?"

Melanie shrugged. "It wouldn't matter. I have decided that he is the man I'm going to marry. No matter how many times he leaves the village." Her expression was one of willful determination. "He'll come back for me."

"And you know this how?"

"Are you deliberately trying to discourage me, Caro?" Melanie rasped. "I thought you'd be happy for me."

"Forgive me. I am not trying to discourage you. I'm trying to save you from heartache. O'Ghill has to be at least as old as O'Malley and the other men in the duke's guard."

"Do *you* know how old they are?" Melanie asked pointedly.

"Er…no. But from my conversations with O'Malley, I would say nearly thirty summers."

"Just what I need, a man with experience."

This time Caroline bit her tongue to keep from saying that Uncle Bertram was not likely to accept an offer for Melanie's hand from someone nearly fourteen years her senior. Then again, he might. Hadn't Caroline's father spoken to her and indicated should Mr. Humbolt offer for her hand, he would accept? She may be wrong about Uncle Bertram.

"Are you determined to smother my dreams because yours did not come true?"

Devasted at the reminder that her dreams had been shattered, she struggled not to give in to the thoughts of what might have been had the man she loved and had promised to marry returned. David and Neil had given their lives, the ultimate sacrifice, shattering her world and her heart.

Caroline had not given a thought to marrying since that day—until O'Malley unlocked her door, and she took notice of a man for the first time in four years. Now was not the time to dwell on her attraction to his deep voice and green eyes, or his kindness when he'd noticed she was cold and slipped out of his frockcoat, wrapping it around her. His scent tantalized her. She sighed and realized she was as hopeless as Melanie.

She shoved those thoughts aside to assure her cousin, "I would never squash your dreams, Melanie. I love you and only want the best for you. I am sorry if you have taken my advice the wrong way. I want only your happiness. If O'Ghill is who you want, Melanie, then I hope he returns your feelings and speaks to Uncle Bertram to offer for your hand."

Mollified, her cousin gave a regal nod. "Thank you."

"Melanie! Caro!" Caroline smiled as her uncle walked toward them from the barn. "You are not overdoing it, I hope, Caro."

"Not at all. Having a reason to be up and about this morning, instead of contemplating my circumstances, has done wonders for me."

"Washing the sheets?" Melanie squeaked. "You must be joking."

Caroline shook her head. "I miss having someone to chat with while doing the household chores. Mum and I always did them together."

Her uncle cleared his throat. "O'Malley left something for you last night, but I thought it best to wait until now to give it to you."

"Oh?" A frisson of anticipation swept up from her toes. "I cannot imagine what it would be."

The vicar reached into his waistcoat pocket and said, "Hold out your hand, Caro."

She did as she was told and felt her heart clench when he placed her mother's locket and father's pocket watch in her upturned hand. Tears welled up and spilled over. "How? When?"

"I did not press O'Malley for particulars, as he needed to return to his duties at Summerfield Chase."

"Did he say anything?" she rasped.

Her uncle nodded. "He said, 'The lass will be needing these.'"

She was overwhelmed with emotion: gratitude to O'Malley for retrieving the only tangible thing she had left of her parents, and longing to speak to him one more time, if only to thank the man. "Does he ever come into the village?"

"All of the duke's men take turns on patrol riding from the baron's estate to the village and back. They rotate, though I cannot say when he will be riding into town, especially after what

O'Ghill just told me. We may not see any of the duke's guard for quite some time."

"What did O'Ghill have to say?" Melanie asked.

"Your mother will need to hear this, too. Why don't we go inside and see if she has our tea ready?"

"We have one more sheet to hang," Caroline told him. "We'll be right in."

When he walked into the house, Melanie turned to Caroline. "Whatever it is cannot be good if no one from Summerfield Chase will be coming to the village for a while. Trouble must be headed our way…again."

They hung the last of the bed linens and carried the basket and clothes pegs inside. Storing them in the alcove just inside the back door, Melanie and Caroline paused before walking into the kitchen. Melanie held her finger to her lips, and they both stood listening to the conversation her father and mother were having in the parlor.

"I refuse to leave the vicarage and hide out at Summerfield Chase. How could you even suggest such a thing, Bertram? Do you not know me at all?"

"Dearest, I'm thinking of you, Melanie, Caro, and Olivia. If you do not go, how will I be able to convince them to?"

"We should send them without me. I am your wife and will stand by your side, as I have always done. Your parishioners need your guidance, especially if that vile man is headed our way!"

"O'Ghill will be returning in half an hour to escort you, Melanie, Caro, and Olivia to the baron's home. You will not stay here!"

"I am not leaving, but I agree that the girls need the protection of the duke's guard. Anderson is a blight on society and should never have been set free!"

Her husband finally agreed, "Fine. We'll just send Melanie and Caro with Olivia. They will be safer there."

Melanie tugged on Caroline's arm and they walked into the kitchen. Her mother walked in from the parlor and smiled.

"There you are. Thank you for hanging out the linens. With the soft breeze and warmer temperatures, they will be dry in an hour or two."

"We'll help you put them back on the beds when you are ready, Mum."

Her mother glanced over her shoulder and back. "You and Caroline will not have time to do that. You will be too busy packing."

"Packing?" Caroline asked, though she knew what her uncle intended. "But I just arrived."

"Circumstances have necessitated that we send Melanie, Olivia, and you to stay with the baron and baroness," her aunt said.

"Whyever would you suggest such a thing?" Melanie asked. "It is not as if we were close friends... We aren't even in the same social class!"

"That is not the point," the vicar said. "The three of you will be safer there."

Melanie moved closer to Caroline and linked arms with her. "We are not leaving you, Mum. Did you forget our conversation while we laundered the linens? You spoke of the care baskets we would help you deliver to those who are in need."

Her mother sighed. "Of course not, darling, but you need to learn to be flexible. I will handle that myself tomorrow."

"It will take more than half the morning to do so," her daughter protested. "What about your meeting with the new mothers at the inn? Olivia and I always help the mums by jiggling fussy babes and playing games with their little ones. Besides, Caroline was looking forward to joining us, weren't you, Caro?"

"To be honest, I was, Aunt Josephine," Caroline replied. "It has been so long since I have ventured out of our house to do more than visit the apothecaries." She could not keep the sadness from her voice, but fought and managed to hold back the tears pricking her eyes. Drawing in a deep breath, she slowly exhaled and counted. Counting helped steady her when she was upset.

"Bertram, I do hate to change my mind, but there is so much that we were to do in the next few days," Aunt Josephine said. "With the overabundance of rain recently, and the first crops of the season drowning, rotting in the field, so many in our congregation need our assistance. As long as Melanie and Caro stay together and do not wander off—"

The vicar interrupted, "Are you asking for a repeat of what happened a few weeks ago? Melanie and Olivia were with Mrs. Garahan, for Heaven's sake, about to take tea at the inn, when they were lured into that carriage. What is to say that Anderson will not do so again?"

"He fooled me once," Melanie said. "It will not happen a second time."

"I have learned to trust no one but family," Caroline added. "The exception would be to trust one of the duke's guard. I put my trust in O'Malley and O'Ghill and arrived safely here. I would trust them again in a heartbeat."

Before the vicar could respond, Aunt Josephine said, "Melanie, check the tea—it has to have steeped sufficiently by now."

"What can I do to help?" Caroline asked.

"Be a dear and stir the soup while I put the bread in the oven. We'll have the hearty soup and fresh bread for supper this evening."

When they'd done as Aunt Josephine asked, the vicar nodded to the three of them. "Have a seat."

Melanie and Caroline sat. "If you make me leave, Papa, I swear I will sneak out and walk back to the village!" Melanie said.

"You wouldn't!" her mother exclaimed.

"If there was one good thing that I learned from being abducted," Melanie said, "it is how to distract one's captors by screaming at the top of my lungs, before kicking them where it will do the most damage."

"Melanie!" her mother scolded, sounding appalled.

Melanie smiled. "Cornelius let us practice kicking him, but you taught us his last lesson, Caro...where to hit our target to bring a man to his knees."

"My brother wanted us to be safe," Caroline quickly explained. "As he would not be around to protect us when he joined his regiment."

Melanie laid a hand on Caroline's arm. "A lesson I put to good use."

"Really, Melanie," the vicar said, "this is hardly polite conversation over tea."

"But necessary," her mother said, "especially if they are going to be staying in the village."

⯈⯈⯈⯇⯇⯇

O'GHILL STOOD OUTSIDE the blacksmith's home, disbelief roaring through him as he stared at Miss Coleman. She refused the offer of protection! He scrubbed a hand over his face. "Do ye not remember what happened last time, lass? 'Twas yer kind heart and Melanie's that pulled the two of ye into that blasted carriage!"

"O'Ghill is right, Olivia," her father told her. "You need to accompany him back to Summerfield Chase. The guard will protect you and Melanie."

"What of Caroline? Shouldn't she be protected too, now that she is part of the Chessy family here in the village?"

"Aye. She will be coming as well," O'Ghill said.

To his shock, Olivia stamped her foot, turned to her father, and said, "I am not going."

What in the bloody hell was wrong with the lass? He remembered her tears, and Melanie's, when he and Garahan rescued them. He had wanted to wring the necks of the bloody bastards involved in their kidnapping and put bruises on them. O'Ghill nearly had, until Garahan reminded him of the pledge the men in the duke's guard had made. Even though O'Ghill was not a member of the guard, they *were* his kin, and he had accompanied Garahan on a rescue mission. Therefore, he had felt obliged to honor the pledge.

O'Ghill argued with Miss Coleman, but to no avail. The lass had brought on tears, pleading with her da to let her stay home with him in the village. The blacksmith agreed, and for the life of him, O'Ghill could not understand why the man had.

Resolved to convince the vicar's wife, daughter, and niece to accept the baron's offer, he made his way to the vicarage. He knocked on the door, and as soon as he was bidden to enter, he could tell from the expressions on the lasses' faces that they too had refused. What in the bloody hell was wrong with these women? Melanie was the one who'd swooned when Garahan mentioned his injury, and she had not even seen the blood! They were not as strong as his cousin's new bride, Prudence, though they seemed to think so.

He turned to the vicar's wife. "Are ye certain, Mrs. Chessy?"

She nodded. "We have so much to do, taking care of those who are in need right now. The first crop planted was destroyed by the recent heavy rainfall, and without our assistance temporarily filling their larders with food, they will go hungry. Bertram cannot possibly manage his flock without our help."

Melanie lifted her chin and glared at him—*glared*! He thought the lass was taken with him, and would readily agree with whatever he told her to do. Apparently, he'd misjudged the lass. "I see Olivia has not agreed either," he said.

O'Ghill grunted. "Coleman was ready to send her, but her tears stopped him." He stared at Melanie and then Caroline. "I do not suppose either of ye used that same feminine trick on the good vicar, did ye?"

Their fierce frowns and dry eyes answered his question.

A short while later, O'Ghill returned—alone—with verbal messages from the vicar and the blacksmith—he was to relay their thanks to the baron, but the women would not be accepting the baron's generous offer of protection at Summerfield Chase.

Bloody *fecking* hell!

CHAPTER NINE

O'MALLEY COULD NOT believe that not one of the lasses would leave their homes. Even with the threat of that bleeding bugger Anderson headed their way! Had they lost the good sense the Lord gave them? Did they not remember what they'd gone through? He shuddered, recalling the detailed report Garahan and O'Ghill had relayed to the baron. Every word had felt like a knife slashing deep. No woman should ever have to face what they had. How could they have forgotten so quickly?

He struggled not to shout that their fathers should have laid down the law and made them leave with O'Ghill. A glance around the room at those gathered and he sensed he was not alone in his opinion. "What of Miss Gillingham?" he asked. "Surely the only reason she stayed behind was because of her cousin."

O'Ghill shook his head. "Ye would have thought with all she'd encountered at the pawnshop, and then faced when the blackguard falsely accused her of stealing to the Watch, that she would have come willingly. But she refused, too."

O'Malley could not hide his surprise. "What did she have to say?"

"She would not leave her aunt and cousin to handle all of their duties without her. They were her family now, and she would stand strong with them."

O'Malley cursed beneath his breath.

Summerfield nodded. "I heartily agree."

The baron's even tone surprised O'Malley. "Are ye not in the least upset that the lasses refused to leave their homes?"

"If it was your mother, would she have left?" Summerfield asked.

O'Malley snorted. "Not on yer life—begging yer pardon, yer lordship."

"No need, O'Malley. You are always free to speak your mind and do not have to continue to beg my pardon," the baron replied. "You and the others have earned my respect, and that of my cousins, along with the right to speak freely."

As one the group nodded, and Flaherty sighed. "'Twas a heavy burden constantly worrying I'd be saying the wrong thing at the wrong time, yer lordship. I'm not used to dealing with Polite Society."

Garahan agreed and thanked the baron. "'Twill make our job easier if we did not have to constantly watch what we say to ye."

Summerfield's eyes widened. "Do you mean to tell me that you haven't been speaking freely since the day you accompanied Phoebe and me here?"

O'Malley shrugged. "Flaherty's right. We aren't used to mingling with the *ton*. We were born and raised to work our family's farms back home. Each of us has a talent that we used, hoping to lighten our parents' load, but in the end, we had to no choice but to come to England. The promise of coin to send home to ease our family's burden was a lure we could not refuse."

The baron met O'Malley's gaze first, then that of Garahan, Flaherty, and O'Ghill. "My apologies, men. I would not have purposely made your job protecting my wife harder than it already has been."

"Ye haven't—well, except for yer strict order to set a specific time when we practice to keep our bare-knuckle skills sharp." O'Malley glanced at his cousins. When each one of them nodded, he told Summerfield, "As Irishmen, 'tis ingrained in our blood to watch what we say and to whom we speak. But we have never been treated with anything but respect since we were hired by His Grace. We're thankful, and grateful."

"Aye," Garahan said. "And we will do whatever necessary to continue to protect his family."

"Do not forget that ye are included in our protection, yer lordship," Flaherty said.

"Even though I'm not employed by the duke," O'Ghill said, "ye have me word of honor to protect yerself and yer family with me life, yer lordship. Me cousin's vow to the duke became me own when I showed up on yer doorstep, and ye treated me as if I were a part of their number."

"Ye are, ye bleeding *eedjit*," Garahan reminded him. "Ye're our blood, therefore a part of us."

O'Ghill snorted and locked gazes with O'Malley. "Even the sainted O'Malley clan?"

O'Malley shook his head. "Aye, ye bugger, or have ye forgotten me ma was a Garahan before she married me da?"

"Distant cousin," O'Ghill reminded him. "Being as that is the case, I'd best hang around and lend a hand until Anderson shows his ugly mug." He cracked his knuckles, then turned and met the baron's steady gaze. "That is, if it is acceptable to ye, yer lordship."

"More than," Summerfield replied. "I'm glad to have you back, O'Ghill. Now that that has been settled, what are we going to do to protect the vicar's family and the blacksmith's daughter?"

O'Malley said, "We need a man in the village to protect them. As the lasses trust Killian, and Garahan's needed here, O'Ghill should be the one to guard them."

Summerfield agreed. "Excellent notion. With the added number of our footmen, and the sharpshooters from our tenant farmers, we shall be ready to fire the first volley across Anderson's bow."

Garahan chuckled. "I'm thinking ye mean over his horse's head, as we aren't at sea, yer lordship."

The baron frowned. "It is a figure of speech."

"Faith, we know it. But none of us are seamen," Flaherty added. "We're tied to the earth."

Summerfield shook his head, chuckling. "I did encourage you to speak freely, didn't I?"

"That ye did," O'Malley reminded him.

"Fair enough," the baron said before turning back to O'Ghill. "I'll pay for a room for you at the inn."

"Not necessary, yer lordship. Coleman offered meals and a bunk to bed down on at his shop anytime, if I lend a hand when he needs it."

"I'll also send you with enough coin to eat during your stay," Summerfield said.

"Thank ye, but again, 'tisn't necessary," O'Ghill told him. "Mrs. Chessy said I'm welcome to eat with them any time, as she can never repay me for bringing her daughter back safe and sound."

"Well then, it appears I have picked the man for the job. Is there anything you can think of that you need before you leave?"

O'Ghill frowned. "A note from yerself stating I'm temporarily on assignment working for ye, and that the lasses need to obey me." He rubbed his chin and continued, "There's a slight chance they may take umbrage at the fact that while they're under me protection, they need to listen to me."

O'Malley listened to the exchange and felt his temper simmering. *He* should be the one to protect Miss Gillingham—not O'Ghill. The vision of the feisty lass at the hands of the kidnapper, should he return, had him curling his hands into tight fists. When he realized it, he relaxed and flexed them. Now was not the time to feel territorial where the lass was concerned. Her safety was as important to him as that of the baron's family and the others who would be in Anderson's sights. *The fecking bastard!*

"Can you think of anything I have forgotten, O'Malley?"

The baron's question brought his thoughts back to where they should be, focused on the volatile situation about to explode, if and when the kidnapper returned to attempt another abduction. The blighter should have remained in custody and never been allowed to leave with Prinny. The ramifications of the man having been released, and solely because of his position in the bloody *ton*, weighed heavy on O'Malley. "I'm thinking O'Ghill may need assistance."

"In yer dreams," O'Ghill grumbled. "I'm well able to handle four women."

Garahan snorted with laughter. "Aye, but none of the ones ye're to protect have set their sights on marrying ye…except for one."

O'Ghill's face lost all expression as he grabbed for his cousin, but Garahan was quick on his feet and evaded him. "Ye'll want to watch what ye say, Garahan."

"And ye'll need to watch what comes out of yer gob around that lass," Garahan reminded him. "She's too young for the likes of ye."

"Have I said I'm interested?" O'Ghill demanded.

"Not in so many words." O'Ghill nodded, and Garahan added, "'Tis in yer eyes every time ye look at the lass."

"She's too young!" O'Ghill shot back.

"Aye, glad to hear ye realize it," O'Malley said before their words could escalate into something more. "Now then, I'm thinking we can either send one of the footmen with experience helping our guard, or one of the tenant farmers."

"I have heard that Stanbridge's eldest son is handy with a short-barreled pistol and rifle," Summerfield said.

"'Tisn't saying much, yer lordship," O'Ghill mumbled. "Anyone can fire a blunderbuss."

"Ah, but a rifle takes more skill, wouldn't you agree?" the baron asked.

O'Ghill grudgingly agreed. "Very well. Where do I find the man?"

"The Stanbridge family works his lordship's tenant farm closest to the village," O'Malley answered. He slowly smiled. "I heard recently that Melanie Chessy was enamored of the lad."

He was pleased to see O'Ghill's reaction—the fierce frown and the tightly balled fists at his sides.

O'Ghill ignored him and turned to Summerfield. "I'll be needing another missive from ye then, yer lordship, as I'm not an official member of yer guard and not every one of yer tenants knows me."

The baron returned to his desk, sat down, and penned the missives. He blotted and sanded them, and handed them to O'Ghill. "If you run into any problems, although I cannot imagine that you will, send word."

"Aye, yer lordship." O'Ghill stalked from the room without a word to his cousins.

"Is his anger a concern?" Summerfield asked O'Malley.

"Nay. 'Twill ensure that he keeps his mind on his duty and not the lass."

The baron frowned. "She is only six and ten."

"Aye," O'Malley replied.

"And well he knows it," Garahan said.

"Ye can trust O'Ghill," Flaherty added.

Summerfield drew in a deep breath and slowly exhaled. "Anything else we need to plan for?"

"There is one more thing," O'Malley said.

"Oh, what would that be?"

O'Malley glanced at Garahan, who nodded—they'd spoken of it earlier. "Ye may want to ask King to have one of his men on hand at Newgate, watching to see who, if anyone, visits the squire or his wife."

"Is that all?"

"Nay," Garahan said. "Ask King if he can have someone watch me wife's family. After how they treated Prudence all of her life, I wouldn't trust her sisters or her da."

Summerfield digested the suggestions before agreeing. "Let Timmons know that I have an urgent missive to send to London."

"Aye, yer lordship." O'Malley strode from the room. He was confident that they had considered every possible aspect to control a situation that could very well blow up in their faces.

As his ma had taught him and his brothers when they were small to never underestimate the power of a simple prayer, he said, "Lord, it's O'Malley again." He paused and could not remember if his ma had reminded them to be specific when praying. After all, he had three brothers and four O'Malley cousins. He started over as he covered the distance from the baron's study to the entryway where Timmons would be found this time of day. "Lord, it's *Thomas* O'Malley, the one with the *eedjit* twin, Eamon. Please watch over those we're guarding with our lives."

Timmons looked up at the sound of O'Malley's footsteps, and O'Malley thought of one more bit to add to his prayer: "Especially the feisty redheaded lass with the freckles and spectacles."

Satisfied that he'd remembered everything, and that the Lord would watch over the innocents they were protecting, he passed along the baron's message to the butler. O'Malley thanked him, then retraced his steps to the study, where the footmen were due to report momentarily.

With reinforcements, the duke's guard would be ready, prepared to stop Anderson once and for all! 'Twas a pity, O'Malley thought, that the duke had forbidden the men in his guard to kill those who preyed on His Grace's family. The duke believed in justice and relying on the British courts to handle matters.

But O'Malley believed in a much older form of justice... *An eye for an eye.*

CHAPTER TEN

THE VICAR STARED at his wife for a few moments before speaking. "I trust you realize that when I deem the time has arrived and it is no longer safe for you to be here, I plan to accept the baron's offer of protection...*before* disaster strikes a second time."

Her mouth gaped open, and he realized she had mistakenly thought he had accepted her decision and would not force them to flee to the baron's estate. His wife was partially right—he wouldn't force them, but he would personally *deliver* them to the baron's doorstep!

"Josephine, you do know that I love you and appreciate everything you do as my partner tending to my congregation." Her soft smile was her answer. The vicar continued, "This matter will not be brushed under the rug, nor do I feel it will magically disappear. You must understand that when I feel you are putting our daughter, niece, Olivia, and yourself in danger, I will pack you up, kicking and screaming if needs must, and drive the carriage-load of you to Summerfield Chase myself!"

Instead of the righteous indignation he anticipated, his wife closed the distance between them, wrapped her arms around him, and laid her cheek against his heart. "I love you, Bertram, and promise when you tell me it is time to leave, I will gather the girls—and drag them with me if necessary."

He blew out the breath he'd been holding and slid his arms around her. "I am delighted to hear it, wife."

⟫⟫✕⟪⟪

"WHAT DO YOU think that was all about?" Melanie whispered to Caroline.

"It sounded as if Uncle never intended for us to remain, but compromised. He'll insist on us leaving when it becomes too dangerous for us to stay here."

"What about what Mum said before about helping him?"

Caroline's eyes filled. "My mum would have said and done the same, though I am not certain she would have capitulated as quickly as yours." They watched her aunt and uncle from the back door where they stood with the basket of sweet-smelling folded linens. Caroline hoped to find a man someday who would trust her to make her own decisions, but would be ready to step in when, or if, he felt it necessary in order to protect her. Her heat beat faster, and she wondered… Could O'Malley be that man?

"Papa may be a bit gruff at times," Melanie admitted, "especially when Mum doesn't readily agree with him. But he loves us dearly."

Caroline shifted the laundry basket and deliberately bumped it against the back door, alerting the couple that they were returning from their chore. She was reminded of her parents when her aunt slowly eased out of her uncle's arms. Both couples shared a deep, abiding love and respect for one another. Proof of that was her uncle's agreement to allow them to stay in the village…at least for the time being.

"How long do you think my father will wait before he packs us up and delivers us to the baron's estate?" Melanie asked.

"Until word that Anderson is on his way arrives through the gossip chain that connects London to the inns along North Road," Caroline replied.

Her cousin sighed. "That's what I was afraid of."

"Thank you so much for bringing the linens in." Aunt Josephine smiled and waved them toward the staircase. "I'll be right up to help you make the beds."

"Melanie and I can handle the task," Caroline said. "Weren't you about to put on the kettle when O'Ghill arrived and distracted you?"

"Caro's right, Mum. We will make the beds and be down to join you for a cup, if that is all right with you."

"Thank you, my dears," the vicar rumbled. "We have something we wish to discuss with the two of you when you return."

Melanie led the way up the stairs, holding one end of the basket, while Caroline had the other. "We already know what they want to tell us. Can you think of a way that we can get around going to Summerfield Chase, Caro?"

"Eventually we may have no choice but to go," Caroline said.

"I realize that, but I need to be in the village to say goodbye to Killian when he leaves."

Caroline reached the top of the stairs and tugged on her end of the basket. "When did you start calling him by his given name?"

"Oh, right away," Melanie answered, "though only when it is just the two of us."

Frowning at her cousin, Caroline asked, "Just how often did the two of you meet and speak privately?"

"Not often," Melanie replied, tugging the basket toward her. "And before you ask, no, it was not his idea to meet privately. It was mine!"

"And he agreed with you? Did he not realize that anyone seeing the two of you alone could be cause for gossip, and possibly have forced your father to demand that O'Ghill marry you to save your reputation?"

Melanie giggled. "Of course not, silly. That was *my* plan."

"You would be consigning yourself to a life of unhappiness if O'Ghill does not care for you in that way. He is a grown man, and I cannot see him as one who would appreciate being trapped, forced into marrying a woman more than a decade younger than him."

"Are you saying that I'm not woman enough?" Melanie demanded.

Caroline bit the end of her tongue. She would have to take back her words and tread carefully, lest her headstrong cousin do something she, and O'Ghill, would regret. "Not at all. There was a young woman in our village who did just what you are suggesting, forcing the man she wanted to marry her. He did so with a blunderbuss pressed to his spine, and a few months later, he slipped away in the middle of the night."

Melanie's eyes widened before narrowing on Caroline. "But he came back, didn't he?"

Caroline shook her head. "He never did. He left behind more than his young wife... Lizzy delivered their babe seven months later."

Her cousin frowned and stared at her hands holding the basket's handle for a few moments. "They anticipated their vows."

"Yes."

"And he left without ever thinking she may be carrying his babe?"

Caroline noted the concern in her cousin's eyes and was relieved. "Aye."

"Did he not have a conscience? How could he leave her without his support, or considering the possibility that she would have his babe to raise on her own?"

"Apparently he did not, as he was never seen again. O'Ghill would ever act in such a way. But neither of us have any idea how he would react with his back to the wall, forced to marry. I told you about Lizzy because I wanted you to open your eyes and realize the world is far from what we've always read in fairytales, Melanie. Lizzy was a kind and a gregarious young woman... She reminded me of you."

"Was?" Melanie whispered.

Caroline's eyes welled with tears. She did not hold them back when she whispered, "Lizzy left her babe on her parents' doorstep in a basket, just like this one, in the middle of the night." The memory of the shock that reverberated through her little village swept through her. "They found her floating facedown in the pond by the church the next morning."

Melanie dropped her hand from her mouth long enough to ask, "And her babe?"

"His grandparents have been raising him these four years past."

"Did the man she coerced into marrying her ever return?"

"He was never seen again."

Melanie squared her shoulders and tossed her head. "A sad tale, Caro, but Killian would never act as that blackhearted man did." She tugged the basket out of Caroline's grasp and walked into the first bedchamber.

Knowing her cousin's mercurial temperament, Caroline followed her without a word. In silence they made the first bed, and the next two. When she could not stand the silent treatment another moment, Caroline said, "It would break my heart to lose you. I treasure your friendship, Melanie."

Her cousin was still miffed, but her temper had cooled. "I know that, but it bothers me that you thought you had to share such a tale of woe with me, thinking I am not old enough to understand the ramifications of what could happen if I encouraged Killian."

"Though it upset you, I would tell you again in a heartbeat if I thought it would sway you from running away with him."

"What makes you think he hasn't already asked?"

Caroline's mouth opened and closed without her uttering a sound.

Melanie swept past her, leaving the empty basket behind. With a heavy sigh, Caroline mumbled to herself, "That was my warning not to interfere, but I will press her until she confides if O'Ghill has asked her to run away." She shook her head at the thought, disbelieving it. Caroline had had to learn how to judge a person's character quickly after her father died. Sadly, she knew firsthand that there were those bent on taking advantage of a young woman alone, caring for her desperately ill mother.

Melanie may have grown up since the last time I was here, but I still have four years of life experience on her and will not let her toss hers away...or throw herself at O'Ghill, hoping he will catch her with open arms.

Resolved, she picked up the basket and headed down the stairs to the discussion she knew would revolve around O'Ghill and the danger headed their way.

Everyone was seated around the kitchen table after she stored the basket in the alcove.

"Thank you for taking care of that, Caro. Melanie should have put the basket away and not left it to you to do."

"I don't mind, Aunt Josephine," Caroline replied, taking a seat where a steaming cup of tea waited for her. "Thank you for the tea."

Her uncle passed the pitcher of cream. She thanked him and added a dollop to her teacup. Stirring it, she lifted her gaze to meet Melanie's, but her cousin quickly looked away. It would obviously take some time before she was ready to see reason.

"Now then, my dears," the vicar began. "We have discussed the situation fully while you were making the beds and have come to an agreement."

Melanie set down her teacup, and Caroline did the same. "What did you and Mum agree on?"

"When I feel the situation has become unsafe," her father answered, "you and Caroline will retrieve the bags you will have already packed with essentials for a sennight, and get in the carriage without a word of complaint or dissention."

"I see," Melanie murmured.

"Furthermore, you will not utter one complaint when I deliver the three of you into the baron's care and the protection of the duke's guard." Melanie opened her mouth, and her father raised his hand in the air. "The topic is closed. There will be no further discussion, nor will there be any hysterics when the moment arrives. In this I will be obeyed!"

Caroline marveled at the forceful tone her uncle used, as he so rarely had to employ it. Afraid to speak before her cousin had the opportunity to, she nodded. She saw the relief in his eyes.

"Although I may have disagreed earlier when O'Ghill was here," Aunt Josephine said, "your father and I are in full agreement in this. Neither of us will bargain when your lives—and Olivia's—are in danger."

"Yes, Papa," Melanie eventually said. "Caro and I will pack a bag after we finish our tea. Papa?"

Caroline ached at the frustration in the vicar's gaze. She sensed it had more to do with the horror of Melanie's abduction than anything else. He must have felt so helpless.

"Yes?" he replied.

"I'm sorry, Papa. I truly do not try to vex you."

His loud sigh had his wife pressing her lips together to keep from speaking, though Caroline noted the mischievous glint in her aunt's eyes and knew she had something to say. "I pray that it is a happy accident, daughter."

Melanie ducked her head and stared at her hands instead of her father. "I truly am sorry."

He cleared his throat. "Now then, we shall speak no more of vexing and disagreeing, understood?"

The chorus of yeses seemed to please him, and Caroline let go of the breath she had held waiting for the situation to be resolved. Thankfully it had, because Heaven only knew what the morrow would bring.

<hr>

CHAPTER ELEVEN

CAROLINE AND MELANIE were hitching the horse up to their carriage when the sound of hoofbeats pounding up the road reached them.

"Who is in such a hurry that they would gallop through the village?" Melanie asked.

"Someone on urgent business, no doubt," Caroline answered.

"Come on!" Melanie grabbed Caroline's hand and tugged her along as she raced toward the back of the house. "Hurry!"

Caroline straightened her skirts and brushed a wayward curl off her nose. There was no point in re-pinning the loose knot at the nape of her neck—it would only come undone the next time her cousin grabbed hold of her and dashed about.

The sound of a heavy hand pounding on the front door reverberated through the house.

"O'Ghill," they heard the vicar say. "What brings you here this morning?"

Melanie and Caroline moved swiftly, skirting the kitchen table as they went toward the front of the house.

"Orders from the baron—'tis in his missive. I've already delivered a missive to Mr. Stanbridge and will be delivering one more to Mr. Coleman as well. If ye have any questions, ye can find me at the smithy, where I'll be working for the foreseeable future."

Melanie's fingers tightened around Caroline's wrist. "Mr. Stanbridge?" she whispered. "What on earth does the baron want with him? He has three sons who won't need protection."

"I have no idea," Caroline whispered back. "I only met their son Lyman a few times during my last visit when you introduced him to me."

Melanie glared at her. "I am quite certain the missive has nothing to do with him." She paused. "Why do you suppose O'Ghill will be working for the smithy, when it sounded last night as if he would be working with the duke's guard?"

Caroline shook her head.

Melanie held a finger to her lips as they crept closer to the parlor. She had yet to let go of Caroline, who stumbled behind her.

O'Ghill's head lifted at the sound, and his gaze riveted on Melanie, then swung to Caroline, but he did not speak to either of them. He nodded to the vicar, then turned and mounted his horse to continue to the smithy a short distance up the road.

"Before either of you decide to investigate or eavesdrop on the missive O'Ghill was going to deliver to Mr. Coleman, I suggest you have a seat." The vicar pointed to the settee, waiting for his daughter and Caroline to be seated. "Josephine!"

"Coming, Bertram." His wife descended the staircase and asked, "Who was that at the door?"

"O'Ghill with a message from Baron Summerfield."

She frowned. "Well, what does it say?"

"I was waiting for the three of you to have a seat before I opened it, my dear."

"That was considerate of you." Aunt Josephine sat and waited for her husband to break the wax seal.

"Apparently the baron has sent O'Ghill with a note for Coleman, and me, indicating that O'Ghill and another will be protecting you. That is, until I relent and send you to Summerfield Chase until the danger is over."

"Who else will be protecting us, dear?"

"My guess would be Stanbridge's eldest son—he is a crack shot."

Melanie sagged against Caroline, who put her arm around her cousin. Her uncle took note of his daughter's reaction and frowned. "Wasn't Lyman Stanbridge the young man you spoke of night and day for an entire fortnight?"

"Papa!"

"Well, daughter?"

Melanie's sigh sounded put upon to Caroline, though she would never say as much.

"I may have mentioned his name a time or two," Melanie admitted.

"More like ten times a day," her mother said.

"Now, Mum—"

"Enough," the vicar said. "We have more important matters at hand than whether or not the young man in question—who did *not* show himself at our door to escort you to the harvest dance and left you in tears, refusing to attend without him—is now one of your protectors."

Caroline patted her cousin on the shoulder. "You aren't the only one he is charged with protecting, is she, Uncle?"

He nodded. "Correct. He and O'Ghill will divide their duties protecting the four of you. I would suggest you listen and do whatever they ask of you."

"What exactly do you think they will ask of us, my dear?" his wife asked.

"Most likely their first order will be to insist that you, our daughter, and our niece are not to leave this house unescorted."

"I see. When do you suppose that order will take place?"

"Immediately. Why do you ask?"

"Really, Bertram. Did you not hear me mention Melanie and Caroline will be helping me deliver care baskets to those in need this morning?"

Caroline noted her uncle's momentary confusion before he sighed. "It slipped my mind, given all that has happened since you mentioned it yesterday."

"Well, if we are to deliver all of the baskets in time for us to return and prepare the midday meal, we must leave in the next few minutes."

"Not without your escort."

"O'Ghill said he would be back, Papa," Melanie put in.

Caroline disagreed. "He said he would be at the smithy if Uncle needed him."

"That settles it, then," Aunt Josephine said cheerfully. "Have you hitched the horse to the carriage?"

"We have," Melanie answered.

"It is a lovely day, though it may be cooler riding in the carriage. Why don't you two fetch a shawl?" Turning to her husband, Aunt Josephine said, "We shall see you later, my dear." She motioned them toward the stairs, and they rushed to do her bidding. A few moments later, Melanie and Caroline returned with their wraps and headed to the back door.

"Mum, are you certain we should be leaving?" Melanie asked as she got into the carriage.

"Really, Melanie," her mother admonished her. "Such things should be left up to your father." The distinct sound of the front door opening and shutting reached them as they settled into the carriage. Aunt Josephine took the reins and smiled. "That will have been your father leaving to head to the smithy, no doubt to speak with O'Ghill."

THEY HAD JUST pulled up in front of their first stop on their list when the sound of hoofbeats pounded toward them. The vicar's wife smiled. "I expected O'Ghill a mile or so ago. No matter," she said. "He is just in time to help us deliver the baskets."

She turned and beamed at the frowning O'Ghill. "You are right on time, Mr. O'Ghill—we would appreciate your help making our deliveries."

Caroline noticed that O'Ghill ignored Melanie and her, but not her aunt, who was still smiling as she handed the heavy baskets to him. "I trust that the Stanbridge boy is guarding Olivia this morning," she said.

"Aye."

From his one-word answer, Caroline knew he was frustrated with them already.

"Will you be switching assignments tomorrow, sending the Stanbridge boy to guard us?"

O'Ghill grumbled, "I only just delivered the missive, Mrs. Chessy, when the vicar alerted me to the fact that the three of ye had left the vicarage without protection."

Caroline wondered how her aunt would handle the situation and had to bite her lip to keep from giggling when Aunt Josephine batted her eyelashes at O'Ghill and said, "I do apologize, but Bertram must have forgotten to advise that we had made plans to deliver the first load of baskets to those of our congregation that are in need. They all have little ones who will go hungry without our assistance."

O'Ghill's dark eyes widened. "I would never stop ye from doing yer good deeds, Mrs. Chessy, just ask that ye tell me in the future what yer plans are, so I can make certain ye'll be well protected."

"Of course," she agreed. "Why don't you join us for dinner tonight? Afterward, we can go over our plans for the week."

Caroline noted O'Ghill glancing at her cousin out of the corner of his eye before nodding. "Thank ye for the invitation. I'd be delighted."

All things considered, Caroline was relieved that her aunt had handled O'Ghill in such a way that he was obliged to offer his assistance for such a worthy cause and had not felt compelled to chastise them...especially Aunt Josephine.

Baskets in hand, they approached the first house on the list of many.

CHAPTER TWELVE

O'MALLEY STALKED TOWARD the stables. He could not have envisioned events transpiring the way they had in the last twelve hours. He'd completed the first late night patrol to the village and back, relieved that all was quiet. Never one to take things at face value, he nodded to Garahan, who was guarding the exterior of the baron's house, and headed toward the village for the second trip...just to ensure all was as it should be.

The second time he approached the vicarage, he saw the back door open and a woman rush across the yard to the barn. As the moon slipped from behind a cloud, its shimmering silver beam illuminated the figure. *Bloody hell!* What was the lass doing out of the house at this time of night...and still dressed? Had she not been to bed yet?

O'Malley tried to move slowly so as not to call attention to himself, but the lass must have keen hearing. Her head shot up, and her hand went to her ample breast. *Curse me hide for noticing.* He was close enough that she instantly relaxed her stance, dropping her hand. Dismounting, he walked to the picket fence separating the gardens on either side of the vicarage from the road.

As if in a trance, the lass slowly walked toward the gardens. As she wound her way in and around the herbs and flowers, the hem of her gown brushed against rosemary and lavender, releasing their fragrance into the night. With the fence between them, she asked, "What are you doing here at this hour, O'Malley?"

"I might ask ye the same, lass."

They stared at one another for a few moments before she glanced away. "I couldn't sleep."

Striving to keep the frustration and irritation out of his voice, he leaned over the fence and asked, "So ye decided to take a walk outside. In the middle of the night, without an escort, when there's a good chance a madman is headed this way?"

She lifted a shoulder, and he could not help but notice how the moonlight cooled her fiery locks until they were pale in comparison to the brilliant red that had captured his attention when he first laid eyes on her.

"Do ye have no concern for yer own safety? Is that what had ye traipsing off to the pawnbroker instead of sending a message to yer uncle from the inn?" Before she could form an answer, he continued, "He would have sent me sooner, if ye had."

"Why would he send you?" Caroline asked.

O'Malley straightened to his full height. "I'm head of the duke's guard at Summerfield Chase. The baron sets great stock in Garahan, Flaherty, and meself. He depends upon us to protect Lady Phoebe, and now that they have taken the squire's twin sons under their wing, the lads are included in those we protect."

"Mrs. Garahan's cousins?"

"Aye, lass. The scamps are cousins to Prudence."

A cloud passed over the moon, and for a heartbeat, he could not see her face. They were standing close enough that O'Malley noticed her shivers. The moon emerged, caressing her face once more with its gentle light. Her freckles were darker, while her spectacles cast a shadow over her eyes.

"Best go back in the house, lass. 'Tis damp. Ye'll catch a chill." When she made no move to obey, he added, "'Tisn't safe out here."

"You're out here."

"'Tis me job to patrol to the village and back."

"From what Melanie mentioned, the baron's estate is a few miles from the village. Shouldn't you be concerned that it isn't safe?"

He chuckled. "That's different—"

Before he could say anything more, the lass folded her arms beneath her breasts, calling his attention to them once more. He resisted the urge to let his gaze drop.

"If you are going to say it is because you are a man," Caroline rasped, "do not bother." She turned her back on him and retraced her steps to the barn, mumbling to herself all the while.

O'Malley tied his reins to one of the pickets and whispered to his horse, "Be a good lad." He opened the gate and followed in her footsteps, and was a step behind her when the lass spun around and bumped into him. O'Malley reached out to steady her and felt her trembling. The urge to soothe took hold, and instead of releasing her, he pulled her into his arms.

"O'Malley?"

"Ye have a way of staying on a man's mind, lass."

"I... I do?"

He tucked a loose wave of silken hair behind her ear and traced the tips of his fingers along the curve of her cheek. O'Malley gently tapped a finger beneath her chin until she raised her head and met his gaze. There was little color except varying shades of gray at midnight, but he recalled with clarity the vibrant red of her wavy hair, and that the sprinkling of freckles across the bridge of her nose and apples of her cheeks were pale brown. Drawn to her, he gave in to need and lowered his mouth to hers, pausing when their lips were a breath apart.

She whispered, "Thank you."

He chuckled. "Ah, lass, I haven't kissed ye yet."

Her soft laughter tied his guts into a hard knot. "Thank you for retrieving Mum's locket and my father's watch."

O'Malley splayed one hand against the middle of her back and drew her closer. "Ye're welcome, lass." He settled his lips on hers, pressing firmly while drinking in the soft feel of her supple mouth. Her lips warmed by degrees, and he inhaled the subtle scent of rosemary and lavender that clung to her from brushing against the herbs in the garden. Tasting the tangy-tart essence of her, he wanted more. *Needed* more.

He abruptly ended the kiss, carefully easing her out of his embrace, until he was holding her upper arms once more. "Ye pack a punch, lass."

"A punch?"

"Aye, feels as if ye just delivered an uppercut beneath me jaw." He shook his head and rubbed his hands up and down her arms. "Ye need to go inside—ye're cold to the touch."

Hands to her lips, she continued to stare without speaking.

Concern filled him. He knew he hadn't asked permission to kiss her, but he had paused. She could have pushed away. "Are ye wanting an apology?"

She shook her head.

"Well then, that's something." It dawned on him that it had taken the lass a few moments to realize she was being kissed before the stiffness left her. When it had, she melted against him, kissing him back. "I have to ask ye, and I'm meaning no disrespect, but am I the first to kiss yer sweet lips?"

Her eyes filled. "Nay."

Moved by her tears, instead of feeling jealous that he wasn't the first to kiss her, O'Malley rasped, "I did not mean to rush ye, lass. Forgive me."

When she burrowed into his embrace, he said, "I have to continue on me patrol. Flaherty's waiting to relieve me."

She gently pushed against him until he released her. "I'm sorry. I do not know what came over me."

O'Malley did not want to rattle the lass more than he already had by telling her he knew what had drawn her to his embrace. "Go on inside now, and bolt the door behind ye. The good vicar would have heart palpitations if he knew ye were wandering in his gardens at this hour."

She laid a hand on his forearm, and he felt pinpricks of heat through his coat sleeve. Did she realize her touch branded him as hers?

"Goodnight, O'Malley."

This time he let her go, waiting until she opened the door and he heard the bolt slide into place. He may not have been the first man to kiss her, but by God, he would see to it that he would be the *only* man from this moment forward!

He untied the reins, mounted his horse, and rode through the village. Half a mile out, he nudged his horse from a walk to a trot. The road ahead had a few dips that were not a problem by the light of day, but could be treacherous at night. When they reached the part of the road he knew was smooth, he leaned close to his horse's ear and promised, "There's a cup of oats waiting for ye, laddie." As if the gelding understood, he increased his pace to a fast trot.

Horse and rider rode the rest of the way to Summerfield Chase in silence, attuned to the shadows on the road and the forest creatures that roamed along the very edge where the fields met the woods. The hoot of an owl had him smiling. A mile away from the stables, he heard the call of a nightbird.

Pulling on the reins as he reached the stables, he rubbed a hand on his gelding's neck and dismounted. After leading the animal into the barn, he rubbed the horse down, watered him, and gave him the promised cup of oats. All the while O'Malley's thoughts were tangled, twisting him up with images of kissing the lass and tumbling down with her onto—

He called on his steely control and set those thoughts aside. Miss Caroline Gillingham was an innocent. O'Malley had no business thinking of her that way. With the trouble headed to their door, he had no business thinking of her at all. He had a vow to keep, and nothing would stop him from doing so.

A SHORT WHILE later, it was his turn to grab a few hours of sleep. Lying on his back staring at the ceiling, he knew that he would never be able to forget the feel of the lass, her smile, or her generous curves. He closed his eyes but could not stop thinking of her, so he started counting all of the bare-knuckle bouts he'd won to become champion. Finally, he was able to put the lass from his mind and steal a few hours of much-needed sleep.

A shout woke him. He sat up and ran a hand over his face as the call sounded closer this time. "O'Malley?"

"Aye, coming!" He tossed the covers aside, grabbed his frockcoat where he'd left it over the back of a chair, and headed for the door.

Garahan collided with him in the doorway. "O'Ghill sent word. Melanie and Caroline are missing!"

"They cannot have gotten far." He squinted at the horizon and saw the sun had barely broken over it. "The lass was in the garden about four hours ago."

Garahan grabbed him by the shoulder and bit out, "How in the bloody hell would ye know?"

"I was talking to her."

He let go of his cousin and shoved him backward. "Ye were supposed to be on patrol!"

O'Malley glared at Garahan. "I haven't even cleared the sleep from me eyes, and ye're thinking to tell me how to do me job?"

Flaherty joined them, his face unreadable. "Argue later. We have got to find the lasses."

Garahan put his foot out to trip O'Malley, who anticipated the move and leapt over his cousin's foot. "Ye're a predictable *eedjit*, Ryan."

"*Feck* that! What in the bloody hell were ye doing talking to Miss Gillingham at midnight?"

"Telling her she had no business heading to the barn at that hour and to go inside!" O'Malley curled his hand into a tight fist, but instead of tossing the punch his cousin deserved, he hit himself in the forehead…twice.

Garahan chuckled. "So it's like that, is it?"

"Like what?" O'Malley grumbled.

"She's got ye twisted up into knots so tight ye don't know whether to shake some sense into her or to kiss the breath out of her."

O'Malley snorted. "Something like that."

Flaherty raised his eyes heavenward and groaned. "*Feck* me, not another one."

Garahan put his arm around O'Malley's shoulders and said, "Now that yer head is clear, did ye see the lass go into the house?"

"Do ye think I'd leave without seeing for meself that she not only walked into the vicarage, but waited to hear the bolt slide into place and lock?"

Garahan grunted in response.

"What else did O'Ghill's missive say?" O'Malley asked.

"Mrs. Chessy heard a door close an hour or so ago, but thought she'd dreamt it."

"Where in the hell would the lasses be going before dawn?" O'Malley mumbled.

Flaherty rolled his eyes. "I have an idea where they've gone."

"Let's hear it, Dillon," O'Malley said.

"Me cousin Nora still likes to sneak out at dawn and head to the meadow." When his cousins stared at him, Flaherty shrugged, "Did ye forget about morning dew?"

O'Malley yanked on his hair. "Bugger it, Flaherty, just spit it out!"

Garahan groaned. "Ye could have the right of it, Dillon. Me cousins Siobhan, Brigid, and Aisling used to sneak out to a certain spot in one of the fields where a particular clump of wildflowers grew. They'd bathe their faces in the morning dew."

O'Malley was incredulous. "How old were they, and what in the bloody hell they would they do that for?"

Flaherty shook his head. "If ye don't recall that morning dew has been blessed by the *fae* and is sure to help a lass attract the man of her dreams, then ye've been gone from home too long."

"I didn't forget," O'Malley barked. "I never believed it."

"I'll stay here and speak to his lordship," Garahan said. "Send

Flaherty back if ye don't find them in the fields behind the graveyard."

Jaw set, O'Malley nodded. "We will split up and enter the village from different directions. We will find them!"

CHAPTER THIRTEEN

CAROLINE WIPED THE cool water from her face and laughed. "You did not just kick water in my face!"

To prove her wrong, Melanie did it again, this time wetting the front of Caroline's gown until it clung to her curves. Taking off her spectacles to wipe the lenses so she could see, Caroline asked, "What are you, twelve?"

To her surprise, her cousin spun around and plopped down in the middle of the stream. "Just because I am a month shy of turning seven and ten does not mean I have forgotten how to have fun!"

Caroline could not believe her younger cousin was sitting in the stream! As the sun began to warm the air around them, she was able to see the delight on Melanie's face as she dipped her hands in the water and poured it over herself. Her joy was a subtle reminder of all that Caroline had forgotten in the last few years. There had been no time for tea with friends, nor walks to the shops and back. No time for frivolity of any kind, no time to lose herself in one of her favorite books, nor to pause long enough in her task of weeding the herb garden to bend her head to the fragrant plants and inhale their soothing scents. War, death, and illness had driven every feeling but duty from her soul.

"It seems I *have* quite forgotten, Melanie."

As the words left her mouth, her cousin reached up, grabbed

Caroline's wrist, and yanked her down beside her. Shocked by the action, Caroline did not move fast enough to turn so she would land on her bottom—her cheek hit a rock hidden beneath the flowing water. Sputtering, she sat up.

"I'm sorry, Caro... Oh, Lord, you're bleeding!"

Caroline didn't feel anything for a few moments. Then the shock wore off and pain lanced through the left side of her face. She cupped her cheek in her hand and felt a warmth instead of the chill of the water. Lowering her hand, she stared at the blood smeared on her fingers.

"Do not move," Melanie ordered her as she stood, lifted her gown, and ripped a length of fabric from her chemise. Quickly folding it, she placed it on the gash in her cousin's cheek.

The injury began to throb, and Caroline lifted her gaze to meet Melanie's. Her cousin had been bright with laughter a moment before, but now Melanie shed silent tears as she attempted to stanch the flow of blood from Caroline's wound.

Neither of them realized that the blood had run down Melanie's arm and spread onto the front of her damp gown, nor that the deep wound in Caroline's face had slowly bled onto the front of hers. The wet fabric spread the blood until they both were covered with it.

"I can't stop the bleeding, Caro! What should I do?"

Caroline knew from tales of her brother's fatal head wound that the face and head bled profusely. She needed to pay attention and not let her thoughts wander.

"Caroline!" Melanie's sharp tone had Caroline lifting her gaze to meet the guilt-laced fear on her cousin's face.

"Help me stand up, Melanie. I need you to rip a wide band from my gown—not my chemise; the fabric is not as tightly woven." Melanie quickly did as she was instructed and folded the material into a thick square. "That should work," Caroline murmured. Her head felt just a bit woozy. "Hand it to me and help me out of the stream. We need to get back to the vicarage."

"Yes," Melanie agreed. "Mum will know what to do. Lean on

me, Caro."

Resisting the urge to close her eyes and sit down, Caroline let herself be led out of the water. When her cousin steered her toward the third field they had ventured to in order to dip their toes in the stream, her strength was fading and she stumbled. "Leave me here, Melanie, and go for help."

Melanie started crying again and wiped the back of her hand over her forehead, leaving a smear of blood behind. "I am not leaving you, Caro!"

"I don't think I can walk much farther. My head feels light and my stomach queasy."

"Lean on me," Melanie told her. "Together we will walk back to the vicarage—if we follow the road, it'll be faster."

Caroline wobbled and leaned a bit more of her weight on her cousin. In her heart, she knew neither of them would make it that far. Her cousin was shorter and had a slender build. Melanie would not be able bear Caroline's full weight, but Caroline was too occupied keeping the fabric pressed to her cheek to argue. Sticky, wet warmth trickled between her fingers, over the back of her hand and down to her elbow, which she braced against her ribs. While her cousin spoke of the tarts they would be baking when they reached the vicarage, a worrisome thought plagued Caroline: just how much blood could a person lose before it became fatal?

O'MALLEY SLOWED AS he was about to ride past the vicarage. The vicar stood on the front steps and rushed to speak with him. "O'Ghill went in the direction of the church," the older man said. "Melanie is fond of walking through the fields beyond the graveyard."

"Aye, that's what Garahan told us."

The urgent need to find Caroline and Melanie overwhelmed

O'Malley. He needed to leave now! But the vicar laid a hand to his arm, delaying him further. "There's a stream just past the third field—my daughter is fond of wading there."

O'Malley nodded. "Which way is quicker, the fields or the road?"

"The road. The stream is two miles ahead on the right. Find them and bring them home safely, O'Malley."

He didn't bother to answer.

The vicar released his arm. "I promise to keep them under lock and key until the danger has passed!"

"As ye're a man of the cloth, I know ye'll be keeping yer word."

O'Malley urged his horse into a fast trot until they reached the last home. "Hurry, laddie, we have to rescue the lasses." He gave the gelding his head and leaned over the animal's neck, murmuring encouragement and promises of carrots, oats, and apples when they found the women.

Rounding the bend in the road, he blinked—they were up ahead of him. As he drew closer, he ground his teeth together. Whoever had tried to murder the lasses would not live to see another day! He could not believe they hadn't heard him approaching. "Melanie! Lass!"

Melanie looked up. Her face was stained with tears. Blood was smeared across her forehead. The bodice of her gown was soaked with it. Had she had been stabbed or shot? He couldn't tell from this distance.

"Hurry! Caro's hurt."

O'Malley could not believe the vicar's daughter was not asking for help for herself when she was covered in blood. He took a closer look at Caroline, whose gown was saturated in it, too. But the lass had bright crimson trickling down her arm. He urged more speed from his horse.

He reached the women and leapt off his horse.

"I can't hold Caro up any longer." Melanie released her hold and let O'Malley lift Caroline into his arms. When her head lolled to one side, the makeshift bandage slid from the lass's fingers, and bright red blood welled up and spilled out of a deep gash on her face.

"Quick now, Miss Chessy—reach into me coat pocket. There's a clean cravat. Fold it up and hand it to me." Melanie did as he asked, all the while crying, prompting O'Malley to ask, "Who attacked ye?"

She looked up at Thomas with wide, tear-filled eyes. "*Attacked* us?"

He wanted to shout the question, but knew the vicar's daughter would not react well to being yelled at—the poor lass had been through enough trauma a few weeks ago and again today. He would not add to what she had to be feeling right now. "Where are ye hurt? Were ye stabbed or shot?"

"Stabbed?"

His anger roared to the surface, but he kept a tight lid on it. "Aye."

"Shot?"

"'Tis a simple question—if ye do not know, just say so."

"Neither. We were in the stream. Caro has forgotten how to enjoy life and have fun," Melanie rasped. "I tugged her so she would sit down in the stream with me. I...pulled her off balance. She didn't have time to turn around so she would be sitting..."

Her voice trailed off, and O'Malley knew what had happened. "She landed on her face."

Melanie nodded. "I didn't notice the rock until she lifted her face, holding a hand to her cheek."

"Yer damp gowns soaked up the blood while ye were trying to tend to her wound."

Melanie looked down, saw the blood, and swayed on her feet. "Melanie!"

The familiar deep voice had O'Malley shouting, "O'Ghill! Get yer *arse* over here!"

His cousin ran toward them. "God in Heaven! Melanie, who attacked ye?"

The vicar's daughter turned toward O'Ghill's voice. "Killian?"

"Aye, lass. I'm here." O'Ghill reached her side in time to catch her before she swooned at his feet. "Who attacked ye? Did they shoot ye? Where are ye hurt?"

She didn't answer. O'Ghill put the question to O'Malley. "What happened, Thomas? Did ye see either of the men who did this?"

O'Malley shook his head, with a glance down to make certain the fabric was still firmly pressed against the lass's face. "According to Melanie, they were in the stream—"

"What in the bloody hell for? 'Tisn't warm enough for a swim!" The sound of pounding hoofs had them looking toward the horse and rider gaining on them. "Flaherty! Move yer *arse!*" O'Ghill shouted.

Melanie opened her eyes and stared up at him. "You found us."

"I would not have had to," O'Ghill grumbled, "if ye had stayed put tending to yer chores, instead of gallivanting off to play in the stream like children." Melanie sobbed, and O'Ghill cursed under his breath.

Flaherty dismounted and looked from one woman to the other. "Shot?"

O'Malley shook his head, set Caroline on his horse, mounted behind her, and pulled her onto his lap. "The dampness of their gowns spread the blood from Caroline's wound. We need to get her back to the vicarage and have her wound tended to. 'Tis deep."

The men knew without asking that Caroline had lost a lot of blood. Her wound needed to be sewn back together.

"Flaherty, let O'Ghill ride in front of ye, holding the lass."

His cousin nodded. "Me horse can handle the extra weight for the short distance to the vicarage."

The men set off for the vicarage with their precious burdens in their laps.

CHAPTER FOURTEEN

WHEN THEY ARRIVED, Olivia was standing by the front door, waiting with Mrs. Chessy. The twin expressions of horror on their faces were telling—the two women had assumed what O'Malley and the others had. Before he could tell them not to worry, Mrs. Chessy lifted her chin and pasted a false smile on her face to greet them.

Olivia had a far different reaction—she wavered on her feet as her eyes rolled up in the back of her head. If not for the fast reflexes of Stanbridge, she would have crumpled at their feet. The lad swept her into his arms and followed the vicar's wife into the house. Once inside, Olivia came out of her swoon and Mrs. Chessy told Stanbridge, "Set Olivia on the chair by the window, Lyman." After Stanbridge did as the vicar's wife bade him, she cautioned him to stand by Olivia in case she felt faint again.

O'Malley and O'Ghill, followed by Flaherty, entered the house. O'Malley could not help but notice Mrs. Chessy's stilted movements, nor that her face was a mask of worry, as she glanced from her daughter to her niece and back again.

"I put the kettle on in anticipation of Melanie and Caro returning," she said, "but it appears that we'll need to heat more water." The woman's hands trembled as she took in her daughter's bloodstained gown, and that of her niece's. She started to reach for her daughter, then abruptly noticed the bandage

O'Malley held to her niece's cheek. "I'll ask what happened later. There is so much blood that I cannot discern at a glance—is Caro the only one injured?"

O'Malley answered, "Aye. It appears as though yer daughter was helping her to walk from the stream to the road. When we reached them Melanie fainted, not from injury, but from exhaustion supporting yer niece as they tried to walk home."

"And fear." Melanie, who had been silent the entire ride back to the vicarage, finally spoke. "This is all my fault, Mum."

"We'll talk about it later, dear. Are you able to stand?"

"Yes."

Her mother's sigh of relief was audible. "I need you to put on a large pot of water while I examine Caro's wound." Studying her daughter closely, she hesitated, then asked, "Are you able to do that?"

Before Melanie could answer, O'Ghill spoke up. "I'll fetch the water for ye, and promise to keep an eye on her, Mrs. Chessy."

"Thank you, Killian." There was a sharp intake of breath from behind them. "Olivia, I need your help, too. Please fetch the bandages and my healing herbs from the cupboard in the alcove by the back door."

"Of course, Mrs. Chessy. I'm so sorry—"

"Not now, my dear. We need to take care of Caroline and Melanie."

O'Malley was impressed by the way the older woman took charge. She reminded him of Mrs. O'Toole, the duke's cook at his London town house, and Constance, the cook at Wyndmere Hall. Both women had been instrumental in keeping order among the staff while both residences were under attack a year or so ago.

When Olivia returned with a fresh stack of folded bandages, Mrs. Chessy turned to O'Malley. "Press this on her wound while I wash my hands."

"Aye." He did so and noticed the lass flinch. "Lass, can ye hear me?" Caroline bit her bottom lip, and he knew she had heard him. "Are ye in too much pain to open yer eyes?"

"Dizzy," she answered. "Queasy."

"'Tis expected that ye'd feel that way, given yer injury," he said. "Keep them closed, lass."

The front door swung open, and the vicar stepped inside. "I've brought Dr. Higgins."

O'Malley felt the lass trembling. He leaned close and asked, "Do ye want me to stay?"

Tears gathered among her dark lashes, and he realized she wasn't wearing her spectacles. "Would you, please?"

"Aye." O'Malley turned to the vicar and the physician. "Miss Chessy told us that the lass—er, Miss Gillingham—fell facedown in the stream and hit a rock." Before either man could question him, he added, "The lass said she's dizzy and her stomach is upset."

"To be expected with blood loss—head wounds bleed prodigiously," the physician stated.

"I'm thinking the loss of her glasses may be adding to her dizziness, too," O'Malley said. "They must have slipped off her face when she fell."

"Thank you, O'Malley, Flaherty," the vicar said. "Please thank his lordship—"

Caroline rasped, "Please don't make O'Malley leave, Uncle. I asked him to stay."

"With yer permission, of course," O'Malley said to the vicar.

"I will need someone to hold her still while I cleanse the wound and determine how many stitches it will require to close it," the physician said.

O'Malley frowned at the doctor. In a low voice, he said, "I'm thinking ye may not want to go into any more detail, if ye don't want the lass to paint the room with her bile."

O'Ghill had just entered the room and snorted at his cousin's words. "Best listen to O'Malley. He's been known to empty his guts, if he happens to be nearby when someone else is in the process of doing so. 'Tis a sympathetic reaction, I'm told."

O'Malley was about to curse when he remembered he was in the vicar's home. He grunted instead and watched the lass's lips curve on one side. He leaned down next to her ear and whispered, "Ah, so the idea of me casting up me accounts amuses ye, lass?"

As he'd hoped, both sides of her tempting mouth lifted as she smiled. "You came to my rescue again. Thank you, O'Malley... For everything."

"'Tis me job to protect and defend. Rescuing fair maids comes under the protecting part."

He watched her thick, dark lashes flutter open a smidge more. "I wish I could see your smile, but without my glasses, your face is a blur."

"Ye'd best not be opening them any wider, then, lass. Ye don't want to become dizzy again... It'll make yer stomach churn."

She closed her eyes and sighed. "I hate to ask, but when you have time, would you promise to look for my glasses? It will take weeks if I have to replace them."

"That I will, lass. Now rest while the doctor and yer aunt finish washing up."

True to her word, the lass closed her eyes and was so quiet, O'Malley thought she'd fallen asleep until he positioned himself behind her head, prepared to place his hands on either side of her face to hold her still.

"Will you count the stitches for me, O'Malley?"

He had not planned on actually watching the physician sew her face back together. Now he would have to in order to do as she asked. O'Malley raised his eyes to the ceiling before asking, "Are ye certain ye want to know? I could just say 'twas a few, or more than a few."

Caroline licked her lips, and he followed the path of her tongue as it moved across her plump bottom lip. He stifled a groan, surprised when she answered, "No."

"No?"

"I would rather not have you tell me it was only a few, or more than a few," the lass stated.

Curious as to why, he asked, "Is there a reason ye need to know?"

Her eyes opened wide, searching his face before she squinted, then frowned. "It is *my* face, and I will bear this scar for the rest of my life. When people who have not seen me recently ask what happened, I will be able to tell them what occurred, and how many stitches were needed to close the wound." She dropped her voice to a whisper, adding, "I do not want them to speak of it—it would upset Melanie unduly, as she blames herself, when it wasn't her fault in the least."

She lifted a hand to her cheek, without thinking, and her fingertips brushed against O'Malley's. She dropped her hand to her side and continued, "I would rather my aunt and uncle be spared the retelling of something that should not be made much of. Accidents happen in our lives, and how we react is more important than the whys and wherefores. Aside from that, I would rather be the one questioned about what happened, as I was there, and will be able to tell anyone who asks the exact number of stitches required to set my face to rights."

Her aunt must have heard what they were discussing. Mrs. Chessy walked over to stand at Caroline's side. "Surely you don't mean that, my dear."

"I most certainly do. I remember those poor men returning to our village with scars and missing limbs after the Battle of Salamanca." Caroline's voice broke, but the brave lass never shed a tear.

Giving her and her aunt a few minutes to calm themselves, he changed the subject. "Well now, Miss Gillingham, do ye mean to tell me that if I asked to escort ye to tea at the inn, ye would refuse to go with me because of a paltry wound to yer lovely face?"

She blinked and stared up at him in disbelief. Then she closed her eyes and sighed. "I would never subject you to such public scrutiny."

He wondered why she did not mention the scrutiny *she* would have to face, as most people with visible scars eventually did. "I've gotten to know most of the shop keeps, as well as the innkeeper and his wife, and most are a friendly lot," O'Malley told her. "Besides, I doubt anyone would say a word when I escort ye, as I am head of the duke's guard."

"We need to close the wound on Miss Gillingham's face before infection has a chance to take hold," the doctor said. "Please place your hands gently, but firmly, on either side of her face."

"Aye, doctor." O'Malley was glad the lass had closed her eyes. He looked over his shoulder and frowned at the ghoulish way Melanie and Olivia stared at the lass. He met the intensity of O'Ghill's gaze. O'Ghill understood the unspoken request and escorted them from the room. Mrs. Chessy stayed behind as chaperone—not that he felt they needed one. They were in the vicarage, after all.

The lass flinched the first time the physician's needle pierced the skin of her swollen cheek. O'Malley wished he could take her place. He'd been sewn back together more times than he could recall and was immune to the discomfort.

He felt when she clenched her jaw against the pain, and heard the soft rush of air as she tried to use her breathing to control the pain. "Easy, lass—halfway there." She opened her eyes. The tears that welled up unmanned him. "Close yer eyes, lass, and focus on the sound of me voice."

When his words did not seem to help, he struggled to think of something—anything—that would take Caroline's mind off the jab of the needle and pull of the boiled threads. Finally, he thought of the times Ma would rock him after she had had to stitch up one wound or another. When she would rock, she would start to hum, and then she would softly sing.

He began to hum softly at first, and he noticed the lass relax her jaw. Encouraged, and since no one told him to be quiet, he began to sing the lullaby that was as familiar to him as Ma's warm brown eyes, and Da's brilliant green ones.

By the time Dr. Higgins had tied off the last knot, the lass was breathing quietly and on the verge of sleep. The physician reached for the ointment and bandage. "Now then, O'Malley, please lift Miss Gillingham up so I can wrap this thin strip of linen around her head to keep the bandage in place."

The lass opened her eyes and began to breathe rapidly. "Easy now, *mo chroí*—ye won't want to disturb the doctor's fine stitches," O'Malley said. "Now do ye?"

"I didn't realize he would have to cover half of my face with a bandage and hold it in place with a linen strip," she murmured.

"Ye need to cover yer wound for a few days, lass, and not be worried about it slipping off."

"I... Well..." she murmured. "I had no idea, but I suppose you must be right."

"Place that pillow beneath her head, would you, O'Malley?"

"Aye, Dr. Higgins." O'Malley did as the physician asked, grateful that the lass had closed her eyes once more.

"Mrs. Chessy, I'd like to leave instructions with you, if I may."

"Of course, Dr. Higgins."

"O'Malley?" Caroline whispered.

He leaned closer. "Aye, lass?"

"Could you stay a little longer?"

"I wish I could, but I need to get back to me post." Her tears would be the undoing of him if they continued to fall. "Let me see if I can convince O'Ghill to take me shift for an hour or two. That way, his lordship and his family will be protected."

She placed her hand on his forearm. "Never mind, O'Malley. Mayhap when it is your turn to patrol to our village and back, you might stop in and visit for a few moments."

"That I can do, lass." He lifted her hand to his lips and pressed a feather-soft kiss to the back of it. The coolness of her hand had him wishing he could stay long enough to hold her while she cried. He sensed she was holding on to her control for his sake, mayhap because she was used to keeping her tears to herself. A mixture of sadness and pride filled him. Caroline Gillingham was a lass he would be proud to claim as his own.

Claim as his own?

His head spun at the thought that just popped into his brain. Examining it from all angles, he realized that his heart was certain, and had been from the moment he unlocked the door to her room at the inn and she stared up at him. His mind slowly warmed to the idea. He'd need to speak to Garahan, to ask for suggestions as to how to go about courting the lass. Ma would split a gut, she'd be so happy—and surprised—that O'Malley would even consider courting a lass. He hadn't since he left Ireland.

His decision made, he gave a slight tug on her hand until she met his gaze. "Promise ye'll do whatever the physician tells ye to, and that ye won't argue with yer aunt when she's standing beside ye, tapping her toe waiting for ye to finish every drop of the calves' foot jelly ye'll no doubt be eating for the next few days."

Caroline made a face, as if she recalled how vile the remedy tasted. The freckles on her scrunched-up nose distracted him. "I promise."

He nodded. "Then I'll be leaving ye in the excellent care of Dr. Higgins and yer aunt."

"You promise to stop by tomorrow?"

He rubbed his chin and went over the patrols for tomorrow in his head. "If I can convince Flaherty to take me midnight shift, I could take his early morning shift—not the dawn shift."

The lass flinched in pain before thanking him. He wished he could take the pain away, but she would have to navigate the road to recovery and all that went with it. He would be able to visit with her, but as he did not possess a magic wand, or crock of gold, he would be unable to take her pain as his own.

He pushed aside the feeling of helplessness and turned to the vicar's wife. "Would ye mind if I knocked on yer door tomorrow after breakfast, Mrs. Chessy?"

"Not at all, O'Malley. Caro will be looking forward to seeing you."

"Thank ye, Mrs. Chessy. Lass?"

Caroline opened her eyes. "Yes?"

"Twenty," he rasped.

She frowned for a moment and then understood he referred to the number of stitches. "I will have no trouble remembering the number, as it's my age."

Though he had not asked outright, he was relieved that she was older than he thought her to be. "When is yer birthday, lass?"

"In a few weeks."

"Rest now, lass."

"I will. Thank you, O'Malley." She started to close her eyes, and he breathed a sigh of relief now that the worst was over.

"Ye're more than welcome, *mo chroi*."

Her eyes opened and met his. "You said that before. What does that mean?"

"Me heart."

The lass's mouth fell open, and she made an endearing humming sound before she whispered, "Your heart?"

He grinned. "Aye, lass."

She smiled. "Goodbye, *mo chroi*."

O'Malley was still smiling when he thanked the physician and made his way outside. Flaherty's horse was missing. He hadn't noticed his cousin leaving, but Flaherty must have made the decision to report back to his lordship. The lasses had been found, safe and more or less sound. Flaherty would no doubt explain why O'Malley had needed to stay.

"I'll be courting the lass," he told his gelding as he mounted. "Sweeping her off her feet."

"Does that mean ye intend to marry her?" O'Ghill asked, walking toward him.

Bugger it—O'Malley hadn't heard his cousin approaching. "I suppose it does."

O'Ghill grinned. "Well now, I wouldn't celebrate until ye're certain the lass will have ye."

His words were like a blow to the solar plexus, but O'Malley managed not to show how deeply they affected him. "The lass is partial to me."

"We'll see how she feels about ye in the morning."

O'Malley grunted. "Do ye have anything I need to report to his lordship?"

"Nay."

O'Malley stared at his cousin for a few moments before saying what had to be said, though it irked him to do so. "Thank ye for staying on to help watch over the lasses, Killian. It means more than ye know, that ye'd willingly step in to a job ye didn't ask for—working with the likes of me."

O'Ghill snorted with laughter. "Well now, 'tis pure pleasure working with one of the *sainted* O'Malleys again."

O'Malley shook his head. Leave it to O'Ghill to take the heartfelt thanks he'd offered and make light of it. He was chuckling to himself as he rode back to Summerfield Chase.

CHAPTER FIFTEEN

"**W**HAT DO YE mean, no one has seen or heard from Anderson?" O'Malley could not believe both King's and Coventry's men had lost track of the man.

The baron frowned. "I just sent off two missives asking that question. Obviously, our current course of action does not change simply because Anderson managed to elude the men following him. We will not pull back on our protection detail, nor will we relax our vigil."

"I'm relieved to hear ye say as much, yer lordship. If ye had suggested it, I would have talked ye out of it. We'll need to be on guard. Anderson may have stopped along the way and changed his mode of transportation, possibly even disguised himself."

The baron clasped his hands behind his back and paced in front of the terrace doors.

O'Malley followed Summerfield with his eyes, taking it all in: the frustration in his lordship's steps. The taut muscles in his face. The baron paused to watch his wife lying on the fainting couch, prompting O'Malley to wonder at which point the baron had known he would give his life for Lady Phoebe. When she had been abducted en route to Sussex, and Summerfield, himself, and the others had rescued her? If not that, was it the bravery she displayed attempting to free the baron when he was kidnapped? Whichever event, it had been the catalyst that brought the two of them together, determined to marry...no matter who objected.

Although O'Malley worked for the baron, he did not feel comfortable asking such a personal question.

He was relieved when the baron gave in to Lady Phoebe's request to sit on the terrace, and had two footmen carry the couch downstairs to place on the terrace overlooking their gardens. Her ladyship had been far too pale since her injury.

As O'Malley studied the lady he had sworn to protect, and would give his life for, his worry abated. She was recovering from her injury, wrapped in a blanket to keep the slight breeze from giving her a chill, soaking up the late spring sunshine.

He curled his hands into fists at his sides, thinking of another woman who'd recently been injured, although not by the blackguard he suspected was headed toward their village of Summerfield-on-Eden...but by her exuberant younger cousin.

O'Malley was about so say how well her ladyship looked when the baron spun around and walked over to stand beside him. "How was Miss Gillingham feeling when you stopped to check in on her and Miss Chessy earlier this morning?"

"Miss Chessy was helping her ma in the kitchen when I arrived. Miss Gillingham was on the settee, where she apparently spent the night...sitting up."

"Did they physician advise her not to lie down?"

"I asked her the same question. She said she was afraid she would roll over and press on her cheek."

"Ah, understandable, but not conducive to a good night's rest. How did she look to you?

O'Malley swallowed the words on the tip of his tongue. He was certain the baron did not want to know that the pain lingered in her soft gray eyes, cooling the warmth he had grown accustomed to seeing. "The swelling has gone down, and there's a bit of bruising."

Summerfield nodded. "The vicar and Mrs. Chessy will summon the physician if they suspect there is a hint of infection or if their niece is not healing as expected. Was Miss Gillingham happy to see you this morning?"

"Aye, yer lordship. Poor lass started to smile, then had to bite on her lip to keep from doing so. The doctor warned that she has to be careful not to move her facial muscles too much until the rest of the swelling goes down. It tugs on the threads and could open one of the stitches."

"Best be cautious picking topics to speak about when you see her tomorrow," the baron advised.

O'Malley hesitated. "I was not planning to see her tomorrow, since I already switched a shift with Flaherty to fit a quick visit into me patrol to the village and back this morning. I won't be shirking me duty to make a habit of visiting when I should be attending to me job."

"What if I ordered you to?" Summerfield asked quietly.

O'Malley's shoulders slumped. There was no way he could ignore a direct order. "Do ye mind if I ask why ye would?"

The baron laid a hand on O'Malley's shoulder. "Because I see the same look in your eyes when you speak of Miss Gillingham that I used to see reflected back at me in my looking glass after meeting Phoebe." Dropping his hand, he said, "We cannot ignore what our hearts tell us any more than we can ignore a cry for help when we have the ability to lend our aid. Every one of the married men in the duke's guard have managed to balance their duty to His Grace with their wives and babes. I see no reason you could not do the same."

O'Malley was shaking his head. "'Tisn't like that at all, yer lordship." How could he put into words the muddled feelings he felt where the lass was concerned? *Protective. Dazzled. Frustrated. Charmed.* "Ye see, I was after making the lass smile to take her mind off the scar she's worrying she'll have."

"How exactly did you hope to make her forget? By visiting her whenever time allowed?"

"I was thinking to discuss it with ye first, but I have asked her to tea at the inn when she's able to remove the bandage. The wrapping is cumbersome and would have all heads turning to gawk at the poor lass, whispering about what happened to her and speculating as to what the scar will look like."

"So, you are concerned for what others may say about her and how they may treat her."

O'Malley frowned, then admitted, "Aye, that's part of it."

"I see. And when you visited with her this morning, you promised to take her to tea as soon as the bandage comes off. It sounds as if you have feelings for her and are, in your own way, courting Miss Gillingham."

The knock on the door interrupted O'Malley's reply.

"Enter."

"Begging yer pardon, yer lordship, but I could not help but overhear ye speaking of Caroline and me cousin," O'Ghill said as he joined O'Malley and the baron.

"Do you have information about Miss Gillingham?" Summerfield said.

O'Ghill locked gazes with O'Malley. When O'Malley shook his head, O'Ghill ignored the warning, grinned, and said, "Me cousin intends to sweep Caroline off her feet and marry her."

The baron looked at O'Ghill and then O'Malley. "Congratulations, O'Malley. When do you plan to ask Miss Gillingham?"

"I haven't begun to court the lass yet!"

"Best get to it, O'Malley," the baron warned. "With Anderson giving King and Coventry's men the slip, he could arrive here any day. Don't you want her to have the protection of your name?"

"Aye," O'Ghill agreed. "Ye'll not be wanting yer intended to be in the thick of things, now would ye?"

O'Malley groaned. "I'd best be at me post, yer lordship."

To his frustration, O'Ghill followed him out of the room. Giving in to the emotion, O'Malley shoved his cousin with his shoulder. O'Ghill snorted with laughter as he followed O'Malley down the hallway.

"Ye won't be laughing if Anderson gets his hands on Melanie again," O'Malley warned.

O'Ghill's face lost all expression. "He'll be a dead man walking if he touches one hair on her head."

"Are ye planning to court Melanie?"

"She's too young."

Turning the tables on his irritating cousin, O'Malley agreed, "Aye, but yer heart knows what it wants, despite her age, O'Ghill. What are ye going to do about it?"

"I'll be staying until Anderson makes his move, and we capture the bloody bugger. That's it."

"That doesn't answer me question about Miss Chessy," O'Malley said.

O'Ghill kept pace as O'Malley walked toward the door to the servants' side of the house and yanked it open. "What do ye expect me to do?"

O'Malley spun around and got right in his cousin's face. "Tell the lass how ye feel! Life is too short to let the other half of yer heart slip away from ye because of a small thing like her age. Did ye forget there are plenty of lasses back home who marry at the same age?"

"Not as many as in our parents' time," O'Ghill reminded him. "Besides, why didn't ye say this to his lordship? Have ye even told Caroline how ye feel?"

"In a way." O'Malley figured the midnight kiss they'd shared should have spoken volumes to the lass. "I'm thinking the vicar's daughter knows her heart. I've seen the way she looks at ye when she thinks no one's looking."

Killian shoved Thomas into the wall. "And I noticed the way Caroline watches yerself when ye aren't paying her any mind."

A warmth slowly seeped into O'Malley's gut and wrapped around his heart. "Her eyes are the color of morning mist. I have to watch meself, else I get lost in their soft gray depths."

"Ye'd best be following yer own advice, O'Malley, before the lass slips out of yer hands."

"What if she thinks I'm only courting her because she was injured?"

"Why in the bloody hell would she think that?" O'Ghill demanded.

"I was trying to distract her to keep her from thinking about her stitches and asked her to tea. 'Tis a concern that she'll try to hide in the vicarage even after she heals."

"Ah, then ye don't feel more than friendship for the lass?" O'Ghill asked.

O'Malley groaned. "I cannot close me eyes at night without seeing her soft smile, her glorious red head, freckles, and spectacles. I can't decide if I want to claim her, or if I love her."

"Ah, so ye do have feelings for Caroline."

"Aye. They've got me twisted up inside."

"How deep a hold does she have on ye?" O'Ghill asked.

O'Malley had to admit, "Down to me bones."

"Ye're in love, boy-o."

O'Malley snorted. "How would I know? I've never felt this way before." When O'Ghill moved to stand in his way, O'Malley elbowed him aside. "I'm late for me shift on the rooftop. Why aren't ye in town guarding the vicarage?"

"His lordship decided we needed to rotate shifts there as well. Did he not mention it?"

O'Malley grumbled, "We spoke of other things."

"Ah, that explains it. He knew I would be telling ye," O'Ghill replied. "When ye have the village patrol, ye'll be staying at the smithy, and I'll return here to take yer post for the day."

O'Malley's eyes nearly bugged out of his head. He would be able to see the lass and keep her spirits up while she healed. Gut-punched, he rasped, "Thank ye, Killian."

O'Ghill nodded. "Me pleasure, Thomas."

They parted, going their separate ways. O'Malley could not wait to stop at the vicarage and speak with the woman who had yet to realize she held his heart in her hands.

CHAPTER SIXTEEN

O'MALLEY KEPT HIS horse at a trot through the heavily wooded section as he neared the village. He was anxious to see how the lass fared this morning. Hopefully, she had been able to sleep.

He hadn't. The worry that they had not heard from Coventry or King, after the missive advising that their quarry was headed north, plagued him. It had been two days without a word. The baron expected to receive an update soon. Until then, they would continue with their shifts in the village, guarding the vicar's wife, daughter, and niece, and the blacksmith's daughter. At Summerfield Chase, they would continue their increased protection guarding Lady Phoebe, Prudence and her twin cousins, and the female staff members.

Vigilant, he scanned the area on either side of the road, slowing his gelding's pace as they rode past the heaviest section of forest. Satisfied that all was as it should be, O'Malley rode to the spot where he'd found Melanie and the lass, and followed the well-worn path that led to the stream where Miss Gillingham had been injured. He planned to find and return her spectacles.

Up until his cousin Darby Garahan had suffered an injury to one eye, O'Malley had not given much thought to his vision. After Ryan Garahan shared the news about his brother's loss of sight, it had never been far from O'Malley's mind. Knowing that it was possible the lass's dizziness and queasiness were due to her lack of spectacles, he had to do what he could to help her. He had promised to look for them. So look he would.

Slowing his mount's pace to a walk, O'Malley noticed clumps of wildflowers on either side of the path. He'd pick them after he found what he was looking for. He tilted his head to one side, listening for the musical sound of water flowing over rocks. Knowing the lass could have lost her spectacles anywhere between here and the stream itself, he dismounted. It would do no good to find them only to step on them.

He scanned the ground as he led his horse deeper into the woods. Around a bend in the path, the stream meandered along its way, happily flowing over rocks and around branches that had fallen long ago. He closed his eyes and listened to the soothing sound, until his horse nudged his arm, calling his attention back to the task at hand.

"Right ye are, laddie. There's a lass who will be delighted when we find and return her lenses. Why don't ye nibble on the patch of grass on the other side of that boulder while I search in and around the stream?"

The sun's rays glinted off the water where the trees thinned out. O'Malley searched there first, knowing that as long as the lenses were intact, they would reflect the sunlight, making them easier to spot. Though he was tempted to remove his boots, he didn't want to risk slicing the bottom of his foot on a sharp rock. The duke's guard could not afford to be a man down at this crucial point.

He hopped from rock to stump to fallen tree and back, making his way down the stream until he noticed something white under the water. Bending down, O'Malley carefully scooped out what appeared to be a length of torn fabric. Quite thin and soft. Though the fabric had been underwater for more than a day, the faint rusty-red stain remained. *Blood!*

Moving a rock in the streambed, he freed the fabric, wrung it out, and tucked it in the pocket of his frockcoat. He straightened and was about to step on the next large rock poking out of the water when he noticed the outline of what had to be the lass's spectacles!

He reached down and carefully pulled them out of the water, hoping the lenses were still intact. If not, he would see if he could locate them too. The frames were bent, and he carefully manipulated them back into shape. Other than that, her spectacles were in one piece. Elated that Caroline would be able to see clearly again, he tucked them in the pocket of his waistcoat, turned, and made his way back along the edge of the stream.

"Time to pick a few flowers," O'Malley told his horse. He used to bring clutches of wildflowers from their fields home to his ma. She'd always set them in her best pitcher and put them on the windowsill facing east, so the sunlight would shine on the flowers every morning. He slipped the knife from its sheath on his belt to cut the flowers.

Holding the long-ago memory close to his heart, he wondered what Ma would think of Miss Gillingham.

Soon he had enough flowers to divide between Mrs. Chessy, Melanie, and Caroline. He added a few more, on the outside chance that Olivia would be at the vicarage when he arrived.

More than pleased that he'd been successful, he whistled to his gelding, who was a few feet away from where he'd left him grazing, drinking from the stream. "The lass will be happy that we found her spectacles—and picked flowers for *all* of the lasses."

Before he mounted, he wiped the blade clean on the hem of his coat and tucked it into the sheath. O'Malley had carried the two blades since leaving home—one on his belt, and one in his boot. He only carried his rapier when they had been under threat of attack. 'Twas his favorite blade other than his knives.

"Off we go, laddie." In the saddle, he leaned down to remind the animal, "There'll be oats waiting for ye at the vicarage." His horse's ears twitched as he headed back along the path. Reaching the road, O'Malley urged the horse into a trot and then faster, eager to return the spectacles to the lass.

"O'Malley!"

He looked up and waved to the vicar as he reined in his horse and dismounted.

"I see you come bearing gifts. Mrs. Chessy is fond of flowers."

O'Malley grinned and patted his waistcoat pocket. "That's not all. I found yer niece's spectacles.

The vicar sighed. "Poor Caro. This will cheer her up."

"Did something happen?"

"She did not sleep well. Mrs. Chessy and I took turns checking on her last night. Tonight we are hoping she will sleep upstairs in Melanie's room. When I went out to the barn a little while ago, she was in sore need of a nap."

"'Tisn't quite ten o'clock in the morning," O'Malley told him.

"Time is not the issue here—her needing rest is."

O'Malley nodded. "I see yer point. Mayhap a wee spot of tea and something sweet, and a small clutch of wildflowers, will improve her disposition. She cannot help but feel things more deeply, as she is grieving. I know I did when we lost me Uncle Patrick."

Vicar Chessy studied O'Malley for a few moments before agreeing, "Wise words, and ones that should be in the front of my mind, given the number of years I have been tending more than one flock." He patted O'Malley on the back and said, "Why don't you head into the house, while I settle your horse in the barn?"

"I promised him a cup of oats, if ye have them."

"An excellent treat to have for your horse. Would he like a carrot as well?"

"Ye'll be spoiling him, vicar. Thank ye."

O'Malley was about to knock on the front door when the vicar called out, "I believe Josephine baked cream tarts early this morning in anticipation of having guests for midmorning tea."

O'Malley grinned. "I shall tell her ye'll be right in."

"Aye, just as soon as I take care of your mount for you. Hurry, Caro could use some cheering up."

He raised his hand to knock on the door, but it swung open

before he could. "There you are, O'Malley." Mrs. Chessy appeared relieved to see him. "We have been trying to think of ways to distract Caro all morning. She's a bit unsettled and too quiet. She did not sleep well last night."

"Aye, that's what the vicar said. He told me to come in and deliver me flowers…and something the lass needs that just might lighten her mood."

"Oh?" the vicar's wife said. "And what might that be?"

"Ye'll see. I want to surprise her."

He stood in the doorway to the parlor and felt the sadness coming off the lass in waves. Her head was leaning against a pillow, and her eyes were closed. Wondering if she was awake, he approached the settee, watching for a sign that she heard his footsteps. When a tear fell from the corner of her eye, he called to her, "Lass?"

Her eyes shot open, and she turned to face him. "O'Malley! I thought something came up and you weren't going able to stop by this morning."

"As a matter of fact, something did come up." He reached into his waistcoat pocket and withdrew her spectacles.

She squinted, and then her face relaxed. "You found them? Were you able to find both lenses?"

"Aye, they were still in the frames, intact. Hold still, and I'll put them on ye." Carefully, as if she were fragile as glass, he slipped them onto her face. Fortunately, the gash was just below her cheekbone, parallel to her jaw line. "This may not work, lass—the bandage is a bit bulky." As he said those words, a puff of air brushed against his lips and he realized how close their faces were. His gaze riveted to her soft gray eyes, which widened, then she blinked twice.

He swallowed the desire tearing up his throat. "Forgive me, lass. I was trying to see if they'd fit. Mayhap we can ask Mrs. Chessy if we can use a thinner bandage, as there doesn't seem to be any seepage from yer wound."

"I…" She paused and licked her lips, drawing his gaze to the plump bottom one. The urge to nibble on it had him by the *bollocks*. He cleared his throat and eased back as Mrs. Chessy entered the parlor with a tea tray.

"You found her spectacles!" The vicar's wife set the tray on a side table and walked over to where Caroline was seated. "You must feel better, dear, being able to see clearly again."

"Thank you for finding them, O'Malley."

"Ye're welcome, lass." He turned and found Mrs. Chessy studying him. Trying to ignore the intensity in her gaze, he asked, "Do ye think we can change out her bandage for a thinner one?"

She nodded. "Her spectacles would fit better. O'Malley, would you kindly fetch a bandage from the stack on the table by the window? I decided to keep them handy."

"I haven't washed me hands yet, and they were in the stream."

"There's hot water in the pitcher on the sideboard and a round of soap next to the wash bowl."

"I'll be right back." O'Malley washed his hands thoroughly, then dried them and walked into the parlor. Locating the stack of folded linens, he selected two from the top and brought them to the vicar's wife. "Is this what ye had in mind?"

"Yes, that will do nicely." Turning back to her niece, she untied the thin strip of linen the physician had wrapped around Caroline's head to secure the bandage to her face. "The ointment Dr. Higgins applied to your wound seems to have helped, Caro. The redness and swelling are all but gone."

The expression on the lass's lovely face blossomed from hesitant to happy. "I'm relieved to hear that. Thank you, Aunt Josephine. I confess, I was worried about the possibility of infection."

"We'll hold off tending to your wound until after you and O'Malley share a nice cup of tea." Mrs. Chessy smiled, adding, "And we'll stuff him with a few of my cream tarts before we send him on his way. What do you say to that, Caro?"

O'Malley was transfixed watching the expressions flit across the lass's face. Her smile was not hampered by the swelling, which had all but disappeared. Relief swept up from the soles of his boots. He hated to see her suffering.

"I'm not sure how many tarts O'Malley could consume," she said.

He chuckled at the idea that he could have as many tarts as he could eat. If he had been a lad of ten years, he would have taken them up on the suggestion just to see how many his gut could hold. But he was nearly thirty, a man who had taught himself to control his appetite for food...and more. "It would be me pleasure to eat one or two of yer tarts, Mrs. Chessy, but me ma taught me not to be too greedy where sweets are concerned." He let his gaze settle on the lass for a heartbeat, staring at his lips. He turned and smiled at the vicar's wife. "She also taught me not to overstay me welcome."

While he watched, Mrs. Chessy replaced the thick bandage with a thin one and retied the strip around her niece's head to keep it in place. He handed Caroline's aunt the spectacles and let her place them on the lass's face. He was not certain he could do so without trailing his fingertips along the curve of her uninjured cheek, or touching a few of her enchanting freckles, or testing the firmness of her plump bottom lip.

"There," Mrs. Chessy said. "How is that, Caro?"

Caroline smiled, then grimaced. "I keep forgetting that I have to be cautious smiling."

"Well now, lass, I'm thinking it's wonderful news that ye feel like smiling. Ye'll learn yer limits while ye're healing. Take it from me. I know."

"I'd better serve our tea before it's tepid," Mrs. Chessy remarked.

She started to rise from her seat next to the settee, but O'Malley stopped her. "I've just washed me hands—let me bring the tea tray over to ye."

"Thank you, O'Malley."

He placed the tray on the table next to the settee and watched the lass's graceful movements as she accepted the teacup and saucer from her aunt, setting it within reach on the table, so she could take the small plate with two cream tarts on it. Without pausing, she handed it to O'Malley. "Thank you, Aunt Josephine."

"Oh, that plate is for you, Caro—you need to keep your strength up while you heal." She then squeezed four tarts on another plate and handed it to O'Malley.

Eyes wide, he grinned. "Thank ye kindly. I'm certain Ma wouldn't mind if I accepted yer generosity…just this once."

The vicar's wife beamed as she passed him a cup of tea and kept up a steady conversation while they sipped from their cups and nibbled on her delicious tarts.

O'Malley could not help but sneak glances at the lovely red-headed lass. She was prettier every time he saw her. Her bravery almost made up for her stubbornness. He chuckled when he realized why he admired her stubborn quality—it reminded him of his ma.

The room had gone quiet. He blinked and tore his gaze away from Caroline. "Forgive me—I was lost in thought."

Mrs. Chessy's smile widened. "I was saying how grateful we are that you were able to visit this morning. You have managed a small miracle and perked our Caro up. She was so despondent before you arrived."

"'Twas the spectacles," he replied.

"And the flowers," Mrs. Chessy said. "They are lovely."

O'Malley glanced around the room, but did not see the flowers.

"There were so many, I had to put them in a large pitcher of water in the kitchen."

"Once I started gathering them, I decided I'd better pick enough for ye to share between the four of ye."

Mrs. Chessy tilted her head to one side. "Four?" She laughed delightedly. "O'Malley, you are so thoughtful. Thank you. I will be sure that Olivia receives her flowers and knows that you thought of her, too. Melanie is visiting with her this morning."

"Me pleasure, Mrs. Chessy."

O'Malley could not help stealing another long look at the lass. Her freckles were distracting him…again. He closed his eyes and drew in a deep breath. When he opened them, the lass was staring at him. The longing in her eyes pulled at him. Thank God that he wasn't alone in his attraction.

"I need to resume me patrol. O'Ghill and I will be sharing duties here in the village," he told the women. "I will return this evening for the overnight shift."

"Will you be staying at the smithy?" Mrs. Chessy asked.

"Aye." He rose to his feet and extended his hand to the lass, who stared at it for a moment before putting her hand in his. "Thank ye for the delightful company, Miss Gillingham." His eyes never left hers as he tilted her hand to press his lips to the back of it. The dreamy expression on her face had his heart making plans before his head realized it. He released her hand and advised, "Sleep if ye can. Ye'll heal faster." He smiled at the vicar's wife. "Thank ye for the tea and tarts—they were delicious."

"You are welcome. Thank you for lifting Caro's spirits and finding her spectacles."

"Me pleasure. I'll see ye this evening."

He ordered his feet to walk to the door, though he wanted to stay.

Outside, he walked over to the barn. The vicar was no longer there, but O'Malley's horse had been pampered while he was inside. It was time to stop by the smithy and speak to Coleman. He thought about returning for Miss Coleman's flowers, then decided against it. 'Twas better if he let Mrs. Chessy give her the flowers. He did not want the blacksmith to get the wrong idea. His only intention was the lift the spirits of the women he was protecting.

A short while later, he was riding out of the village. He hoped a missive from either King or Coventry arrived while he was there. Even without advance notice, Anderson would not have the opportunity to sneak into the village or onto the baron's property. They had more than enough men spread out and around Summerfield-on-Eden and Summerfield Chase.

He could not wait to get his hands on the bloody bastard and give him a taste of what it felt like to be abducted and held against his will. And for the bloody hell of it, he'd enjoy roughing him up. Oh, he wouldn't break any *large* bones, mayhap snap a few fingers and Anderson's nose. He'd have to think about which would be the proper message that would get through to the bugger.

O'Malley thought he would ask what Garahan thought, then abruptly changed his mind. His cousin had a score to settle with Anderson for stabbing him in the back. Whatever Garahan wanted to do to the lord would no doubt be breaking his vow to the duke. O'Malley wouldn't blame Garahan if he beat the man to within an inch of his life. Hell, he'd hold his coat. But if the man wasn't strong enough to handle the beating, he may die, and every man in the guard had agreed to injure, not kill, their prisoners. O'Malley would never want to be the cause of Garahan being banned from the guard.

Approaching the edge of the baron's property, he followed the road leading to the stables. O'Malley decided that he would ask Flaherty, who would be a bit more levelheaded. As luck would have it, Flaherty was waiting for him when he rode up. The fierce frown on his face had O'Malley on alert. "What's happened?"

"His lordship is waiting for ye. A missive arrived while ye were on patrol."

"Did he disclose what the contents were?" O'Malley asked.

"Nay, he wanted to wait until ye arrived."

One of the stable lads rushed over. "I'll take care of him for you, O'Malley."

"Thank ye. Oh, I promised him—"

"A cup of oats," the young man said with a grin. "We all know your gelding is partial to them."

Smiling, O'Malley fell into step beside his cousin. "Where's

Garahan?"

"Guarding the interior while ye were on patrol," Flaherty said. "From the expression on his lordship's face, the news was not expected."

The two men strode to the back entrance and entered the house, not surprised to find Garahan pacing in the long hallway between the back door and the kitchen.

"About time ye got back," he grumbled. "We've been waiting."

"His lordship gave me leave to have tea with the lass to see how she was feeling this morning," O'Malley said.

Garahan raked a hand through his dark hair, making it stand on end. "And how is she?"

"I found her spectacles in the stream."

"Broken, no doubt," Garahan remarked.

"Nay, nary a scratch. She was elated, though I could see smiling pulled at the stitches in her cheek."

Flaherty grimaced. "Poor lass." He shoved O'Malley with his shoulder and asked, "Did ye tell her?"

"Nay, there wasn't time."

"Ye had to have been there for nearly an hour," Flaherty said.

"That's time enough," Garahan interrupted. "His lordship's waiting."

The three men greeted Mrs. Green, who glanced over her shoulder and smiled, all the while stirring the large pot on the stove. "I'll save a bit of this berry jam for the afternoon scones."

Garahan sighed, Flaherty smiled, and O'Malley replied, "Ye're a treasure to be sure, Mrs. Green. The lot of us are grateful to ye for feeding us…especially when ye're baking scones."

Her delighted laughter bounced against the walls of the kitchen and surrounded them like a hug from home. If the baron's news was what O'Malley anticipated—Anderson being spotted closer to the Borderlands—they would need this small bit of comfort to remind them what was important in life and why they'd chosen to step into the role of protector. The news would mean a change in plans, and he wouldn't be able to do more than wave to the lass as he passed the vicarage when—make that *if*— he had the village patrol.

As they strode through the door to the main part of the house, he decided that he'd suggest to the baron that they try once more to convince the vicar that it was imperative Mrs. Chessy and the others seek the safety of Summerfield Chase. He could not imagine the lass being out of his sight when danger was headed toward the village.

Experience taught him collateral damage happened on the battlefield, in skirmishes, and during everyday life. The lass would be a target, and in the line of fire, as long as she was near Melanie and Olivia. Which she no doubt would be while she remained at the vicarage. He needed to think of a way to convince her and the others to accept the baron's offer.

Mayhap it was time to enlist Garahan's wife. Prudence had been the main target when Anderson abducted the women. Surely, she would be able to think of a reason to urge them to take the offer of protection.

Lord willing…

CHAPTER SEVENTEEN

O'MALLEY KNOCKED AND was bidden to enter, followed by Garahan and Flaherty. The baron acknowledged the men and turned to O'Malley. "How is Miss Gillingham this morning?"

"Once she put her spectacles on, much improved, yer lordship. Without them it was as if she had two injuries instead of just one. Not to ignore the seriousness of the gash in her cheek, but 'twill heal, while her eyesight will not improve without spectacles."

Summerfield's lips twitched. "I'm happy to hear that you found and returned her lenses to her. Your long-winded answer to my question has me wondering if Mrs. Chessy invited you to tea and served her cream tarts. She is quite famous for them at gatherings in the village."

O'Malley could not keep from grinning. "They were delicious."

"I can only imagine, as I have not yet had the opportunity to taste one. The last three times she baked and set out her tarts on the table for the baked goods at the church fair, they were gone in minutes."

"I could put in a good word for ye, yer lordship. Mayhap she'll surprise ye and drop off a plate of her tarts."

Summerfield's eyes narrowed as if he were considering it. "Thank you for the offer, but I believe I will wait my turn like the rest of the villagers do." He glanced at the men surrounding him and said, "I received a message from Coventry. It's good news. Tremayne and Masterson have been working undercover, feeding Anderson false information, delaying him. Extreme secrecy was used, given the recent charges leveled against the man. The captain did not want to rouse suspicion of their activity, which was why Coventry's last report mentioned his men had lost Anderson's trail." The baron's jaw clenched, then relaxed. "Apparently Coventry has reason to believe there is a break in communication somewhere along the line."

Garahan bit out, "Anderson is paying someone!"

O'Malley asked, "Is he still headed this way?"

"Aye," Summerfield replied. "Coventry believes between Tremayne and Masterson spoon-feeding Anderson conflicting and distracting information, he could hold off the inevitable for a sennight, possibly a fortnight."

Flaherty frowned. "Not if the man travels by horse."

The baron shook his head. "Not a concern. Rumor has it Anderson insists on traveling everywhere via coach, due to an aversion to horses."

O'Malley smiled. "Well now, he'll be keeping to North Road for most of the journey. The roads leading from North Road to Summerfield-on-Eden are less traveled and narrower. Could add a day or so to his journey."

"Don't forget stopping every twenty miles to change horses," Flaherty said.

Garahan snorted. "He'll probably stop for tea."

Flaherty snickered. "And a meal at every stop."

Summerfield nodded. "Anderson never developed an affinity for horses, other than whipping them when they fall off the pace pulling his carriage."

"Just one more thing to dislike about the man," Flaherty mumbled.

"I don't dislike the man." Garahan's voice sounded strained. He narrowed his eyes until they were unholy, near-black slits burning with anger. "I *hate* the man!"

"Hate is a strong word, Ryan," Flaherty replied.

"I've every reason to hate the man for what he did to me wife, Melanie, and Olivia…and what he intended to do! The bloody bugger stabbed me in the back. I nearly bled out!"

"But ye didn't, thanks to O'Ghill's quick action," O'Malley reminded his cousin. "I'm not trying to diminish what he did, but we need to remain neutral while defending the duke and his family."

Garahan's eyes burned with anger. "Are ye saying ye'd be able to remain neutral if Miss Gillingham were the one yanked into that carriage, abducted right from under the noses of the innkeeper in the village? If that doesn't bother ye, imagine she's miles away, and ye don't know where she is."

O'Malley got the picture with surprising clarity. He understood without having the lass's name dragged into it. "I'm imagining it, and I'd be angry, too, but—"

Garahan's voice lowered to a rasp. "Then ye finally find her trail and are only a few hours behind the kidnappers. Ye pull into the innyard and recognize the carriage reportedly seen right before she went missing… And then ye hear her scream, and ye don't know if it's because the bloody bastard who took her is laying his hands on her or if he's—"

O'Malley's blood ran cold. "Enough! Ye made yer point." He turned to face the baron. "Forgive me cousin for interrupting what ye were trying to tell us, yer lordship. I'll make sure he soaks his head in the horse trough." He glared at Garahan, then continued, "With a sennight or more before Anderson arrives, and the assurance that Tremayne and Masterson are following at a distance, we'll have the time to practice our patrols with the men we've added to our number."

Garahan snorted. "We could use a half-dozen more men, preferably ones able to handle a pistol or a rifle. But will it change the fact that the bastard has set his sights on me wife and the others again?"

"Aye, because this time, he will not escape answering for his crimes quite so quickly…or easily," the baron said. He waited a beat before saying, "We shall increase our patrols and add another six men. O'Malley, I'd like you to ride to the village. Speak to Coleman and his daughter first and have them meet you at the vicarage. You and O'Ghill need to convince the women to accept my offer."

When O'Malley remained silent, Summerfield added, "I'm leaving the details up to you. Word the request however you need to. I will not feel at ease until you have convinced the ladies to seek shelter here at Summerfield Chase. It is not safe for them to remain in the village."

"Aye," Garahan agreed. "Too many places ripe for ambush."

"A sharpshooters' paradise," Flaherty added.

"Once Anderson discovers they are not in the village," the baron continued, "he will focus his attentions here." His face lost all expression. "And we will be waiting for him."

"I'll do me best," O'Malley said. "but I warn ye, the lass—er, Miss Gillingham is quite stubborn."

The baron rubbed his eyes. "What about Miss Chessy?"

O'Malley shook his head. "Just as stubborn, I'm afraid."

"And Miss Coleman?"

"I think she and the vicar's wife have softer attitudes toward being told what to do," O'Malley admitted.

"Meaning they'll be reasonable?" Flaherty asked.

Garahan grunted.

"Do you believe they will be?" the baron asked O'Malley.

"Aye."

Summerfield inclined his head. "Excellent. See to it. Now then, Garahan, mayhap you could ask your wife if she could encourage the women to come. I'd ask Phoebe, but she is still on bed rest and I do not want her getting too involved."

When Garahan did not answer right away, which was not normal for him, O'Malley sensed his cousin was worried about his wife leaving the grounds of the estate. "Prudence could pen a note to Mrs. Chessy inviting the women here for tea," he suggested.

Flaherty nodded. "Once they are here, we'll keep them!"

Garahan grinned, and the baron sputtered, "You cannot simply keep them. That's what Anderson did!"

"Aye, but he had nefarious intentions," O'Malley said. "We'd just be offering them to tea and to stay for an extended visit." He considered the ramifications and added, "It would probably be best *not* to mention the length of the visit in Prudence's note to the vicar's wife."

"We'll spring it on them once yer wife and her ladyship ply them with tea and scones or some of Mrs. Green's fancy iced teacakes," Flaherty added.

"Ye should ensure Percy and Phineas are included in their visit," Garahan said. "Those two could charm the birds out of the trees."

The baron smiled. "Men, it appears as if we have a plan."

CHAPTER EIGHTEEN

O'MALLEY REINED IN his horse in front of the smithy and dismounted. He bloody well hoped Coleman would be agreeable to sending his daughter to the baron's estate to ensure her safety. If he had to, he'd be stating hard facts to remind the man how his daughter had been abducted just a few storefronts down from his forge!

Coleman lifted his head and waved to O'Malley through the open double doors as he was tying the reins to a post outside. "Aren't you early for the midmorning patrol?"

"We're changing it up a bit," O'Malley answered as he stepped into the shop. "'Tis the best way to keep everyone on their toes." The blacksmith nodded as he worked the bellows, breathing life back into the fire. O'Malley watched for a moment, then said, "His lordship asked me to speak to ye and yer daughter this morning...at the vicarage."

Coleman's head snapped up, and his eyes blazed. "Is it about is that blackhearted bastard?"

O'Malley had a split-second warning. It was all he needed as Coleman's meaty fists pounded into the wooden support post a hairsbreadth from his face. Impressed by the force of the lightning-fast blows, he waited a beat before saying, "Yer jabs are a thing of beauty. Why haven't you taken Garahan up on his offer to spar with us? We'd welcome the chance to go a few rounds with ye."

Coleman scrubbed his hands over his face, ignoring the blood seeping from his split knuckles. "I haven't had the time. Every spring there's always a glut of repair work…plow blades and tools need straightening and sharpening. We seem to grow rocks around here. Don't get me wrong, they're a bonus when building stone fences, but are hell on the blade of a plow and the tines of a pitchfork."

"I remember well, as I grew up on a farm in County Wexford. We were always building rock walls from those we turned up with the plow."

Coleman nodded. "Please tell his lordship that I'm grateful for O'Ghill and the Stanbridge boy guarding my Olivia and Melanie. I have tried to keep an eye on my daughter, but with all this work"—he swept his hand toward the stack of tools and blades beside the forge—"I've been struggling to do both. The men are a godsend." He frowned. "Olivia and Melanie have been friends since birth, and both look for trouble…or are apt to wander off if the notion takes hold of them. I still cannot believe that Melanie got it in her head that she and Olivia needed to wash their faces with morning dew in the field beyond the graveyard the other morning. And all because of fairytales they'd heard when they were little girls."

"The lasses will need to be cautious of the *tween* times," O'Malley warned. "The fae prefer those times."

"What is that?"

"'Tis more *when* than what," O'Malley said. "The veil between worlds is thin at certain times of the day—the between hours, when it's easier to slip into the faery realm. Just as it is at certain times of the year."

Coleman shook his head. "Now you are starting to sound like my daughter and the vicar's." He glanced at his forge again and shook his head. "I can't leave to go to the vicarage and leave the fire untended. The chance of a spark igniting is too great. I wouldn't risk the safety of my daughter, or anyone in the village.

I am more than happy to help, but you need to catch me before dawn, before I light my forge, or wait until after I bank the fire for the night."

O'Malley nodded. "Do I have yer permission to escort yer daughter there?"

"Aye, if you tell me the reason, and whether or not it has to do with Anderson."

"It does," O'Malley replied. "His lordship feels the safest place for yer daughter and the vicar's family is Summerfield Chase."

"Isn't Olivia safer now that the Stanbridge boy and O'Ghill are sharing the duty guarding them?"

"They are," O'Malley replied. "We understand that neither yerself nor the vicar can neglect yer duties to hover around yer daughters."

The blacksmith studied O'Malley for a few moments. "Has something occurred that I need to know about?"

"Anderson is being closely watched. I can say no more."

"I'll kill him if he comes near Olivia!"

"And hang for the murder of a member of the *ton*?" O'Malley could not believe the widowed blacksmith would do that. "She'd be an orphan then. Ye'd leave yer daughter without her da?" Coleman fell silent, and O'Malley knew his question had hit home. "Leave Anderson to us."

The blacksmith nodded. "She can go with you to the vicarage, but she may not leave the village without my permission."

"Ye have me word on it. Thank ye." They shook hands, and O'Malley walked around the back of the building to Coleman's house to knock on the door.

O'GHILL REINED IN his horse in front of the vicarage, dismounted, and tied off the reins on the wooden fence. He opened the gate and walked to the front door. At the sound of rustling behind him, he looked over his shoulder in time to see his horse gently lipping at the vicar's flowers. "Ye cannot be eating those!"

His horse didn't bother to lift his head…or stop. O'Ghill mumbled about horses, and hardheaded females, while he untied the reins to lead his flower-nibbling horse toward the barn. "I cannot trust ye not to keep eating those blooms. Ye'll have to stay in the barn until I deliver Mrs. Garahan's invitation."

Soft laughter filtered out through the partially closed barn door. Intrigued by the sound, which was growing closer by the moment, O'Ghill slowed his steps and waited. He didn't have to wait long before the barn door burst open and the owner of the laughter ran into him.

He caught Melanie as she bounced off his chest, preventing her from landing on her backside. "Where are ye off to in such a hurry, lass?"

Wide, guileless blue eyes latched on to his. She all but melted against him. "I knew you'd come back for me." Without a hint of what she intended, the lass wrapped her arms around his neck and held on for dear life.

O'Ghill slid his hands to her wrists and, as gently as possible, pried her loose. "What are ye thinking, lass? 'Tis the middle of the morning, and anyone could be looking out the window or walking toward the barn."

When she didn't answer him, he steeled himself to ignore the lass and walked toward the house. The front door opened as he was poised to knock. Had the vicar's wife been watching through the window? Should he tell her what happened in front of the barn just now, or wait for her to ask?

Bollocks! He had no time for schoolgirl games.

"I have a message for ye from Mrs. Garahan." At the concern on Mrs. Chessy's face, he added, "'Tis more in the way of an invitation."

"Thank you, O'Ghill. Why don't you come in and visit with Caro while I read the message? I may need to pen a reply."

"I can deliver a verbal message for ye, if ye like."

"That is so kind of you. Please. Come into the parlor." He followed behind the vicar's wife. "Caro, O'Ghill just arrived with a message for me—won't you keep him company while I read it?"

"Of course, Aunt. Good morning, Killian. I hope it is good news that you bring."

"I wouldn't be knowing." Now, he could guess, but he wouldn't be mentioning that fact to the lass. He glanced at her bandage. "How are ye feeling this morning?"

"A little better, thank you." Her eyes seemed clearer.

"I'm pleased to hear it, Caroline." He turned to the vicar's wife and said, "I'll wait outside for yer reply, Mrs. Chessy."

"That won't be necessary. I would love to accept Mrs. Garahan's invitation on behalf of my daughter, my niece, and myself," she replied. "We would be delighted to take tea with her this afternoon."

Caroline's choked cry had O'Ghill turning around to face her. "What's wrong?"

"Aunt Josephine, I can't go anywhere. Especially to Summerfield Chase! My face is still bandaged and would cause no end of speculation as to how horrific the scar will be."

Mrs. Chessy sighed, and Caroline said, "I shall be fine while you enjoy taking tea with Mrs. Garahan, Aunt. Lyman Stanbridge is still on guard."

Mrs. Chessy sighed. "I'm afraid we cannot go, O'Ghill. Please send our regrets."

He nodded and bade them goodbye. The baron would not be happy that the invitation had been turned down. He could understand why, but still, Summerfield would not be pleased. Mayhap O'Malley would have better luck with Olivia.

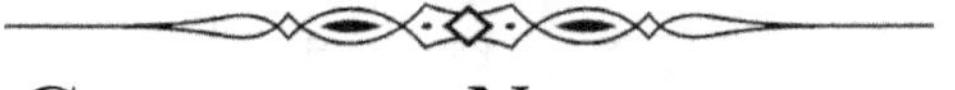

CHAPTER NINETEEN

O'MALLEY SENSED THE tension before he entered the parlor. A glance at the lass's worried expression had him needing to fix whatever was bothering her. He walked over to the settee and crouched down in front of her. "Are ye feeling poorly this morning, lass?"

Caroline twisted her hands together before lifting her gaze. "I am fine, thank you."

Something was definitely wrong. "Do ye need me to interfere on yer behalf?"

That question had her head popping up. "No thank you."

"I cannot fix whatever is wrong if ye don't confide in me."

Caroline lowered her gaze to her lap once more.

O'Malley stood up and stared at Melanie, then let his gaze rest on her mother. "Is there anything I need to be knowing? Has someone been speaking ill about Miss Gillingham? I'd be happy to have a word or two with whoever has the lass on the verge of tears."

"O'Malley, please," Caroline said. "It's nothing. I'm feeling out of sorts. Would you excuse me, please? I need to lie down."

"Do ye need someone to accompany ye, in case ye swoon?"

She shook her head and walked to the staircase. He was not convinced that she wouldn't faint halfway up.

"If one of ye will not follow the lass to make sure she won't swoon and fall down the stairs, I will."

Olivia rushed to the stairs and accompanied Caroline the rest of the way. Satisfied that she would come to no harm on his watch, O'Malley turned to Melanie. "Can ye not see she's not just worrying about her injury, but still grieving for her ma?"

"I'll be right back." Melanie darted across the room and up the stairs.

"Thank you, O'Malley. Melanie has not been herself since..." Mrs. Chessy's voice trailed off.

He sighed. "I can well understand that, and ye'd be right to treat her with care, but can ye not see that yer daughter needs to do the same for her cousin? When I first met Miss Gillingham, she was full of fire with a quick wit. She's changed in just a few short days."

The vicar's wife nodded. "Ever since she was injured." She walked over and placed a hand on O'Malley's arm. "At first I thought it was the physician's reply when he was here a little while ago. Caro asked him if it was the depth of her cut that required so many stitches."

O'Malley frowned. "What did Dr. Higgins say?"

"He added extra stitches, and kept them as tiny and uniform as possible, so the scarring would not be as raised and puckered."

He swore under his breath. "In me experience, physicians do not always consider a patient's feelings, as they are more concerned with healing them." From the way Mrs. Chessy's eyes darted to the staircase and back, he sensed there was something more she had yet to tell him.

"I think it might have to do with the invitation O'Ghill delivered from Mrs. Garahan," she explained. "I assumed Caro would want to go to tea with us."

"Ah, but she still has the bandage covering her face. The lass would feel self-conscious."

Mrs. Chessy's shoulders slumped. "To be honest, all I had been thinking was that it would be a pleasant diversion. Just what Melanie, Olivia, and Caro needed. I never gave a thought to her stitches. She has seemed to be handling her injury and recovery as if they were of no consequence."

"Sure and it's yerselves she's putting before her own wants and needs. Can ye not see that? She's lost the last of her family and does not want to give any of ye a reason to regret opening yer home to her."

The vicar's wife had the grace to look embarrassed.

"The lass may not have said it aloud," O'Malley continued, "but I am willing to wager she's worrying about the scar that will be left behind when Dr. Higgins removes the threads."

Frowning at him, Mrs. Chessy reminded him, "We're still dealing with my daughter's nightmares about the abduction."

O'Malley sighed. "Forgive me. I did not mean to dismiss what happened to yer daughter. I'm trying to help ye see that both lasses need your help. I may not have been there when Garahan and O'Ghill rescued yer daughter, Olivia, and Mrs. Garahan, but me cousins spoke highly of yer daughter's courage. 'Tis a mile wide. Ye should be proud."

The knock on the door interrupted their conversation.

"Excuse me." The vicar's wife walked out of the room to answer the door. "O'Ghill. Olivia and Melanie are upstairs with Caro. O'Malley is in the parlor."

"I wanted to ask if ye have changed yer mind about coming to Summerfield Chase this afternoon to tea."

"I haven't. I was too hasty accepting the invitation and should have asked Caro before accepting for her. Please extend my thanks, and let Mrs. Garahan know that once Caro's stitches are removed, we would be delighted to accept, if Mrs. Garahan's invitation is still open."

"I understand, Mrs. Chessy. I am certain that the invitation will be open."

O'Malley rose to take his leave. "Would you please tell the lass I was asking after her? I need to convey yer regrets to Mrs. Garahan."

"Did ye forget ye are to remain in town when ye have the

village patrol?" O'Ghill asked. "I'll speak to Garahan's wife and see ye in the morning."

O'Malley's spirits lifted at the thought of being close to the lass. If only she weren't feeling poorly, he would have had a chance to speak to her before going on his rounds in the village. "I had other things on me mind."

O'Ghill chuckled. "'Tis the reason I stopped here to remind ye." He bade them goodbye and left.

O'Malley turned toward the stairs when he heard footsteps—two distinct sets of footfalls, not three. He did not have to look to the stairs to note that the lass had chosen to remain upstairs. "Do ye need me to fetch Dr. Higgins for ye, Mrs. Chessy? I'll be passing by his house on me rounds."

"I think all my niece needs is to rest quietly. She mentioned being used to being on her own. My sister-in-law must have been bedridden for longer than either Bertram or I were aware of."

O'Malley digested that information. "Do ye think she'd enjoy a chance to sit outside, maybe walk in yer gardens or to the barn and back? When my rounds have me swinging back again, I could stop for a brief visit."

"I have a feeling Caro would enjoy that immensely."

"When ye check on her, please ask her, and let her know I'll be stopping by this afternoon."

"In time for tea?" the vicar's wife asked.

"I would not want to put ye to any trouble, Mrs. Chessy—mayhap before teatime. That way, I should be able to convince her to take a short walk with me."

"What if she is unsteady on her feet?"

"Not to worry; with her arm linked through mine, ye have me word I will not let her fall." He paused on the front step, as he realized no one had mentioned the lass's former suitor a second time. Was he still a worry? "Forgive me, Mrs. Chessy, I've been meaning to ask—has Miss Gillingham heard from Mr. Humbolt?"

"Caro has not received any letters since she arrived. Although from what she confided about his behavior when he called on her, right after her mother passed, I cannot imagine that he would."

O'Malley had a gut feeling that the lass had not heard the last of Humbolt, especially if the man heard through the grapevine that she was living with an uncle who had connections to members of the *ton*. The bloody bastard would no doubt follow the trail of growing coin from Summerfield-on-Eden, all the way to Wyndmere Hall!

"Will ye let me know if she does hear from the man? It might be important, given their last conversation. I do not trust a man who cannot keep his word. The lass has been through so much already."

Mrs. Chessy's eyes welled. "Has she told you about David?"

"Is he another cousin?"

She shook her head and blinked away her tears. "My nephew Cornelius, her older brother, had a close group of friends growing up. They purchased their colors within a sennight of one another."

O'Malley had a feeling he was about to hear something he would not like.

"David Bantry was a soft-spoken young man, closer to my nephew than the others. He and Cornelius joined the same regiment." She paused and placed a hand over her heart. "They gave their lives for king and country fighting on the Iberian Peninsula."

He sensed David was more than a family friend to Caroline. In order to better understand the lass, he had to know, had to ask, "Was there an understanding between Bantry and Miss Gillingham?"

"Yes. Before he left, he asked Caro to wait for him," the vicar's wife replied. "They planned to court and marry when he returned...after the war."

His heart hurt for the lass. "I cannot fathom the pain the lass has suffered these last few years, not only the loss of her brother, but the man she was promised to, her da, and now her ma." His eyes searched the older woman's face. "How much pain can one heart endure? How does one cope?"

Mrs. Chessy reached for his hand, and at the soft gasp behind him, O'Malley glanced over his shoulder toward the stairs, where Melanie stood transfixed. He sighed. He had not wanted anyone to know how deep his feelings for the lass went...yet. Baron Summerfield knew of O'Malley's intentions, but he had yet to tell the duke.

"Prayer and faith have always helped Bertram and me through our trials and tribulations."

O'Malley stared into Mrs. Chessy's compassion-filled eyes. "'Tis something Ma has said to me on more than one occasion." He turned and met Melanie's questioning gaze as she and Olivia walked toward where he stood. "Have ye spoken to yer cousin?"

Melanie nodded. "I have. Did O'Ghill leave?"

"Aye. He'll return tomorrow morning to relieve me."

Olivia tugged on her arm. "You can speak with O'Ghill tomorrow. Come on, Melanie!" she urged. "We have something to *do* at my house."

From the way Olivia stressed the word, O'Malley had a feeling neither of them were about to mention what it was. The exasperated expression on Melanie's face spoke volumes, and he knew neither would speak of it—at least to him or Melanie's mother.

"Melanie."

She paused mid-step. "Yes, Mum?"

"You and Olivia may speak in the kitchen...or on the back steps. You are not to run off without one of the men accompanying you."

Mrs. Chessy's firm voice had her daughter responding quickly. "Yes, Mum."

"I'll wait for Stanbridge outside," O'Malley said. "I'll take me leave of ye now. If ye need me, give a shout."

"I rarely need to raise my voice, but I will if it's an emergency. Thank you, O'Malley."

He nodded to the vicar's wife and took his leave, then walked around the perimeter of the property and back toward the barn. It was larger than he'd realized, but he was still well within hearing range. He checked on his gelding, pleased the animal was contentedly grazing in the small enclosure attached to the barn. "We'll be leaving as soon as Stanbridge returns." O'Malley stroked the horse's neck and scratched behind his ear, chuckling when the animal leaned into his hand. "Ye'd follow me anywhere as long as I keep scratching yer favorite spot and ladling out a cupful of oats a few times a day."

Stanbridge hailed him as he rode up to the barn. "Where's O'Ghill?"

"The baron asked him to switch assignments for the rest of today. He'll be back in the morning."

The younger man nodded and reported, "All's quiet."

"As it should be," O'Malley replied. "Melanie and Olivia are out back. The lass is upstairs resting."

"And Mrs. Chessy?" Stanbridge asked.

"She was in the parlor a few moments ago, but mentioned baking."

"Is there anything else I need to know?"

"From the way Melanie and Olivia have been whispering since I arrived, they are planning something. Ye'd best keep a close eye on those two."

Stanbridge frowned. "It's mostly Melanie's doing. Olivia would never even think of half of the trouble those two seem to get into on their own."

O'Malley had a feeling the young man was enamored of Olivia and was not willing to believe that she was capable of any wrongdoing. The pair would be a good match.

He let his horse out of the small enclosure by the barn and mounted. "I'll return shortly. Don't forget that we have enlisted lads around the village as messengers. Use the signal I taught ye. One of them is bound to hear yer short, sharp whistle and will find me."

"I won't forget."

More than pleased with how the eldest of the Stanbridge sons was adapting to guard duty, O'Malley began his patrol of the village, and the roads leading to and from the baron's home. Pleased that it was still quiet, he reversed direction when he reached the blacksmith's shop.

Stanbridge hailed him as he approached the vicarage again. "Anything happening that I need to know about?"

O'Malley grinned. "'Tis the question I usually ask. Nay. Still quiet. Where are the lasses and Mrs. Chessy?"

"Take a deep breath and you tell me," Stanbridge said.

Judging from his wide smile, O'Malley would wager the younger man had been given a taste of whatever smelled like Heaven. "Tarts or scones?"

"Both. The tarts have yet to cool. The scone I had was delicious. Oh, Caroline is still resting."

"Upstairs?"

"Aye. Mrs. Chessy had Melanie and Olivia check on her while they were baking."

Unease settled into O'Malley's gut. He'd have to ask to speak to the lass. No matter if he had to have all three of the women upstairs in order to protect the lass's reputation—he would find out why she was still hiding in the bedchamber.

O'Malley was poised to knock when he saw Melanie grab Olivia by the hand and drag her around the side of the house. At the last second, Olivia looked over her shoulder, then stumbled, but righted herself.

"Go after them," O'Malley ordered Stanbridge. "I'll stay with Mrs. Chessy and Caroline."

Stanbridge took off and caught up with the women before they reached the open field behind the blacksmith's barn. Watching the way he dismounted and stalked over to Melanie, O'Malley knew the lad would handle the situation.

O'Malley knocked on the back door and opened it to find the kitchen empty. "Mrs. Chessy?" When she didn't answer, he followed the sound of voices to the bottom of the stairs and called her a second time.

"O'Malley?" The vicar's wife appeared at the top of the stairs. "Didn't Melanie tell you I where I was?"

"Stanbridge just chased after Melanie and Olivia—they were headed toward the meadow."

"But I told Melanie that I wanted her to arrange a plate of cream tarts and set them aside for Baron Summerfield. I remembered your mentioning he hasn't had the pleasure of sampling them yet and thought he would enjoy them."

"Thank ye, Mrs. Chessy. Now about yer daughter—"

"O'Malley?"

He turned around and saw Olivia standing in the doorway to the kitchen, wringing her hands. "Where's Melanie? Is Stanbridge outside?"

"She…er… Well, you see…" She dropped her hands to her sides. "This is all my fault. She loves raspberries, and I wanted to show her that the raspberries growing in the thicket at the edge of our yard were almost ready to pick. She said the ones near the marsh would be then, too."

"What does that have to do with Stanbridge?" O'Malley asked.

Olivia glanced at Mrs. Chessy before she answered, "Melanie may have smacked his horse on his hindquarters."

O'Malley was beyond irritated with the vicar's stubborn daughter, but remembered to keep his voice devoid of emotion. "And?"

"I grabbed the reins and held on tight."

"Do ye mean to tell me that ye were on his horse at the time? Ye could have fallen off and been knocked senseless! Where is his horse now?"

"I rubbed him down and left him in the barn. I wanted him to cool off a little more before I gave him a drink."

"Thank ye, lass. 'Twas the right thing to do if his horse was lathered from the run. But what about Melanie and Stanbridge?"

She snuck another glance at Mrs. Chessy before answering, "She kicked Lyman hard, in the knee, and ran toward the marsh."

"Mrs. Chessy, is Caroline well enough to walk to the smithy?"

"Yes, why?"

"I need yer word that ye'll escort Olivia and Caroline to the smithy while I go after Stanbridge and Melanie. Will ye do that for me?"

"Yes. Right away. Caro?" she called out, rushing to the stairs.

The lass appeared at the top of the stairs, her riot of red curls tumbling around her shoulders, falling to her waist. Her face was pale as parchment, and her gray eyes huge behind her spectacles. "I overheard what Olivia said. Of course I'll go with you, but I need to pin my hair up—"

O'Malley nearly swallowed his tongue, her beauty so beguiled him. He managed to get a hold of himself and clear his throat to say, "No time. Yer cousin is headed to the marsh. I cannot risk another near drowning."

Hand to her abundant breast—not that O'Malley was staring, but how could he not notice when she placed her hand there?—Caroline said, "Aunt Josephine, I cannot let anyone see me in such *dishabille*. Please explain it to O'Malley."

"I'm afraid O'Malley is right," Mrs. Chessy replied. "I have no idea what has gotten into my daughter's head, but we cannot take a chance that she'll do something so foolish as to head to the marsh to pick berries. She knows that in the spring the ground is always soggy. The mud positively seems to grab hold of your boots."

The lass, God love her, was braiding her hair as she descended the stairs. "Quickly now." O'Malley ushered the women out the back door. "I can't wait for ye to walk there. I need yer word that ye'll not stop to speak to anyone. The smithy is just a short walk from here. I'll whistle for yer da, Olivia. He'll understand the meaning. Though he cannot leave his fire, he'll be waiting for ye."

Mrs. Chessy lifted her chin. "You have my word, O'Malley."

"We promise, O'Malley," the lass said. "Please hurry and bring Melanie back."

"And Lyman," Olivia added, worry creasing her brow.

"I will," he promised. "Now go!"

O'Malley leapt into the saddle and whistled as he approached the smithy. Coleman appeared in the open doorway to his shop, and O'Malley shouted, "Stanbridge is chasing after Melanie. She'd headed to the marsh. Yer daughter, Mrs. Chessy, and the lass are walking this way. They gave their word to come straight here."

"They'll keep it," Coleman told him. "Go!"

O'Malley put his head down and gave his gelding his head as he turned onto the well-worn path just past the blacksmith's house. "God help me, the vicar's daughter is more trouble than Lady Phoebe ever was!"

He did not have time to hare after the young woman, but what other choice was there? She could have left Stanbridge incapacitated, especially if she kicked his knee from the side. Did she not realize he and Stanbridge had a bloody duty to perform? Although that duty entailed guarding the lasses with his life, it was also paramount that he protect and ensure the safety of the baron, his family, staff, tenant farmers, and every blessed villager in Summerfield-on-Eden.

"She better not have fallen in that bloody pond." He covered the distance quickly on horseback and saw Stanbridge ahead of him about to enter the marsh. He called out, "Stanbridge! Grab hold of me hand." O'Malley slowed down and pulled Stanbridge onto his horse behind him. "Hang on."

"It's wetter than usual," the younger man warned. "Stick to the path."

O'Malley did for a few minutes before asking, "How far ahead of ye is she?"

"Not too—"

The splash and cry for help had O'Malley's gut twisting with worry. "Can she swim?"

"Nay. Hurry!"

O'Malley raced toward the edge of the water, leapt off his horse, and scanned the pond. Seeing the top of Melanie's head, he dove in. Striking out with strong strokes, he reached her as she slid beneath the surface. He dove down and grabbed hold of her arm, pulling her to the surface. "I've got ye."

She sputtered and spat out a mouthful of water before her eyes locked on him. "Thank you."

"Ye're safe now, lass."

Stanbridge was there to pull her out of the water. "Sit here while I fetch O'Malley's horse." She shook her head and slowly stood. She trembled, but managed to stand without aid.

O'Malley climbed out of the water and brushed the water out of his eyes. "Are ye all right, Melanie? Did ye swallow any water?"

"I spat the water out. I'm fine."

"Ye've no more in yer belly?" When she shook her head, he turned toward Stanbridge, who had a hold of the reins to his horse. "Thank ye, lad. Get on. I'll lift Melanie up to ye." He turned to Melanie. "Do not even *think* about running again."

She had the grace to flush before she inclined her head. Stanbridge wrapped his arms around Melanie and warned her to be still. It took longer to reach the smithy leading the horse back, but O'Malley did not want to take the chance that the vicar's daughter would do something else foolish. It was his duty to bring her back.

No one spoke until Mrs. Chessy waved to them from the front door of Coleman's house. "O'Malley! Stanbridge!" Her eyes welled with tears as she rushed toward them. "Thank you! Thank you both for bringing Melanie safely back."

"Why were you worried? I'm fine, Mum," Melanie replied.

"She's a bit damp and bedraggled," O'Malley said.

"But uninjured," Stanbridge added.

Mrs. Chessy let her gaze drift from the top of Melanie's head to the tips of her toes. "Your willfulness and stubborn pride injured Lyman and could have gotten you killed! What were you thinking? You cannot swim! Have you absolutely no concern for others? I thought your father and I taught you to respect life, not disregard it."

"Melanie!" Olivia rushed out of her house and stopped before she reached the horse. She watched Stanbridge dismount. "Lyman, thank you for going after my best friend."

"Thank O'Malley. I would never have reached her in time when she fell in the pond." Stanbridge turned to glare at Melanie. "Someone thought it would be funny to kick me in the knee to keep me from following her."

"I'm sorry to have caused so much trouble," Melanie said.

"But you'd do it again in a heartbeat, wouldn't you?" Stanbridge asked. She didn't answer, prompting him to add, "When are you going to grow up and start acting your age?"

Tears welled up, but Melanie blinked them away. "You are right, Lyman, and I am sorry to have kicked you so hard, but I was mad."

"Melanie Alexandra Chessy, that is absolutely inexcusable," the vicar's wife interrupted. "You have much to atone for, and will have plenty of time to do it. Your father and I will discuss this later."

O'Malley noticed Caroline standing in the open doorway and wondered if she had finally been able to set aside her fear of being ostracized for her disfigurement—not in his eyes, but her own.

"I'm not a child," Melanie protested. "And I refuse to be treated as one!"

Caroline stepped out of the house and walked over to where her cousin still sat atop O'Malley's horse. "Come inside, Mellie. Olivia and I have filled the slipper tub for you. Your mum has had the water warming to brew a pot of tea."

At the lass's soft tone, Melanie lost all defiance.

"I'll help ye down," O'Malley said.

"No thank you, I can manage."

After Melanie dismounted, Caroline held out her hand and pulled her cousin to her side. "You'll feel better after a nice, hot soak in the tub." The lass glanced over her shoulder at Olivia, who nodded.

"Lyman," Olivia said, "I have a poultice Mrs. Chessy helped me prepare with herbs from our garden. It'll help with the swelling in your knee."

Stanbridge stared at Olivia. But instead of thanking her, he chastised her: "When will you stop letting Melanie Chessy lead you around by the nose?"

O'Malley wanted to smack the lad on the back of his thick head. "The lass just offered to take care of ye, and ye're going to lecture her? Did yer ma not teach ye any manners?"

Stanbridge stiffened as if he'd been struck. "I beg your pardon, Olivia."

O'Malley asked, "Would ye mind fetching the poultice ye prepared, Olivia? Stanbridge can borrow me horse and have his ma see to his knee. It'll save time if she doesn't have to prepare a poultice herself."

"I didn't mean to snap at you, Olivia," Stanbridge apologized. "I was angry with Melanie. When I heard the splash, all I could think was she couldn't swim…and when she cried for help…"

His voice trailed off, and O'Malley was pleased that the younger man seemed to be searching for the right words to say.

"I should never have taken it out on you, Olivia. Please say you'll forgive me?"

Olivia bit her lip and nodded. "You are forgiven. I'll get the poultice and be right back."

"I'll help you, Olivia." Mrs. Chessy accompanied her into the house.

O'Malley gave in and cuffed Stanbridge in the back of the head—not as hard as his da would have done, but hard enough to get the younger man's attention. "Well done, lad. Think before ye speak next time. Without Olivia racing to the vicarage for help, I would not have gotten to either of ye in time to pull Melanie out of the pond. I owe Olivia me thanks as well."

"You both put your lives on the line for my daughter and the others," the blacksmith said. "Thank you."

Olivia rushed out of the house and handed Stanbridge a jar with the warm poultice in it. "It may look a little odd and a tad bit slimy, but it is supposed to look like that. It's the comfrey root, which will help with the swelling and any bruising."

This time Stanbridge's reaction was what it should be. "Thank you, Olivia. I'm grateful. Please thank Mrs. Chessy for me." He mounted the horse and rode off. Before either O'Malley or Coleman could speak, Olivia ran to the house and closed the door behind her.

Summing up what he'd observed, O'Malley said, "Ye might want to speak to Stanbridge about letting him court yer daughter."

Coleman stared at O'Malley for a few moments, then shook his head. "She's not old enough."

"Lasses back home marry by the time they're seven and ten. When is her birthday?"

The blacksmith ignored O'Malley's question. "I'm not ready for her to marry."

"I'm told a da never is."

"Wait until you have a daughter of your own," Coleman warned.

O'Malley nodded and followed him into the smithy to the room where he stashed a spare set of clothes. While he changed, he thought about Coleman's prediction, which planted the image of a babe with flame-red hair, wide gray eyes, and the lass's sweet smile. "I'm not sure I can wait."

CHAPTER TWENTY

A FEW DAYS later, O'Malley was on patrol in the village again. Though his lordship had given him leave to stop by and visit with the lass, that had been before the recent missives going back and forth between London.

He felt the warmth of the sun on his back as the faint breeze caressed his face. It was a fine day. Finer still because he would see Caroline. Lord willing, he could get her alone long enough to satisfy the overwhelming need to kiss her again.

Shoving the need deep, he sighed. 'Twas more than that, he admitted—he enjoyed her company and was looking forward to seeing the lass without the bandage. Though he'd become used to seeing it, in another few days, the physician would be removing the threads as well.

A double-edged sword, he mused. He knew the lass was anticipating it, while at the same time, he sensed—nay, knew— she dreaded seeing the scar she would carry for the rest of her days. He should introduce her to Tremayne, the former lieutenant in the dragoons who carried a scar from forehead to chin from the slash of a saber. He'd survived the near-killing blow, though the prominent scar had ended his engagement.

Putting himself in Tremayne's place helped O'Malley to understand a bit more of what the lass was feeling and would be facing. After they apprehended Anderson—and they would—he would introduce the two. Gryffyn Tremayne bore the good looks of his forebears with his coal-black hair, a startling contrast to his green eyes. No matter—O'Malley knew the lass was partial to him. Their midnight kiss had spoken volumes.

O'Malley needed to get her alone and speak to her, tell her what was in his heart, and had been, since the day at the inn. The bold way she'd rushed out of her room had had him smiling. He'd automatically grabbed hold of her to steady her and keep her from falling. Their eyes met, and he'd been snared by the winsome lass with wavy red hair, freckles sprinkled on her face— as if by faeries—and eyes the color of morning mist enhanced by her spectacles.

Mine!

He'd thought it then. He was thinking it now. She was the only woman for him, and if he did not tell her that soon, he'd lose her once she got a maggot in her head that she should spend the rest of her life hiding because of her scarred face.

If Caroline had hit any other part of her head on that rock in the stream, her injury could have been one no physician could heal. He'd be reminding the lass of that, and though it would pain him to bring it up, he'd be blunt and tell her that Melanie's brush with disaster should be a stark reminder to all of them just how uncertain, and at times far too short, life could be. But then, the lass had already experienced that, hadn't she?

Reminding her about her cousin was far kinder than speaking of her da's illness and passing, or her mother's. 'Twas why he had spoken to the baron, who had sent missives to the duke and the earl. Thank God for fast horses. They'd delivered their communi- cations between Summerfield Chase, the Lake District, and Sussex. O'Malley now had the blessing of the duke, the earl, and the baron, with the assurance that the vows he planned to take with the lass would not compromise the one he'd sworn to His Grace.

O'Malley would ask for, and receive, the vicar's approval today. By teatime, he would ask Caroline for her hand in marriage. She would shed a few tears of happiness and say yes, right before he pulled her into his embrace and sealed their words with a kiss that would fog her lenses.

For a heartbeat, he wondered if she would be the last hurdle, then dismissed the idea. He would not let the lass destroy what happiness they could find because she doubted he would still love her because of her scar. By God, he would convince her that she loved him, too! They would be taking that walk in the vicar's garden a little later in the day, where he would confess what was in his heart.

Inhaling deeply, he smiled. The stubborn lass was no match for O'Malley when he aimed his considerable charm her way.

All was right in his world as he continued on the road to the village. The sun seemed brighter and the breeze softer now that he'd settled the matter of the lass in his mind. He loved this time of year—it always gave one hope after the cold of winter. Flowers bloomed in bright profusion along the sides of the road, in the meadows, as well as in gardens around the village.

The road he traveled was as familiar as the one back home. He'd ridden this patrol countless times, and could point out the section of stone fence with gaps in it, the cottage with the worn roof, both of which were on the baron's list to be repaired. Up ahead was the copse of fir trees so dense, it was nearly pitch black beneath them. O'Malley reached the spot where the trees grew thick along the road, winding around the outskirts of the village, before they would thin out again, the landmark indicating he was but a short distance from the vicarage.

Approaching the vicar's home, O'Malley reined in, surprised to see a horse and carriage in front of the barn. He frowned. It wasn't the vicar's carriage. Guts in a knot, he urged his horse toward the barn. Stanbridge was nowhere in sight. There was no reason for him to abandon his post! *Bloody hell*, he and O'Ghill had trusted the lad, had spoken to him more than once about the seriousness of the situation with Anderson, and the probability he would come after the women. O'Malley had specifically warned

Stanbridge that under no circumstances should he admit visitors into the vicarage without O'Malley's or O'Ghill's knowledge and approval.

He dismounted, tied his horse to one of the posts of the enclosure, and stormed up to the front door. Intent on rescuing the lasses inside, he pounded on the door. Before he could turn the knob, the door swung open.

"O'Malley!" Stanbridge's guilty expression had O'Malley's hackles rising. "I can explain."

"There's nothing to explain. Ye disobeyed orders. No one is allowed to visit without me approval, or O'Ghill's."

"O'Malley?" Mrs. Chessy walked toward him. "Come and meet Mr. Humbolt. You remember us talking about him. Nelson and Agatha had high hopes he would offer for Caroline's hand."

He remembered, and had meant to track down the blackguard to pummel him for what the man had said to Caroline. He would leave Humbolt with a reminder that he'd never forget for the way he'd treated the lass in her darkest hour.

Without waiting to be introduced, O'Malley strode into the parlor. The lass's eyes were tear-filled and red-rimmed. Her pale-as-flour face called attention to the dark stitches on her cheek. He tried to contain his anger, but her tears had him seeing red!

Incensed, he spun around to face the uninvited guest. "What did ye say to the lass?"

The man blanched at the anger and the pointed question. "What concern is it of yours?"

O'Malley closed the distance between them. "We can handle this one of two ways: ye answer me question, or I toss ye out on yer head."

Mrs. Chessy rushed over to them. "But O'Malley, this is Mr. Humbolt. He's—"

"Nothing to the lass!" O'Malley wanted to plant his fist in the man's face to wipe the superior look off it. After the lass had confided what happened the last time this blackguard showed his face, Humbolt deserved to feel the sharp edge of O'Malley's anger…and the power of his fists. "He disrespected Caroline and maligned her character." He glared at the shorter man and growled, "Ye're leaving. Now!"

The vicar's wife wrung her hands together. "O'Malley, don't you think Mr. Humbolt deserves the opportunity to explain?"

"Nay." He turned back to the man who'd reduced the lass to tears…again. "Well? Will ye answer me question?"

O'Malley gave the man credit for standing his ground, but Humbolt was a fool to do so. It only took a moment to sum up his weaknesses. Too many to list. The widower was no match for O'Malley.

He glanced at the lass and was instantly captivated by the change in her expression. Gratitude, instead of fear, shone in her mist-gray eyes. He wanted more than that from her, but he would not press right now. "I'll be right back, lass. I need to remove the rubbish from the parlor."

"Tell him that we're betrothed, Caroline!" the bag of wind demanded.

The lass darted a look at Humbolt before meeting O'Malley's confident gaze. "We were never betrothed."

"You are mine!"

Humbolt's roar had the lass curling into a tight ball, and she tried to hide in the corner of the settee.

O'Malley's control snapped. He reached for Humbolt's cravat and twisted it. The man's face turned beet red, and his eyes bulged in their sockets. Unable to trust his voice to speak, lest he say something that would have the lass and Mrs. Chessy cringing in fear, O'Malley tossed Humbolt toward the front door. When the man tripped over his own feet, O'Malley lifted him up by the back of his coat and shoved him toward the front door.

O'Malley had enough sense to shut the door behind him. Outside, he shook Humbolt until the man's teeth clacked together and he went lax in Thomas's grip. "Do not ever come near the lass again! If ye so much as even *think* me intended's name, I'll know, and will chase ye down and make ye wish ye were never born."

The sound of water dripping had O'Malley looking down. He quickly extended his arm, stepped back, and checked his boots to ensure they weren't wet. Pleasure ripped through him. He'd literally scared the piss out of the bugger. Stepping over the puddle, he tightened his grip on the back of Humbolt's coat and carried him to his carriage. Shoving him toward it, O'Malley stared down at the man, crossed his arms, and waited. He did not need to say another word. Humbolt scrambled into his carriage and, with the crack of his whip, got his horses moving toward the barn. Visibly shaking, the man maneuvered his carriage around until it faced the road.

The carriage passed by the spot where O'Malley stood. The wild-eyed expression in the older man's eyes lifted his spirits. He waited until the carriage disappeared before going back inside. Mrs. Chessy was speaking quietly to the lass, while Melanie and Olivia bustled about in the kitchen. No doubt tea was in order. If he were home in Ireland, his ma would have had the whiskey out and ready to pour.

Caroline's eyes met his. He could see the remnants of her tears, and it gutted him. He walked over to her. "I did not mean to make ye cry, lass. I apologize for letting me temper get the better of me. He won't bother ye again." She nodded, and he asked, "Was the man lack-witted? 'Twould explain why he thought ye'd want to speak to him again."

It was Mrs. Chessy who answered. "Apparently, Mr. Humbolt got wind of Bertram's connection to Baron Summerfield."

O'Malley sighed. "And through the baron, he discovered the connection to the earl, and His Grace. Both of who, by the by, would have done exactly what I just did." Which reminded him of the puddle on the front steps. "May I borrow a bucket?"

"Of course, but why would you need one?" the vicar's wife asked.

O'Malley could not hold back his grin. "I need to rinse yer front steps. Seems Humbolt got the message loud and clear enough to scare the—" He cleared his throat. "I'd best leave it at that."

Mrs. Chessy's eyes were bright with laughter. "I see. Thank you for taking care of that chore for me."

He nodded to the vicar's wife and turned back to the lass. "I'm sorry ye had to endure whatever he said to ye. I know it must have been cruel, because he refused to tell me. I won't press ye. I'll be alerting his lordship and the rest of the guard to add Humbolt to the list of those who are not allowed anywhere near ye, lass."

Caroline bit her bottom lip and rasped, "He was surprised to see my injury, and he made a few derogatory comments before telling me how it would turn his stomach to have to see my fractured hatchet face across the breakfast table every morning."

O'Malley wanted to jump on his horse and chase after the bleeding bastard! But the lass's feelings needed soothing. When she bit her plump bottom lip a second time, need rushed through him. He wanted to soothe her lip with the tip of his tongue before he pressed his mouth to hers. Passion and desire twisted inside of him, forcing him to grind his back teeth in frustration.

The lass had just been insulted by the man who had already stomped on her grieving heart the last time he dared to show his face at her home. "I'll make certain he never bothers ye again. After I speak to the vicar, I'll be needing to have a word with ye. Would ye feel up to taking a walk with me in the vicar's gardens this afternoon?"

"I would like that, Thomas."

Looking deep into her eyes, he leaned down and brushed a kiss to her forehead. "Well then, lass, best get yer rest now."

"I'll be looking forward to it." The way her eyes lit, as if from within, enchanted him. The need to enfold her in his arms threatened his control.

He cleared his throat. "I'll just get that bucket." He nodded to the women and walked through the house to the kitchen on his way to the back door.

"It is hanging on the tree by the pump," Mrs. Chessy called out. "Just outside the back door."

His heart was pounding by the time he'd filled the bucket. Caroline was hard to resist, but he could not just grab the lass and haul off and kiss her, especially in front of her aunt, even if the untested passion in Caroline's eyes begged him to. Need wreaked havoc with his control, his heart, and his head. Was this what his brothers, Sean and Michael, and his cousins went through when they realized they'd met the woman who held the other half of their heart?

He attended to the task of cleaning the front steps. Three full buckets of water took care of the lingering odor. By the time he finished, he realized the only thing that would ease the pain in his gut was the lass's promise to marry him. That and kissing the breath out of her until she went limp in his arms. He needed to speak to the vicar at once! Composing a list in his mind, he added that item to the top:

Ask the vicar for Caroline's hand. He could court her after they wed.

Make love to the lass...

No! Not yet! Speak to the vicar, bloody hell! That was already on his list.

Kiss the lass senseless. That he could do after the vicar granted him permission.

Make love to the lass...

Bugger it! Not yet!

Vow to love, honor, and protect the lass for the rest of his days.

Kiss the breath out of the lass after they exchanged vows. Then...and only then, would he be able to make love to the lass. *Finally!*

With the list complete, his plans firmly in mind, he returned the bucket and opened the back door. "Mrs. Chessy? Me boots are wet, so I won't be coming inside."

"Be right there!" The vicar's wife hurried to the back door. "Thank you, O'Malley. You are more than welcome to remove your boots and have a cup of tea with us."

"Thank ye, but I have to return to me duties. How is the lass?"

Worry evident in her eyes, she apologized, "I'm so sorry that I did not notice how upset Caro was. All I could think was that Humbolt had changed his mind and would offer for her. Thank you for interfering when you did, O'Malley."

"Would ye do me a favor, Mrs. Chessy?"

"Of course."

"Do not let anyone else in yer house."

"I won't," she promised.

"I need to speak to the vicar—will I find him at the church?"

Mrs. Chessy studied him for a moment before her smile bloomed. "Bertram will be so pleased, O'Malley. We could not ask for a man worthier of Caro than you. I have noticed the way she looks at you, and you look at her when you think no one is watching."

Her reaction surprised him. He had thought she might be resistant, since the lass had only been living with them for a fortnight. "Thank ye, Mrs. Chessy. Would ye please tell the lass that I'll be stopping by later for a short visit...in the garden?"

"Of course." Her smile faded as she confided, "I cannot believe that I trusted Humbolt. Thank you for reminding me that *she* did not trust the man. I had completely forgotten what Caro confided about his actions after Agatha passed. A few days in the stocks or pillory would do the man a world of good. No one has the right to disrespect or demean another the way he did to our Caro."

"He won't ever do so again," O'Malley promised. "Ye have me word on that. I'll be passing that information along to the rest of the guard. Between the three of us and O'Ghill, we'll get the word out. Humbolt won't be able to enter the village without a sending up a hue and a cry."

Mrs. Chessy's eyes filled, but she blinked away her tears. "If you hurry and speak to Bertram now, he can have the banns read on Sunday."

Gratitude filled him. "Thank ye for approving of me, even though all ye know of me is that I have been in the right time at the right place to rescue yer daughter and yer niece."

"I know love when I see it. Sparks fly every time you two are in the same room. You'd better be going. My husband will be delighted to have you marry our niece. I know I am. Do not forget to tell Caro that I told you about David. It has been a few years, but the heart heals in its own time, and cannot be rushed. Will you wait for her if she is not ready to marry?"

"I'll wait for as long as it takes for the lass to accept me offer."

Mrs. Chessy surprised O'Malley by placing a hand to his cheek. "I cannot wait to welcome you to the family, Thomas."

He grinned. "Thank ye, Mrs. Chessy. I…er…need to return to me duties after I speak to the vicar. I'll be by again this afternoon."

"I'll let Caro know."

"Thank ye." He closed the back door and noticed Stanbridge standing at the edge of the property. He walked over to him. "I hope ye realize, by the way I dispatched with that blackguard, that he is never allowed near Caroline again."

"Aye, O'Malley. I'm not used to saying no to Mrs. Chessy. It won't happen again. Before you feel it necessary to remind me, I do know how to follow orders and will not let anyone sway me again."

O'Malley studied Stanbridge's earnest expression. "Even if it's yer ma or da?"

The younger man clenched his jaw, relaxed it, and said, "I will tell my parents what happened so they will understand why I will obey orders from you or O'Ghill over theirs."

"Well then, I'll leave ye to yer post." O'Malley retraced his steps to where he'd tethered his horse. "Time to speak to me future uncle-in-law." Scratching the animal behind his ears, he added, "Then we'll make the rounds again. Are ye ready?" His gelding ignored him until O'Malley pulled a carrot out of his pocket. "I got this for ye earlier and forgot to give it to ye... If ye're not wanting it—"

His horse nipped the carrot from his fingers and ate it.

O'Malley chuckled. "There's a lad. On our way to the church, we need to stop at the inn. I need to ensure that the blackguard's carriage is not still in the vicinity. I'm thinking Humbolt got the message, but he seemed to be a bit of an overconfident blowhard to me. Best to be certain."

The animal lifted his head and whinnied.

O'Malley mounted his horse and headed down the road toward the inn. With his plans for the future mapped out, his heart settled back to its normal beat.

Alert, eyes scanning his surroundings, O'Malley was prepared when the first shot sounded. He ducked to the side. The lead ball hit his shoulder...instead of his head!

He urged his horse to gallop in the direction the shot was fired, dodging the second blast from the tallest fir tree between the vicarage and the inn. Knowing he had seconds to act, he aimed his primed and loaded rifle and fired. The answering cry of pain was music to his ears.

He wasn't surprised to see Stanbridge riding hell for leather toward him. O'Malley nodded toward the large tree. "Sharpshooter's up there. Think I winged him."

The younger man nodded and aimed his rifle at the center of the tree, where O'Malley could just make out the shadow of a man squatting on a branch with his arms wrapped around the trunk. "Climb down, or I'll shoot ye in the arse!" Stanbridge called.

O'Malley snorted with laughter. "Good one, Stanbridge—ye got his attention."

"Don't shoot," the man yelled. "I'm coming down!"

"Toss yer rifle to the ground first!" O'Malley commanded.

They watched the rifle fly out of the branches, followed by the man scurrying down. He jumped the last few feet to the ground, turned, and faced O'Malley and Stanbridge. "Don't shoot!"

"I won't," O'Malley told the prisoner, "if ye tell me who sent ye."

The man glanced around him. "Some nob from London. I won't get the other half of my payment if I don't kill you."

O'Malley sighed and nodded to the man's bleeding hand. "Ye'll be needing a new plan after the constable arrives."

"How did you see me? I was well hidden."

"I was scanning the area—'tis the perfect spot for a sharpshooter to lie in wait for his quarry."

"I was told you would be an easy target," the man mumbled.

"By the nob from London?"

The prisoner nodded.

"None of the men in the duke's guard are an easy target."

The man's Adam's apple bobbed up and down. "Duke?"

"Aye. I'm a member of the Duke of Wyndmere's private guard. Who did ye think ye were shooting at?"

"An Irish drifter."

Stanbridge pulled a length of rope from his pocket and tied the man's hands behind his back, then picked up the rifle. "You'd best let Dr. Higgins remove that lead ball, O'Malley."

O'Malley winced and would later swear he felt the lead ball move. "How do ye know it's still in there?"

The young man shrugged. "From the way you're pressing your arm to your side. What should I do with him?"

"Coleman said we could use the vacant stall in his barn, if need be, while we wait for the constable. We've never had a need to summon the man before now," O'Malley admitted. "I'm told the constable oversees the three villages nearby along with ours."

"Aye. My father has had dealings with him in the past. Says he's a good man," Stanbridge said.

"Are you going to take me to the doctor, too?" the prisoner asked.

"Well now, I may, but first I'll be needing yer name, and the name of the man who hired ye. Otherwise, I might just be letting ye bleed." O'Malley leaned to the side to get a better look at the man's hands, which were tightly bound behind his back. "Ye're bleeding like a stuck pig. Now would be the time to confess what ye know."

O'Malley's words had the desired effect. "Name's Greeley." The prisoner mumbled something, then told O'Malley what he needed to know: "The swell who hired me did not tell me his name, but I overheard someone calling him Anderson."

"How many men did he hire besides yerself?" Greeley stared at his feet, and O'Malley urged, "The sooner we get yer hand taken care of, the less chance of lead poisoning."

The man's head snapped up. "Two others."

O'Malley's mind raced. "Sharpshooters like yerself?"

"Aye."

"Where are they?" Stanbridge asked.

"Blue and Flowers should have reached Summerfield Chase by now and positioned themselves within shooting distance of the house."

"And ye're the only other man Anderson hired?" O'Malley said.

Greeley nodded. "I've been in that tree for the last hour waiting for a giant of a man dressed in black from head to toe patrolling through the village. You fit the bill."

O'Malley narrowed his eyes. "Where's yer horse?"

"I left him tied up in the woods. You'll never find him unless I guide you to him."

O'Malley snorted with laughter. "If that's what ye're thinking, then ye're not as smart as ye think ye are. We'll find yer horse. Stanbridge, take Greeley to the blacksmith's and lock him in."

"But I told you all I know!" Greeley protested.

"Guard him with yer life, Stanbridge. I've got to warn Garahan and the others. If Greeley cooperates and goes willingly, ye can leave him with Coleman long enough to fetch Dr. Higgins."

"Who's Coleman?" Greeley asked.

"The blacksmith. Ye'll want to cooperate," O'Malley advised.

"He has a wicked jab. I had the pleasure of watching him crack more than one of the posts in the smithy by punching them when he was angry."

The prisoner paled, and O'Malley knew he'd gotten his point across.

Stanbridge asked, "What about your shoulder?"

"It'll keep. After ye fetch the physician, tell Coleman ye need to escort Olivia to the vicarage and stay there guarding the women."

"What about the prisoner?"

"Coleman can handle it. He has all manner of sharp weapons, as well as the forge, at his disposal." Greeley keeled over, and O'Malley sighed. "He'll be more cooperative unconscious."

Stanbridge picked the prisoner up and draped him over his saddle.

"Ye're a good man to have at me back, Stanbridge. Thank you."

"When I take Olivia to the vicarage, I'll let Miss Gillingham know that you've been shot."

O'Malley frowned. "Let's just keep this between us." He gave the gelding his head and urged, "Run like the wind, laddie!"

At a gallop, the miles between the village and the baron's home flew by. *Lord, please let me warn the men in time.*

His head felt light, but he dug deep for the reserves he knew he had and could count on. He'd hold out until he alerted the baron and his men, and got Lady Phoebe, Prudence, and the twins to safety.

He whistled as his horse thundered toward the stables. "Two sharpshooters already in place! To yer posts, lads!" He heard the echo of two more whistles, and knew his cousins would find the bleeding bastards. Those with rifles would get into position. Those assigned to gather the women in Lady Phoebe's upstairs sitting room would be on task as well. His rifle again primed and loaded, O'Malley dismounted and ran toward the house.

Summerfield burst out of the back door, and the hair on the

back of O'Malley's neck stood on end. "Sharpshooter! Get down, yer lordship!" He heard the crack of the rifle and used his body as a shield to protect the baron. He jolted as intense heat grazed the side of his head. Ignoring the pain that followed, he spun around, aimed in the direction the shot had been fired, judged the distance, and waited to see movement in the trees on the other side of the stables.

His vision grayed, but he blinked, and it cleared. A branch moved halfway up the tree. O'Malley fired. The scream of agony wasn't as loud as it should have been from that distance. Another shot, oddly muffled, sounded closer to the outbuilding where their quarters were located.

"Get inside, yer lordship!" he shouted. "I'm right behind ye." Numbness crept up his legs. He stumbled.

"O'Malley!" A strong arm wrapped around his back. "I've got ye."

"O'Ghill?"

"Aye."

"Get his lordship inside. I've got to tell Garahan and Flaherty about the sharpshooter in the village before I man me post."

O'Malley's legs gave out as his blood loss hit a critical level. He felt himself being lifted high. His breath whooshed out as his chest hit O'Ghill's shoulder. He started to demand to be put down, but the side of his head banged against O'Ghill's back as the man ran toward the rear entrance, shooting a searing pain through O'Malley's skull.

Fighting to hang on to consciousness, O'Malley rasped, "I can walk."

His cousin jolted to a stop, bent down, and set O'Malley on his feet. "Have at it, boy-o!"

O'Malley wavered, but did not fall. Before he could take a step, his field of vision grayed at the edges and shrank. "Bloody *fecking* hell."

CHAPTER TWENTY-ONE

M RS. CHESSY RUSHED to greet her husband when he walked in the front door an hour after O'Malley had left to meet with him. "Well?"

He bent to press his lips to the middle of her forehead. "I could use a cup of tea and something sweet. How was your morning, my dear?"

"Why don't you tell me about yours?" she urged. "I am certain your morning was far more enlightening than mine."

For a moment the vicar was silent, then he sighed. "Was Melanie difficult again today?"

"Not as much as our unwanted visitor," his wife replied.

"Unwanted? Who was it?" The vicar shook his head. "Don't answer that—tell me where Stanbridge and O'Malley are, and where in Heaven's name they were when you had an unwanted visitor."

Mrs. Chessy wrung her hands and confessed, "It was my fault. I insisted that Stanbridge let Mr. Humbolt in."

"And?" the vicar asked.

"Oh, Bertram! I should never have gone against O'Malley and O'Ghill's orders not to allow anyone inside."

He grasped her hands to still their trembling. "Tell me what happened."

She shuddered and repeated the insults Humbolt had tossed

at their niece. Describing how Caroline tried to shrink and disappear into the settee, her voice wavered. "He even dared to call our Caro hatchet-faced!"

"Where are your guards now?"

She ignored the question. "Don't you have anything you want to tell me about O'Malley?"

"Why would I, when he is supposed to be guarding you, Melanie, and Caro?"

"Because I sent him over to speak to you after he handily dispatched Humbolt. It was good of him to take care of the puddle of—" She met her husband's frustrated gaze and asked, "If he did not ride over to speak with you, then where is he?"

"Was there something urgent O'Malley needed to tell me?" Vicar Chessy asked.

"Yes," his wife said. "Very important."

The heavy pounding on the back door had the vicar stalking through the house. "That had better be O'Malley or Stanbridge. I'll get to the bottom of what happened." He pulled open the door, and Stanbridge rushed inside, tugging Olivia by the hand.

"Vicar! I am so glad you are here. Where are Melanie and Caro?"

"I just walked in the other door. Why don't you ask my wife?"

Stanbridge shook his head. "I do not have time to chase after them."

"What is going on?" the vicar demanded.

"I have orders from O'Malley to ensure that all four women are safely tucked into the vicarage." He gave Olivia a slight nudge to get her feet moving.

"Caro and Melanie are upstairs," the vicar's wife replied. "O'Malley said he'd return this afternoon to speak with Caro and walk in our gardens." She looked at her husband and said, "Surely you know what he wants to speak to her about, Bertram. After all, he was on his way to ask you..." Her voice faded as she noticed the large stain on Stanbridge's coat. "Is that blood?"

"Aye," Stanbridge answered. At the quiet moan of distress, he reached out to steady Olivia. "Maybe you should sit down." He helped her onto one of the kitchen chairs and explained, "Olivia's never seen an injured prisoner before. There was more blood than I'd counted on when Dr. Higgins was taking care of his hand."

"Prisoner?" Bertram asked.

"Who was it, and what happened to his hand?" Mrs. Chessy asked.

"Mum?" Melanie glided down the stairs. "What is all the commotion about?" When her mother did not answer, she turned to her father. "Papa, aren't you a little early for tea? I just came down to put the kettle on." Her eyes riveted on Stanbridge. "Good Lord, is that blood?"

Stanbridge nodded, and Mrs. Chessy asked, "Why did O'Malley order you to bring Olivia here?"

"Safety in numbers. You'll all be in one place when..." His voice trailed off, and as if he realized he'd already said too much, he clamped his lips shut.

He did not count on Olivia speaking out of turn. "O'Malley shot the prisoner. But in all fairness, Greeley's a sharpshooter and shot O'Malley first."

"O'Malley's been shot?"

Everyone turned to stare at the woman standing wide-eyed at the top of the staircase.

"When?" Caroline asked. "How bad is it? Can you take me to him?" Her voice broke, but she held on to her composure.

"You weren't supposed to speak about what happened, Olivia," Stanbridge told her.

"Well then, you should have mentioned that little tidbit on our way over here," Olivia grumbled.

"No more questions!" The volume of the vicar's voice had everyone falling silent and staring at him. "That's better." He locked gazes with Stanbridge. "Where is O'Malley now? How many other men came with this Greeley?"

"Two, and they should be at Summerfield Chase by now. Which is why O'Malley tasked me with delivering the prisoner to the empty stall at the smithy before I went to fetch the physician to take care of his wound."

"And then…?" Olivia prompted him.

Stanbridge raised his eyes to the ceiling. "Then I was to bring Olivia here and stand guard until further notice."

"Stanbridge?" Caroline's voice sounded strained. "Please tell me how O'Malley looked when he rode out of the village."

The young man shook his head. "I am not at liberty to discuss the situation other than to say that Mr. Coleman sent for the constable and is keeping an eye on the prisoner while I'm standing guard here."

Mrs. Chessy drew in a breath and gathered her composure. "Melanie and Olivia, please set the table. Caro, please set out the plate of scones, and another with the teacakes we baked early this morning. Stanbridge, you are welcome to join us for tea."

"I'll be standing guard out back, where I can see the smithy in the distance. I'll breathe easier when I see the constable arriving. That leaves only my most important duty left to do."

Mrs. Chessy was about to ask when the vicar said, "Guarding the women."

"Aye."

"Did you tell Dr. Higgins that O'Malley had been shot?" Mrs. Chessy asked.

"I did. He will be on his way to Summerfield Chase shortly."

"Who will be riding with him for protection?"

"O'Malley and O'Ghill have messengers stationed all around the village. One of the men will accompany the doctor."

"Will another messenger ride out to alert the duke's guard when the constable arrives?"

"Aye. If you'll excuse me, Mrs. Chessy?"

"Yes, of course, Stanbridge. I'll send a cup of tea out—"

"No, thank you. I'll wait until I hear from O'Malley."

The vicar's wife placed her hand on Stanbridge's forearm. "I understand. We are so grateful that you are here guarding our precious girls, Lyman. Thank you."

He nodded and walked out the back door.

WHY HAD HER aunt all of a sudden demanded tea? Caroline's hands trembled, but she did her best to control them. Upended teacakes just might be the trigger to send Melanie and Olivia into a bout of tears. She held hers inside—she would cry later when she found out the full extent of O'Malley's injury and knew that he would recover. With his build, he was such a large target. There was no telling where he could have been hit. Until she knew more, she would pray that he would recover.

Her breath hitched as a dreadful thought occurred. She immediately shoved it aside, refusing to believe the worst.

Finally, the table was set and the tea poured, but the normal camaraderie was absent. Her aunt and uncle drank their tea in silence. Melanie kept staring at Olivia, who kept her head down, staring at her uneaten teacake.

Caroline felt as if she'd go mad if they did not receive word of O'Malley's condition soon. Unable to bear the pall that hung over the room, she rasped, "No one mentioned where O'Malley was shot, or how much blood he lost."

Aunt Josephine reached over to pat Caroline's hand. "No news is good news."

Uncle Bertram cleared his throat and said, "Your aunt is correct. Bad news travels quickly."

"Really, Caro," Melanie added. "Do you think O'Malley would have ridden all the way out to the baron's estate if he was on the verge of collapse?"

Caroline didn't have to think—the answer burst from inside of her. "Yes! I have no doubt O'Ghill would have, too. I have yet to meet Garahan or Flaherty, but if they are anything like

O'Malley and O'Ghill, they would do all in their power to uphold their vow to protect and defend."

Her aunt smiled, and it bothered Caroline.

"Really, Aunt Josephine, I cannot think that is anything to smile about."

"Forgive me, Caro. I was thinking of something else entirely."

Silence descended once more. Caroline had been fearful when her brother and David went off to war, but the fear simmering inside of her now was somehow more volatile than that. Was this how it felt when the man you loved was in danger? Why had it taken his being shot for her to realize how deeply her feelings went? They had been thrown together in a desperate situation from the start, and feelings and emotions were bound to bubble to the surface at some point. Now she knew they weren't based on a volatile situation.

Unlike her feelings for David, which were based on the admiring way he looked at her when he promised to court and marry her when he returned, her feelings for O'Malley were born out the way he'd treated, respected, and protected her. She sighed and admitted to herself that there were also the sparks of desire swirling in the depths of his brilliant green eyes… Desire for her! Caroline had learned all too well how fragile, and precious, life was. In that moment, she promised herself that she would do whatever it took to sneak out of the vicarage tonight and make her way to Summerfield Chase. Nothing and no one would stop her from reaching O'Malley's side!

CHAPTER TWENTY-TWO

"Y E'LL WANT TO step aside, O'Ghill."

O'Malley's cousin shook his head. "God help me, ye're an annoying bugger when ye aren't unconscious."

O'Malley did not need the reminder that he'd not only lost consciousness once, but twice. The first time was right after a lead ball grazed the side of his head when he used his body to protect the baron. The second time was the physician's doing, and the catalyst. He shuddered remembering the pain as Dr. Higgins dug the lead ball out of his shoulder.

His head ached, not from the gouge the lead ball had left behind, but from the scouring of the wound and the bandage wrapped tight around it. The dull throb in his shoulder was all the reminder he needed that between the threads and thick bandage, he would be climbing the ladder one-handed when next he had the rooftop post.

"Ah, O'Malley, you're up and about. Excellent," Summerfield said as he walked in the room.

"'Twill take more than two lead balls to keep me down, yer lordship. Have ye had a report from Stanbridge?"

"Aye. The constable delivered it just now when he loaded the prisoners into his wagon."

"And?" O'Ghill asked before O'Malley could.

"The women are cooperating and have not left the vicarage."

"Are they giving him any trouble?"

"None," the baron replied.

"And ye don't find that curious?" O'Malley asked.

"Not at all. 'Sensible' is what comes to mind," Summerfield said.

"God help me," O'Malley mumbled. "Are ye thinking what I am, O'Ghill?"

The fierce expression on his cousin's face settled the churning in O'Malley's gut. "Aye, Thomas. The quiet before the storm."

"What storm?" the baron asked.

"Melanie," O'Ghill said.

"Caroline," O'Malley answered at the same time.

The baron shook his head. "Thompson and Greeves have been guarding the perimeter of the vicarage since they arrived a few hours ago."

"What about Tremayne and Masterson?" O'Malley asked. "Have ye heard from them yet?"

"They have split up, watching the two roads into the village for a sign of Anderson's carriage."

"And ye're certain the man will not be riding a horse?" O'Ghill asked.

"Aye," the baron replied. "On your advice, men, and as a precaution, aside from the roads leading to and from here, we have men stationed at the head of the graveyard path and the one from the marsh—both of which lead here but are too narrow for a carriage."

"'Tis a relief," O'Malley said, "because ye can travel on foot as well as horseback."

Summerfield's frown was fierce. "I confess, that thought never occurred to me."

O'Ghill and O'Malley shared a look, and O'Ghill drawled, "Well now, that's because ye were born *here*."

The baron ignored the comment.

"With yer permission, yer lordship," O'Malley said, "I need to speak to the vicar."

The baron stared at O'Malley's shoulder, then lifted his eyes to the linen wrapped around his head. "I distinctly heard Dr. Higgins advise you to rest and let your body humors balance out."

"Ye lost a lot of blood, Thomas," O'Ghill said. "I'll deliver a message to him for ye."

O'Malley frowned. "Ye just want an excuse to see the vicar's daughter."

O'Ghill scrubbed a hand over his face. "*Bollocks!* Ye're the one who's after seeing the vicar's niece, while I'm doing me best to stay away from Melanie."

Garahan stuck his head in the open doorway. "Are ye having a family argument without me?"

"'Tisn't an argument," O'Malley grumbled. "Just O'Ghill marking his territory."

Garahan stared at O'Ghill, then O'Malley. "Aren't ye supposed to be lying on the cot resting?"

"Aye," O'Ghill and Summerfield answered at the same time.

"Well then, get yer *arse* on that cot!" Garahan said.

O'Malley's head ached, and his shoulder throbbed, adding to his foul mood. "Did ye forget who's the head of the duke's guard here?"

Garahan opened his mouth to speak but, at the direct look from the baron, fell silent. "I believe that would be *me*, O'Malley," Summerfield replied. "As head of the guard, I am ordering you to do as the physician recommended, and rest for a full twenty-four hours. You will not be on duty. You will eat whatever Mrs. Green sends to you on a tray. And you will not leave this room."

"Yer lordship, I—"

"—*will of course do as you ask.*" He glared at O'Malley. "That's what you were going to say, wasn't it?"

O'Malley knew when he'd been beaten. "Aye, yer lordship."

The baron nodded to his men and walked out.

"Never saw his lordship this upset before," Garahan muttered.

"Must be his worry for Lady Phoebe," O'Ghill said.

"I'm thinking it could be whatever she wanted to speak to him about before ye got shot," Garahan replied.

"Aye," O'Malley agreed. "Mayhap it has to do with the Honeycutts and their trials. Her ladyship is a firm believer in justice, but she may be worrying about how the twins will deal with a guilty verdict."

"'Tis one thing to know yer ma or da has a mean streak a mile wide," Garahan murmured, "but 'tis another entirely when they intentionally strike someone on the back of the head."

"The lads are young enough that they wouldn't understand the nuances of the law, though they know right from wrong," O'Ghill said. "They may understand that justice must prevail, but 'tisn't just about a criminal—'tis their da and ma."

"I wonder if her ladyship is thinking to ask her brother to intervene." All at once, O'Malley felt as if he'd been outside in the sun too long. Heat swept up from the soles of his feet. His face felt as if it were on fire, and his throat was parched. "'Tis gone hot as blazes in here. I…uh, think I'll…"

"Bloody hell!" Garahan pushed away from the doorway, but was too far away to catch O'Malley.

"I've got—Bloody *fecking* hell!" The back of O'Malley's head hit O'Ghill in the face. As blood gushed out of his broken nose, Garahan snorted with laughter.

"I never would have thought to catch him with me face, but at least his head didn't hit the floor."

"Give me a hand, ye bugger. He's burning up."

Mrs. Green screamed from where she stood in the doorway, staring at the blood all over O'Ghill. Garahan swore, while O'Ghill reassured her, "'Tis only a broken nose, Mrs. Green. Would ye mind tossing me one of the linens over there by the pitcher and bowl? I need to lay O'Malley on the cot."

The cook calmed at O'Ghill's quiet tone. She walked into the room and set her tray on the table along the wall. Grabbing the linen, she rushed across the room to hand it to O'Ghill. "Tip your head back."

"Never mind me, 'tis Thomas. A fever's set in." O'Ghill's pronouncement hung in the air for a moment in the silence that followed.

"How long does it take for an infection to set in after a man's been shot?" Garahan asked.

With the bleeding slowing down, O'Ghill walked over to the pile of freshly folded linens. He replaced the saturated one with one from the top, pressing it against his nose. "I'm guessing more than the hour it took from the time the sharpshooter fired that shot to when O'Malley rode up to the stables like the devil was hard at his heels."

"Sometimes five minutes is enough time," Mrs. Green said as she bathed O'Malley's face with cool water from the pitcher. "Garahan, would you please ask the footman to notify Timmons? He'll alert his lordship. O'Ghill, let me take a look at your nose."

"Forget me nose. I've broken it before. Should we be sending for Dr. Higgins?"

The cook agreed. "He needs to know wound fever has set in."

O'Malley thrashed his head from side to side, mumbling.

"What is he saying?" the cook asked.

Garahan had returned and was standing on the threshold in time to hear her question. He walked toward his cousin. "Sounds like he's repeating the same word over and over."

"Caro," O'Ghill said. "'Tis what the vicar and his family call the lass who has a hold of O'Malley's heart. If I were her, I'd want to know he's calling for her." Without asking permission, O'Ghill walked past Garahan, into the hallway, and out the back door straight to the stables.

Flaherty whistled, and O'Ghill turned at the sound. "How's O'Malley?"

"Spiked a fever," O'Ghill told him. "He's calling for the lass."

Flaherty's jaw clenched. "Ye'd best hurry, then. Fetch the lass and bring her here!"

O'Ghill mounted his horse, leaned down, and rasped, "Run, laddie!"

CAROLINE PACED THE confines of the bedchamber until she thought she'd go mad. She had retreated here when she could not handle the inane conversation between Olivia and Melanie another moment. The more time passed, the stronger the worry. She would never be able to wait for the cover of darkness to sneak out of the house.

The uneasy feeling inside of her had grown stronger in the last two hours. Something was wrong with O'Malley...desperately wrong. She could not explain how she knew, but her gut and her heart were in agreement. Mayhap it was a message from her mum in Heaven.

She yanked open the door and started down the stairs when someone pounded on the front door. Everyone was in the kitchen, so she dashed down to answer the door. "Stanbridge? What's happened?"

He stepped aside, and O'Ghill reached for her hand. "O'Malley's in a bad way. He's been calling for ye."

"O'Ghill!" Melanie screeched, rushing toward the front of the house. "Your poor face! Who hit you?"

He ignored her. "Will ye come with me, Caroline?"

"Yes. Of course. Aunt Josephine! Something's wrong. O'Malley needs me."

Caroline's aunt glanced at the sight of O'Ghill's two black eyes and swollen nose, but only for a heartbeat. "Yes. Of course, dear. Please send word as soon as you can. We'll be praying for Thomas!"

Caroline paused on the front steps, staring as O'Ghill mounted his horse. "How am I going to get there?"

He held out his hand, and she let him pull her up onto the

animal behind him. "Hold on tight!" The horse reared up on its hind legs, and Caroline clung to O'Ghill. They took off at a gallop. The wind whipped the pins out of her hair, but she didn't bother with that now. She tucked her head against Killian's broad back and prayed she would be able to help O'Malley.

They kept up the fast pace all the way to the baron's stables. Before she could think to swing her leg over the horse to dismount, O'Ghill plucked her off the animal's back into his arms and sprinted for the back door. "'Tis the wound fever, lass, but I've never seen its like before."

"*Caro!*"

She shivered at the anguished tone of O'Malley's voice. "I'm here, Thomas!" O'Ghill set her on her feet next to the cot where O'Malley thrashed from side to side. She reached for his hand. "Thomas, it's Caro. I'm here. Lie still now. I need to wash my hands, then I will bathe your face. We must bring the fever down."

He ceased moving at the sound of her voice. Relieved, Caroline walked over to the pitcher and bowl and quickly washed. Mrs. Green stood up from where she sat next to the cot and motioned for Caroline to sit there. A moment later, she handed Caroline a cloth. Caroline understood time was of the essence.

She dipped the cloth in the cool water, squeezing most of it out before gently sweeping across O'Malley's forehead to the edge of the bandage, down the sides of his face, and onto his neck, before repeating the movement. When the cloth heated but he had not cooled at all, she asked, "This may sound immodest, but should we remove his shirt? During the worst of Papa's illness, the physician had Mum and me bathing his chest, back, and legs."

"His fever spiked so quickly, I didn't think of it," Mrs. Green admitted. "I knew we had to cool his head, but had to be careful not to wet the bandage covering the wound where the lead ball creased his skull. Then there is the wound in his shoulder. Dr. Higgins had a time of it locating and digging out that lead ball. It is no wonder fever set in."

Caroline's stomach wobbled at the description. She could not fathom the immeasurable pain he must have suffered. Pushing that thought aside, she ignored the queasy feeling in her belly. "O'Ghill, can you sit him up? If we cannot pull his shirt off, you may have to cut it off."

O'Ghill bent down, whipped a blade out of his boot, and sliced the front of O'Malley's cambric shirt.

Caroline ignored the blood seeping through the bandage at his shoulder, and the one wrapped around his head. "Lift him up, and I'll pull the shirt out from underneath him."

They worked as a team for the next hour, O'Ghill lifting O'Malley up so she could bathe his broad back, then laying him down so she could bathe his heavily muscled chest. O'Ghill muttered, "I'm thinking we need to bathe his legs like ye said, Caro."

Exhaustion pulled at her, but she ignored it. She would not stop her ministrations until O'Malley's fever cooled enough to break. "I'll turn my back while you cut his trousers off."

She heard the fabric tearing and sent up another silent prayer. *Dear Lord, please help me bring his fever down. I cannot lose him!*

THE HOURS PASSED with O'Malley caught in the grip of wound fever. Caroline had seen firsthand how devastating the fever was when the first of her brother's friends returned wounded from battle. He had not survived the fever, but by Heaven, O'Malley would!

Time passed in a blur, and she remembered refusing the offer of food, but somehow found herself in the kitchen eating a hearty bowl of stew. She faintly remembered drinking tea and eating something sweet, but could not say what it was. Her heart and mind were concentrating solely on breaking O'Malley's fever. Nothing else mattered! Life would not be so cruel as to take him from her when she'd only just realized how deeply she cared for him.

O'Ghill and Garahan traded places during the night, but she refused to leave O'Malley's side and let Mrs. Green take over for her. Caroline could not say why, other than the gut feeling that if she left him, he would decline further. As it was, every time she got up to change out the water in the bowl, he began moving restlessly. When she brushed the tips of her fingers along the length of his jaw and whispered to him, telling him she was there, he quieted.

Through the long night, she continually prayed that his fever would break, as she willed every ounce of her strength into the man she loved. Losing O'Malley would kill her. She asked for strength when she felt it ebb. Alone for a brief moment, she gave in to despair. Laying her head on O'Malley's chest, she sobbed. "You have to keep fighting the fever! I want that walk in the garden you promised me, and all that the desire in your eyes promised. Please don't leave me, Thomas!"

He roused, grunted, and threw an arm around her. "Faith, but ye're a bossy bit of goods, lass." She gasped and tried to push off his chest to look into his eyes, but he held her in his firm grip. "I've got ye now, lass. I'm not letting ye go."

Caroline cried harder.

"That's it, lass, get it all out of ye." A few minutes later, she heard him groan. She tried to sit up, and this time he let her.

She brushed at her tears with the backs of her hands. "I thought I was too heavy, making you moan like that."

"Nay. 'Twas the idea that I may have I opened the floodgates. Do ye think ye'll be finished crying anytime soon?" She snorted, then covered her mouth with her hands. He reached up, pulled them away from her lips, and pressed a kiss to the back of one and then the other. "Never hide yer feelings from me, lass. Nor yer snorts… 'Tis an adorable sound."

Crying and smiling, she said, "I need to get a fresh cloth." He released her hand, and she slowly stood, stiff from sitting bent over for so long. Biting her lip to keep from groaning herself, she took the small bowl she had been using over to the table along the wall. She exchanged it for an empty one and filled it with cool water. Taking a fresh linen from the pile, she returned to her seat and began her ministrations, the worst of her worry fading as she bathed his face while his red-rimmed green eyes watched her every move. "You're cooler."

O'Ghill returned with a small tray and set it down on the table. "I've brought ye more tea, Caro. Are ye sure I cannot convince ye to try another scone or two?"

"I'll take one," O'Malley rasped.

"Thomas!" O'Ghill rushed to his side and glared at him. "Ye've had Caro weeping for the last few hours. 'Tis about time ye opened yer eyes. We even sent for the vicar!"

O'Malley frowned. "Did I ask ye to marry me already, lass? Me brain's a bit foggy."

Caroline couldn't find her voice, so she shook her head, and O'Ghill grumbled, "We sent for the vicar because there's no priest."

"What in the bloody hell do ye need a priest for?" O'Malley's expression changed. He understood what O'Ghill had not said. "Ah, well now. I'm not dead yet, am I? Can ye give the lass and me a bit of privacy?"

"Ye're only wearing a sheet across yer manly parts, lad. 'Tis one thing when ye're out of yer mind with fever, but another thing altogether when ye're awake," O'Ghill said. "I'll not be leaving the two of ye alone now."

"How long ago did ye send for the vicar?"

"He should be here any moment," O'Ghill replied.

"Best find me a shirt to wear," O'Malley said. "And cover me legs." He reached for Caroline's hand and held tight. "I dreamed a redheaded, bespectacled angel came down from Heaven to bathe my face."

"Angels don't wear spectacles."

He pulled her to him, and she gasped, surprised at his strength when he had been unconscious and burning with fever not fifteen minutes ago.

"Me guardian angel does." When their lips were a breath apart, he rasped, "Spectacles and freckles. Marry me, lass." She hesitated, and he slid a hand around the back of her neck to hold her close as he softly pressed his lips to hers. "I want to be the man to kiss ye awake each morning, and love ye to sleep at night."

How could she say no to him? "Yes, please."

He released his grip on her, and she fell on top of him.

O'Ghill's snort of disapproval echoed behind them. "I thought ye were still weak enough to trust ye alone with Caroline for five minutes while I fetched a shirt for ye."

Ignoring the jibe, O'Malley grinned. "She said yes." O'Ghill shook his head and groaned. O'Malley's brow furrowed as he stared at his cousin's face. "What happened, Killian? Did ye run into a brick wall?"

O'Ghill shouted with laughter. "Aye, that I did, ye bugger—'twas the back of yer hard head! Here, I'll help ye sit up." He slipped the shirt over O'Malley's head, while Caroline tucked the sheet around his legs.

She reached up, thinking to tuck her hair into its pins, and froze.

"Something wrong, lass?" O'Malley asked.

"I seem to have lost my hairpins."

"Must have been on the ride over, Caroline," O'Ghill said. "I'm sure if we ask Prudence or Lady Phoebe, one of them would be more than happy to give ye some."

She brushed her hands over her unruly curls and started to braid them, only to stop when O'Malley's hand covered hers. "I love yer hair. The curlier and wilder the better."

"Well, it is not as if we are going to be married tonight, otherwise—"

"We are, and it's too late to change yer mind, lass. Ye said yes."

She stared at him. "I did not mean that I'd marry you right now."

"Then why did ye say yes?"

"Because I do want to marry you. But you're injured—your fever just broke."

O'Malley ignored the last half of what she just said. "Well now, 'tis a relief. Why do ye want to wait?"

She glanced down at her gown and held her hands next to her sides. "I'm soaked to the skin."

O'Malley's eyes turned a deeper green. "So I see, lass. I can remedy that."

Caroline frowned at him. "I do not see how."

"Ye can take yer—"

"—time, having a cup of tea," O'Ghill interrupted, staring at the doorway behind them. "Thank ye for coming so quickly, vicar."

O'Malley stared at Caroline, and she felt her face heat. Pleased that he was awake and lucid, she turned to the vicar. "Thank you for coming, Uncle. O'Ghill and I were afraid..." Tears welled in her eyes, and her throat tightened. For the life of her, she couldn't utter her fear aloud.

Her shoulders slumped and her uncle hugged her to him. "You have always been a brave woman, Caro. I expected to be praying over O'Malley. I'm happy that is not the case." He urged her to sit down, then turned to O'Malley. "My wife told me you were coming to speak to me earlier today, before you were waylaid."

"Aye."

"She seems to think she knows what you wanted to discuss with me."

"Aye, that she does. Yer wife gave me her blessing and said she was certain you'd be giving yers. Have ye changed yer mind?"

"You haven't asked for it yet," the vicar reminded him.

"Me head's a wee bit foggy still. Not sure if it's from the fever or the lead ball."

"Get to the point, O'Malley," O'Ghill interrupted.

"Aye. I was going to ask if I could court yer niece, Vicar

Chessy. But being as circumstances brought her here to tend to me, I'm not going to ask to court her."

The vicar's lips twitched. "I see."

"Will ye marry us tonight?"

"But you need to rest and recover," Caroline said. "We should wait at least a fortnight before Uncle reads the banns."

"I'll recover faster if ye're the one tending to me, lass."

How could Caroline refuse the man when his voice deepened and his eyes held the promise of kisses, hugs...and more!

"'Tis the truth, vicar," O'Ghill cut in. "When I came to fetch Caroline earlier, we did not think Thomas would pull through. I'm not exaggerating. He was thrashing about, making it difficult for Mrs. Green to bathe his face and neck before Caroline sat down. Once she took over the task, O'Malley quieted considerably."

Caroline's eyes welled with tears, and she let them fall. "He was unconscious when I arrived, but I could not tell if it was from his wounds or the fever. O'Ghill and I worked to bring his fever down. Even though I prayed for God not to, I was not sure if He would hear my prayers and take away another person I love."

"Your aunt and I aren't blind, Caro," her uncle said. "We could see how you two felt about one another. If you believe that O'Malley will not heal if you are not the one taking care of him, say the word, and I'll marry you now."

"Thank you, Uncle. I do not want to take a chance that he will suffer a relapse. Please, marry us now."

He smiled and handed Caroline his handkerchief to blot her tears. "This is not the first marriage I will have performed while the groom is lying on a cot."

"It isn't?"

"I married a handful of soldiers returning from war over the years. Some of them eventually healed to the point where they were on crutches...others did not."

Caroline's throat constricted, but she willed it to relax. O'Malley was awake and seemed stronger by the moment.

"O'Ghill, will you be one of our witnesses?"

"Aye, Caroline, but we'd best be telling his lordship, Garahan, and Flaherty. They're family and will want to act as witnesses, too."

AS IT TURNED out, it was an hour later that Caroline stood beside O'Malley to say her vows. The baron steadied him on one side, while O'Ghill stood on the other. Garahan and Flaherty stood off to the side, slightly behind him, prepared to catch O'Malley if he passed out.

Garbed in the pale blue gown Lady Phoebe insisted that she wear, Caroline felt as if she were in a dream. But when she smiled at Garahan's wife, Prudence, and Lady Phoebe, they immediately smiled back. This was real. She was marrying Thomas O'Malley, head of the duke's guard at Summerfield Chase, with their small group gathered to witness their vow taking.

When her mind drifted, weaving hopes with her dreams, her uncle's words blurred until she heard her name. Caroline repeated her promise to love and cherish O'Malley through sickness and health, in good times and hard. When he repeated those same vows and pulled her close, she sighed and poured everything she felt for him into their first kiss as man and wife.

SHE DIDN'T REMEMBER falling asleep, but woke up in the chair next to O'Malley's cot, surprised to discover she still wore the blue gown.

"Did ye sleep well, lass?"

Caroline blinked and stared at the handsome man smiling at her. She closed her eyes and counted to ten before opening them again. "It wasn't a dream?"

O'Malley chuckled. The warm, rumbling sound felt like warm sun after weeks of rain. "Nay, wife. Now that ye're awake, if ye help me to sit up, I've been suffering, craving another taste of yer sweet lips while I watched ye sleep."

Her gaze dropped to his lips and up again. The merriment in his eyes had her whispering a prayer of thanks while her face heated with embarrassment.

"Never have I seen a blush so becoming on a redheaded lass."

"Oh?" Caroline tried to keep the nip of jealousy out of her tone. "And have you known many redheads, *husband*?" From the way his lips curved, she'd failed in that regard.

"Several. Ye met Flaherty last night; surely ye noticed—"

"Is it morning already?"

"Aye, lass. As I was saying, the Flahertys are all red-haired."

She sighed and lifted a strand of hair that curled around her hand. "This is red. Flaherty's hair is a lovely shade of auburn."

"Since ye're after bedeviling yer poor, injured husband…" He tugged on her hand, and she tumbled onto his chest. "Ah, much better, and right where I'm wanting ye, lass…in me bed."

"'Tis a cot," O'Ghill grumbled from the open doorway. "Ye've not been cleared for relations of any kind! It's me own bad luck to have been assigned the task of keeping ye from injuring yerself further until Dr. Higgins arrives this morning to have another look at ye. And all because ye broke me fecking nose—beg yer pardon, Caroline—and I'm to rest for a few more hours."

Caroline tried to hide her shocked reaction, admitting, "I have heard that expression quite a bit since meeting the two of you."

O'Malley shook his head. "We don't mean to be rude in front of ye, lass."

"I know, you'd much rather wait until my back is turned, or I'm out of hearing."

"Ye've married an intelligent lass, Thomas," O'Ghill said. "Far too good for the likes of ye."

O'Malley tightened his hold on her and sat up. "No one objected last night when we said our vows. 'Tis too late now. I'm keeping her."

O'Ghill grinned. "I'm happy for the pair of ye. Now then, his lordship sent me in to ensure ye kept yer hands to yerself,

O'Malley."

"Well now, how else could I be holding me wife in me arms?"

"Ye wouldn't be."

"Have a heart, Killian. We're wed right and proper, and me wife isn't objecting—" O'Malley's gaze met hers. "Are ye, lass?"

Unable to resist the earnest expression on his face, or the sparkle in his green eyes, she slipped her arms around his neck and kissed him. His mouth was warm. His lips were firm at first, then magically softened as she poured what she felt for him into the kiss.

"O'Ghill! I thought I told you to keep an eye on O'Malley," Baron Summerfield said, entering.

Caroline sighed and leaned back. "It was my fault, your lordship," she confessed. "I have developed this weakness—I just can't keep my lips to myself."

O'Malley frowned. "Ye'd best make certain I'm the only man ye kiss, wife."

"And that is as it should be, O'Malley," Summerfield said. "All joking aside, I'm happy to see that you are much improved this morning. Dr. Higgins will be pleased."

"In that case, kindly excuse us, I have a duty to perform. O'Ghill, please escort his lordship out, and close the door behind ye."

The baron's laugh surprised Caroline. She had been certain he would be insulted. "You remind me of myself, O'Malley."

Her husband smiled. "If I recall, ye were suffering from a head wound at the time, too."

"I had one thought only: protecting Phoebe. When her carriage was surrounded by the kidnappers that night—" The baron drew in a deep breath and slowly exhaled. "And here we are living in the Borderlands, expecting our first babe." His gaze swept from O'Malley to O'Ghill and back again. "This time the tables have been turned, and you're the one with the injured head…and shoulder. Your family has gone above and beyond what my brother-in-law envisioned when he hired you to guard our family. I know I speak for Jared, Edward, and our wives when I say we are in your debt."

"'Tis only a flesh wound, yer lordship. I'll heal."

"Did someone mention healing?" Dr. Higgins asked from where he stood on the threshold. "Mrs. Green said I should just come in." He inclined his head to Caroline. "Good morning, Mrs. O'Malley. I trust our patient had a quiet night."

Caroline tried to sit up, but O'Malley wouldn't allow it. "Dr. Higgins is a married man, lass. I'm sure he'll understand me reluctance to let ye go."

The physician shook his head. "I'm pleased to see you feeling better. I need to change your bandages and assess your wounds. Would everyone but Mrs. O'Malley mind giving us a bit of privacy?"

"Not at all." Summerfield nodded to O'Ghill, who followed behind him and closed the door.

"Now then. I trust you did not do any further damage to your head or shoulder last night," the doctor said.

"I was in pain all night because of it," O'Malley grumbled.

"Shot twice, one would imagine you would be. If not for the head wound, I would have recommended laudanum. Please set your wife free and we'll start with that injury first."

Caroline wrung her hands. "I am so sorry, Thomas! I fell asleep when I should have been taking care of you. Are you in pain now?"

"Aye, lass. Terrible pain."

This was all her fault. She had to fix it. "Is it your head or your shoulder?"

O'Malley snorted with laughter, leaving Caroline totally confused. Her gaze met that of the doctor, who was smiling. "I do not see what is so humorous."

"'Tis yer innocence, wife. Now then, why don't ye have a seat while the good doctor has a look at me head? It doesn't pain me quite as much as it did yesterday."

"A good sign," Dr. Higgins said, unwinding the linen to get a look at the gouge in the side of O'Malley's head. "No inflammation. Excellent."

The doctor tended to the head wound, allowing Caroline to help apply the ointment and bandage. "Now then, let's have a look at your shoulder. I suspect it was the length of time and process of finding the lead ball that had your fever spiking. Your wound was open and susceptible to infection." Dr. Higgins studied the wound. "As I suspected, it's infected. Nothing too serious, or else your fever would not have broken." He turned to Caroline. "I will need your assistance cleaning this out. Can you handle that?"

Ignoring the twinge in her belly, she answered, "Yes, of course. Whatever you need."

"Mrs. Green normally assists me, but as you are O'Malley's wife, and it appears he does not want you to leave the room..." The physician let his words trail off while he locked gazes with O'Malley.

"I'm happy to help," Caroline rushed to assure him. "And would rather not be asked to leave the room, Dr. Higgins." He studied her closely—too closely. "Is something wrong?"

"Not at all—your own wound has healed to the point where I could remove the sutures today, if you like."

She looked at O'Malley, and he nodded. But Caroline wasn't ready. "It can wait until we take care of my husband."

She was surprised that she did not feel lightheaded while she followed the physician's instructions. Her stomach may have wobbled a bit at how deeply the physician was applying the healing ointment, but she managed to stay strong for O'Malley's sake. When the soiled linens and water had been taken care of, the doctor surprised her by saying, "I could use a second pair of hands at times, Mrs. O'Malley, and would be honored if you would think about it."

"I would be happy to help anytime, but am not sure how I would know you needed me."

"You could spend a few hours a day in the small office and

examining room I have at my home."

O'Malley cleared his throat. One glance in his direction, and she remembered she was a married woman now. She would have to ask her husband if he minded. "I will be quite busy for the next week or so caring for Thomas, but will speak to him and see what he thinks. Would that be all right?"

"Wonderful. Thank you, Mrs. O'Malley. Now then, your turn. Please have a seat."

Her heart began to pound. O'Malley reached for her hand. "Why don't I hold on to yer face while Dr. Higgins snips the threads? It won't take but a moment."

"How do you know?"

Her husband smiled. "I've had more than me own fair share of stitches. Quite a few since I hired on with His Grace."

A few snips and uncomfortable tugs later, all of the threads had been removed. "I must say you healed beautifully, Mrs. O'Malley. Care to take a look?"

"No. No, thank you, Dr. Higgins."

The physician didn't ask a second time, but went over the detailed instructions for her husband's continued care. O'Malley thanked the doctor, and Caroline echoed him. "Yes, thank you, Dr. Higgins…for everything. Let me show you to the door."

"Not necessary. I told Mrs. Green I would stop in the kitchen when I was through. She has been waiting to serve you breakfast." Dr. Higgins paused in the doorway. "Send for me if the fever returns, or if the infection worsens."

"I will. Thank you!" she said as the doctor left.

"Come here, wife." O'Malley was about to stand when he remembered: "No pants."

She giggled.

"Do ye find that amusing, lass?"

"Yes, as a matter of fact, I do." She tucked the covers around his legs and cupped his face in her hand. Lowering her lips to his, she kissed him gently and sighed. "Thank you for marrying me."

When he tugged her onto his lap, she willingly went. "'Tis I who should be thanking ye, lass. Ye've made me life feel whole."

She leaned against his broad chest and sighed. "I feel the same way. You're the other half of my heart, Thomas."

"*Mo ghrá,*" he whispered, brushing his lips to her healed cheek.

Caroline sighed. "It sounds lovely, but what does it mean?"

"Me love," he told her.

"Am I your love?"

"Let me show ye, lass." His lips claimed hers in a kiss that had the blood rushing through her veins, her skin tingling from head to toe, and a thousand butterflies fluttering in her belly.

The knock on the door had him groaning. "They won't be leaving us alone for another day, will they?"

She giggled. "That was Dr. Higgins's recommendation."

He laid her forehead against hers and said, "Come in."

"You are looking better by the moment, O'Malley," the cook said, entering. "I've brought your breakfast."

CHAPTER TWENTY-THREE

GARAHAN MET FLAHERTY'S intense gaze, nodded to O'Ghill, and told the baron, "We need O'Malley's take on this."

"I understand your loyalty to him—"

"Begging yer pardon, yer lordship," Garahan interrupted. "Of all people, ye should know how important his opinion on this matter is. He's saved yer life, and that of her ladyship, more than once."

Summerfield walked to the window overlooking the back terrace and stared out at the view beyond. The fainting couch had been carried back inside. Phoebe would not be enjoying the sun on their terrace again until the business with Anderson was over. "I do value his opinion, as I do every one of yours."

"Then why are ye hesitating to bring him in on this?"

The baron spun around, and the stark expression on his face had the men falling silent. "He nearly bled to death. Before you ask how I know, I asked. Dr. Higgins said the chance that the wound healing in his shoulder could become infected again is great. He's recovering, but his body is not fully healed. He married Caroline two days ago—how can you expect me to take a chance with his life?"

The three men frowned. Flaherty spoke up first. "The sixteen of us pledged our lives to His Grace and Lady Persephone. When their twins were born, we vowed to protect them, too."

"When the earl married, we added Lady Aurelia to those we protect," Garahan added. "When yer cousin the viscount married Lady Aurelia's dearest friend Lady Calliope, they were added to our growing list of family and extended family."

"Then there's yerself and Lady Phoebe," O'Ghill said. "I may not have been there with the others when O'Malley was assigned to protect ye, but I was here a few months ago, and stepped in when ye needed me. Thomas may be a royal pain in the *arse*, like the rest of the sainted O'Malleys, but he has a good brain. Ye're foolish to keep him out of this."

The silence that followed O'Ghill's pronouncement hung over the room. Finally, the baron nodded. "What in the bloody hell was I thinking when I asked you men to speak freely?"

Garahan snorted with laughter first. Flaherty and O'Ghill soon joined in. "'Tis one of the reasons we enjoy working for ye, yer lordship," Garahan said. "Ye accept us for who are."

"And Jared doesn't?"

"His Grace does," Garahan replied, "in his own way."

"Ye're more apt to see things from our point of view," Flaherty added.

"Skewed," O'Ghill said with a grin. "Are ye going to send for O'Malley?"

Summerfield shook his head. "I'm expecting King's men to arrive in an hour." He raised his hand when the men started grumbling. Obligingly, they fell silent. "I'll summon him then. King's men have new information for me, and I want O'Malley and the rest of you to be here for the meeting."

Garahan nodded. "We'll be back in an hour with O'Malley."

As PROMISED, AN hour later, the group had gathered around the map of the baron's estate and the surrounding area—the village included—laid out on the baron's desk. Two of Gavin King's most trusted runners stood by, with Thompson pointing to five points on the map. He used the tip of his finger to connect the points using the roads and paths between the points...in the shape of a star. Thompson looked up. "The center is Summerfield Chase, your lordship."

"Anderson is predictable," Greeves said. "He's following the most common route to Summerfield-on-Eden. He hasn't bothered to hide his movements."

Thompson shook his head. "The man still has not guessed who Tremayne is and has followed his advice to the letter, donning what Anderson considers a disguise."

"Which would be?" Summerfield asked.

Thompson shook his head. "He's dressed like a well-to-do squire. Driving his carriage with a pair of matched grays."

"Not much of a disguise," O'Malley muttered.

"Tremayne must be having a good laugh at how gullible Anderson is," Flaherty said.

"Masterson met with us yesterday and told us something of interest," Thompson said.

"Oh?" the baron asked.

"Anderson cannot stomach the sight of Tremayne," Greeves told them.

Garahan curled his hands into fists. "What the *feck* is wrong with the man? Tremayne nearly died from the saber slash to his face!"

Thompson sighed. "Fortunately, Anderson never volunteered to join any of His Majesty's armed forces. Have you heard that Captain Coventry has been trying to recruit another former dragoon?"

"Aye," Garahan replied. "Alasdair Cameron."

Greeves added, "He's recently married—prior to that he was protecting the mysterious Angel of the Streets in London."

"Me brothers James and Darby have met and aided the angel," Garahan told the men. "Darby's wife was rescued by her. He would give his life for her. As would a growing number of men working for the captain and the duke."

"Aye," O'Malley agreed. "Me cousin Emmett and Tremayne are two others."

"Emmett O'Malley?" Summerfield asked.

O'Malley grinned. "From what I've gathered, me cousin is more than intrigued." He turned to Garahan. "Isn't that what ye gathered from Darby's most recent letter?"

His cousin snorted. "Aye, smitten."

"We're getting off topic, men," the baron reminded them. "Now, as to our continued plan of action, we wait for Anderson to make the first move." He nodded at the chorus of "ayes." "O'Ghill, you're to guard the vicar's daughter, while Stanbridge will continue to guard the blacksmith's daughter."

"Aye, yer lordship," O'Ghill replied. "I'll be leaving in a few minutes to return to me post and will pass along the word to Stanbridge."

O'Malley nudged him. "Please send me best, and the lass's, to the vicar and his family. We'll be visiting them as soon as this is settled…or the vicar brings the lasses here to be protected."

"Done," his cousin agreed.

"Now then, as for the rest of you," Summerfield said, "you will coordinate your shifts with Thompson and Greeves. O'Malley, you will be on the interior shift while you continue to heal…starting tomorrow."

"Why not right now?" O'Malley asked.

The baron smiled. "I thought you might want to spend time with your new bride when you weren't out of your mind with fever. When this is finished, and I have a feeling it will be soon, take a few days to become accustomed to being married."

O'Malley grinned. "Sure, and that's a fine idea, yer lordship. Thank ye."

"You're welcome. Now, any questions, men?"

"Where will Tremayne and Masterson be stationed?" Flaherty asked.

"Guarding the perimeter of the vicarage and the blacksmith, in the event O'Ghill and Stanbridge need them," the baron answered. "Anything else?" When everyone remained silent, Summerfield looked from one man to the next. "All of you have my eternal thanks for accepting this assignment. My wife..." His voice trailed off, and O'Malley stepped over to stand beside the baron.

"I think what his lordship is trying to say is that Lady Phoebe is still recovering from the assault, adjusting to her delicate condition." He slowly smiled at Summerfield before telling the men, "Be grateful she's not in full fighting form. She has a wicked right cross, and is a fierce opponent when armed with a brass paperweight and handful of ribbon-wrapped hatpins."

The men were watching the baron closely. When Summerfield grinned, O'Ghill said, "O'Malley, ye're treading a fine line between insubordination and insanity."

"Ye'd be right about that, but his lordship knows I'll protect Lady Phoebe, Prudence, the twins, and me wife to me last breath. If not for me bespectacled guardian angel, I would not be standing in front of ye right now. Life is precious, ofttimes too *fecking* short for some of us."

"Wise words," Summerfield said. "By the by, men, O'Malley did not exaggerate. My wife has a *lethal* right cross."

"Don't be forgetting those hatpins," Flaherty said.

"And brass paperweight," Garahan added.

O'Ghill, Thompson, and Greeves were the first to leave. Flaherty and Garahan followed closely behind. O'Malley was about to take his leave when the baron stopped him. "I almost did not include you in the meeting."

O'Malley frowned. "Have I let ye down in some way, yer lordship?"

Summerfield shook his head. "That was not the problem." He waited a beat before saying, "With the blood loss and infection, I did not think you would pull through and could not accept that you would have died protecting my family."

O'Malley studied the baron. "I knew what the risks were when I signed on to protect His Grace and his family...which has grown by leaps and bounds. Me brother Sean nearly gave his arm. Darby Garahan will not likely recover the sight in his one eye.

The rest of us have been stitched and hobbled back together half a dozen times. A bit stiffer when we rise in the morning, but stout of heart and willing to give our lives for you and your family. Can ye not understand that?"

Summerfield shook his head. "But you'd never even met half of us when Coventry and His Grace formed the guard."

O'Malley grinned at the baron. "Ye became ours to protect when ye fell *arse* over head in love with Lady Phoebe."

The baron threw back his head and roared with laughter. "Bloody hell, O'Malley. You've been more than one of the guard. You've been a friend, giving me advice before I married Phoebe, whether or not I wanted to hear it. So, I'll give you some now. Never fall asleep with hard words between you and your wife. Say you're sorry, whether or not *you* feel you owe her an apology—in her eyes, you do."

"Wise words, yer lordship. Anything else?"

"Two things—first, tell her you love her every day."

"And?" O'Malley asked.

"A happy marriage takes effort on both sides. Sometimes more on your side…other times on your wife's. Do not let others get involved in your squabbles."

O'Malley shook his head. "That's three things, yer lordship."

"So it is. Give Caroline my best."

CHAPTER TWENTY-FOUR

O'MALLEY FOUND HIS wife in the kitchen. "Hungry, lass?"

She whirled around. "From your expression, I'd say the meeting went well."

"Aye. I've been given leave from me duty until tomorrow morning. I have something I want to speak to ye about, if ye'll excuse us, Mrs. Green."

"I'll send a tray up and have the footman leave it outside of your door," the cook said.

"Thank ye." He tugged on his wife's hand. "'Tis important."

"Yes, of course. We'll see you in a little while, Mrs. Green."

The cook just smiled.

"We'll take the back staircase—'tis faster," O'Malley said.

"Are you in a hurry for some reason?"

Her innocence shone like a beacon. "Aye, lass. I'm not after wasting any more time." When she wasn't moving fast enough to suit him, he scooped her into his arms and carried her to the staircase, all the way to their bedchamber on the floor above.

"Open the door, lass." She did as he asked, and he closed the door with the heel of his boot. "Turn the key in the lock."

"This must be a serious conversation if you're going to such extreme measures not to be disturbed."

"Lass, did yer ma speak of what happens in the marriage bed?"

"Yes, of course, a few years ago, after I told her I promised to wait…" Her voice trailed off.

He knew she was remembering her promise to a lad that gave his life in the name of the king. She would always hold his memory in her heart, but O'Malley knew her heart was big enough to hold more love. He intended to fill it. "'Tisn't only that I'm near to bursting with need to make ye mine, lass. Trouble is headed right for us. We need to seal our vows to be truly married in the eyes of the law and the church. Do ye understand?"

She cupped his face in her hand and smiled. "I do. I need to ask you something…a favor."

"Anything."

"Promise you won't be cross with me when I hesitate, or am not doing things the proper way."

From the blush on her face, he knew this was uncomfortable for her. "Ye have me word, Caro-lass. Just so ye know, there is no proper way to make love. There are many, many ways." He held her gaze and kissed her forehead. "I'm going to stand ye by the bed so I can help ye undress. Then I'm hoping ye can help me, because this bandage around me shoulder is a pain in the *arse*." She giggled, as he'd hoped she would. "Turn yer back to me. I'll undo yer buttons."

His wife trembled. Was it anticipation, or fear? A bit of both?

"We'll go slowly." He turned her to face him. "Do ye want me to help ye off with yer gown?"

"Please. Until we can go to the vicarage, I have been borrowing a gown or two. I hope no one notices that Lady Phoebe's gowns are three inches too short on me, and Prudence's are two inches too long."

"If they did, they wouldn't think anything of it, knowing the reasons why." He reached for the hem of the gown and slowly slipped it up and over her head. Her skin glowed like alabaster, pure and white. "May I touch ye, lass?"

She bit her lip and nodded.

He traced the tips of his fingers from the curve of her cheek to the line of her jaw. Her soft gasps encouraged him. "May I kiss ye?"

"Yes…please."

Their lips met, and praise God, she kissed him back. Her moan had him going hard as stone. He had to concentrate to slow his heart rate, or else he'd embarrass himself while they were still clothed!

Nudging her chin up, he gave her a brief peck before tracing the line of her throat with butterfly-soft kisses. He dipped the tip of his tongue in the hollow at the base of her throat to taste her, then inhaled her scent. It clouded his mind, and he hoped he had a similar effect on her. "Lass, are ye ready to let me remove yer chemise?"

She stiffened, and then relaxed when he pulled her close, wrapping his arm around her. The lass was skittish, not ready…yet.

"Would ye like to help me undress first?"

Her soft laughter entranced him. "If you wouldn't mind."

He let her remove his frockcoat. While she unbuttoned his waistcoat, he rasped, "I'm riddled with scars, lass. I hope ye've a strong stomach."

She lifted her eyes to meet his as she carefully slipped it off him. "I have already seen you without a shirt on and never noticed your scars." Lifting to her toes, she pressed her lips to his. "You are so beautiful, Thomas. Would you let me kiss your scars?" When he didn't answer right away, she added, "You kissed mine."

"Fair enough, lass. Are ye certain ye wish to?"

"I am sure."

"Even the one on me *arse*?"

Her mouth opened, and a strangled sound emerged at first. Finally, she managed to ask, "Are you testing me to see how bold I will be?"

"Nay, lass. 'Twas just a question, and an old injury that happened when I was a lad. I goaded me brother Michael into wrestling with me. Unfortunately, we were in the barn at the time. Michael, being older and stronger, flipped me and tossed me against the wall."

"What happened?"

"One of the tines of Da's pitchfork skewered me in the *arse*."

"How old were you?"

"Eight. Michael was ten."

"Did you cry?"

"In front of me older brother? Nay! Michael was horrified. He tossed me over his shoulder and clapped a hand on me hindquarters to slow the bleeding. All the while yelling for Ma as he ran to our cottage."

"You poor little boy."

"Da said I was a brave lad, while Ma… Well, she didn't exactly see it the same way. The both of us were punished."

"But you were hurt."

"Ah, as me Da said at the time, that's what happens when two *eedjits* aren't smart enough to wrestle somewhere safer than the barn where we keep sharp tools."

"I'm not sure quite how to help you remove your shirt."

"One arm at a time."

CAROLINE PULLED THE soft cambric shirt out of his trousers, fascinated by the firm ridge of muscles on his abdomen. Biting her lip, she felt her face flush, but ignored it as she uncovered the beauty of her husband. She had bathed his chest and abdomen two nights ago, but hadn't taken the time to really look at him. She had been consumed with worry, concentrating on bringing his fever down.

But now, she looked her fill. When she had one arm free, she carefully extracted the other. "Would you like me to change your bandage before?" Her eyes met his. "Or after?"

"After," he rasped.

Awed by the sculpted beauty of his heavily muscled physique, she sighed. He moaned as she pressed her lips to the scar below his collarbone. "Do you have any on your back?"

"Aye."

Caroline trailed the tips of her fingers across his pectoral muscles—pleased at his sharp intake of breath and low moan— and counted each and every scar that she kissed. When she reached fifteen, she moved to stand behind him and kissed four more. She couldn't say why, but she needed to kiss the twenti- eth...the same number of stitches it had taken to close the gash on her cheek. He'd counted because she asked him to. So, she counted and kissed all but the last one, which she would do now.

"Almost done," she whispered, and moved to stand in front of him and reach for the placket of his trousers.

His hands covered hers. "Ye don't have to kiss the last one, *mo chroí.*"

She slipped her arms around his waist and stared at his mouth until he took the hint and met her lips halfway. "You kissed *my* scars."

He chuckled. "Ye only have the one."

"You counted the stitches for me while you held my face still. Let me kiss your last scar, Thomas. I need to."

His sigh sounded resigned. When he let his hands fall to his sides, he warned, "Ye've teased and tempted me to the edge of me control, lass. The proof will be standing proudly when ye help me out of me trousers."

She shivered at his words, but remembered her mother's warning that certain parts of a man's body would come as a shock in the marriage bed. Caroline had kissed his chest and back, and would not falter until she kissed his backside. Mentally preparing herself to be shocked, understanding it would be a part of sealing their vows, she wondered if maybe, just maybe, they'd be blessed with a babe. "I'm ready."

At least, she *thought* she had been. Her eyes took in the sight of him standing in front of her, naked. At her gasp, his shaft twitched and her insides tingled. "I...uh...did not know a man's body could do"—she gulped—"that."

He snorted with laughter. "Ye cannot say I did not warn ye, lass."

Caroline clamped her mouth shut. He was right—he had warned her. Digging deep for her courage—after all, they were wed, and their joining would be necessary to complete their vows—she ordered him, "Turn around."

The scar on his buttocks was more pronounced than she'd thought it would be, given how old he was when it happened. As she traced the long-ago wound, the firmness of his muscled backside surprised her. He twitched. Was it at her touch? Her husband had put himself in her hands—there was only one way to find out. "Hold still." She cupped his backside and felt him shiver a heartbeat before she pressed her lips to the long-ago hurt.

His groan was soft, low. "Lass..."

She could not resist testing the taut muscles in front of her. "Is there any spot on you that *isn't* hard?"

He spun around and pulled her to her feet and into his embrace. "Aye, but we'll leave that for yer second lesson...after."

"After?"

"Aye. I cannot hold out much longer."

With the hard length of him throbbing against her belly, she knew he wasn't trying to rush her. She set her uncertainty and fears aside—she trusted him. "Would you help me take my chemise off?"

He didn't waste any time. When she was naked before him, he rasped, "Ye are a beauty beyond compare, Caro-lass. From yer nose to yer toes... Every part of ye. I don't want to hurt ye, or shock ye, but I'm wanting to touch all of ye. Kiss all of ye, like ye kissed me scars."

"All right."

He swept her into his arms and onto the bed, bracing his weight on his good arm so he wouldn't crush her. He lowered himself until they were skin to skin. She marveled that her body took his weight as she cradled the hard planes of his body…and his shaft. "Your strength amazes me. You should be weak from your injuries."

"Yer ministrations and a day to recuperate were all I needed." He studied Caroline as if he were about to devour her. "Where do I start?"

"I've never done this before," she reminded him. "Wherever you think best."

His eyes darkened to a deep forest green. Desire and passion swirled in their depths. "If where I kiss ye makes ye uncomfortable, or doesn't feel right, tell me to stop, and I will."

She nodded, unable to trust that she wouldn't squeak when she opened her mouth.

He took her mouth in a searing, heart-stopping kiss, plundering, tasting until she was writhing beneath him. His lips caressed the column of her throat, the valley between her breasts. The sensations his clever lips and tongue created had her moaning his name over and over. He took her breast into his mouth and suckled her, and she felt the shock of desire and heat all the way to her core.

O'Malley took his time, suckling, nibbling, and kissing. When he paid homage to her other breast, she felt as if she were hurtling toward something she could not quite reach, or understand.

When he moved lower, kissing her belly and hip, she wondered if he truly planned to kiss her all the way to her toes.

"I need to stretch ye, lass, so I'll fit inside ye without giving ye any more pain than our first joining will cause anyway."

Still tingling everywhere he kissed her, she sighed. "I'm not sure I understand."

"Let me show ye." With care, his passion held in check, he slid his fingers from her hips to her core, gently probing and manipulating her.

Sensations bombarded her. Unsure if she was supposed to feel this way, she whispered, "Thomas?"

He understood what she could not put into words. "Aye, lass, that's it—reach for yer pleasure. Don't be afraid. I'm right here."

He kissed her, and the tight ball of tension threatened to burst inside of her. She whimpered when he removed his fingers, until she felt the velvety tip of his shaft pressing against her. "I'll go as slowly as I can, lass."

He entered her, and she felt the walls of her passage pulse around him, urging him onward. She wanted more, but didn't understand what it was she craved. He came to the barrier of her maidenhead and rasped, "I hate having to hurt ye, *mo chroí*—"

"It won't last too long."

"Hold tight to me, *mo ghrá*."

She clung to her husband as he plunged into her, filling her to the hilt. The combination of pleasure and pain stole her breath.

"I'm sorry, lass. It will ease soon." He molded his mouth to hers and rekindled the banked fire inside of her.

"Thomas?"

"That's it, lass. Come with me, *mo ghrá*."

He carried her to the heavens, where she shattered among the stars as he plunged into her one last time and emptied his seed inside of her.

She fell asleep with her head on his heart and his big body wrapped around her.

CHAPTER TWENTY-FIVE

"How much time do we have?"

"Is that yer roundabout way of asking me to make love to ye again then, lass?"

She giggled and shook her head. "You need every ounce of your strength today, Thomas. Please be careful."

"I always am, but now I have even more reason to be." He slid his hand from her waist to her belly. "Ye take care of yerself, and do not overexert yourself, lass. Ye could be carrying our babe."

Her eyes misted behind her lenses, and he had to kiss her just once more. He tucked her against his heart, where she'd spent most of the night nestled while she slept. He knew because he woke up every time she scooted her backside against him. It was a lesson in control, at the cost of sleep, and well worth it to spend the night with her in his arms.

"O'Malley!"

The irritated sound of his cousin's voice echoed in the hall-way outside of their door. "*Shite!* They sent Garahan to pry me from yer arms."

"Let go of yer wife and open the door!"

Caroline snorted with laughter, and O'Malley grinned and kissed the freckles on her nose. "Yer snort is still adorable."

"What's keeping ye, Garahan?"

"Bloody buggering hell!" O'Malley said. "They've sent Flaherty, too."

"If ye don't open the door on the count of three," Garahan growled, "his lordship gave us permission to break it down."

Flaherty scoffed, "I didn't hear him say that."

Caroline dissolved into a fit of giggles.

"I heard that," Garahan grumbled. "Ye had all night, but 'tis time to get to work, boy-o. If I had to leave me wife all soft and warm in our bed, then by God, ye will, too!"

"Garahan's not pleasant in the mornings," O'Malley warned her. "Though a few of Mrs. Green's scones usually soften him up. He's tolerable by midday."

A fist pounded on the door. "Open the *fecking* door, O'Malley." Garahan lowered his voice and said, "On three, Dillon."

O'Malley motioned for Caroline to stand in the corner behind him.

"One, two—"

O'Malley swung the door open on three. Garahan barreled into the room and tripped over his outstretched foot.

Flaherty skidded to a halt and snorted with laughter. "Help me get him on his feet, O'Malley. Then we'll stuff him with scones."

Garahan was on his feet, glowering at O'Malley, until he heard Caroline's muffled laughter. "Faith, forgive me, lass. I didn't realize ye were standing right behind yer husband, or I would not have tried to break the door down. I'd never hurt ye."

She smiled at Garahan and asked, "Do you always wake one another with threats?"

Flaherty laughed and answered, "When it seems prudent." He elbowed Garahan and said, "I wanted to give ye five more minutes, Thomas, but ye know Garahan. Since he and Prudence moved into their new cottage, we have to pry him away from it."

"We had to wait for it to be built," Garahan added. "It was only finished a few weeks ago, and Prudence and I are enjoying our privacy."

"I see, and ye have no problem invading ours?" O'Malley asked.

Caroline slipped her arm around his waist and lifted onto her toes to kiss his cheek. "You'd better go, Thomas. I'll see you when you stop by to check on us."

"So ye'll be spending the day with Prudence and Lady Phoebe?"

"Yes, and Percy and Phineas. I promised."

"Those two will make certain to keep ye on yer toes, lass," Flaherty told her.

"Thank you, Dillon. I'm looking forward to it."

"Watch out," Garahan warned, "they're wily."

"Thank you, Ryan. I'll be sure to keep an eye on them."

When O'Malley didn't make a move toward the door, Garahan growled, "Kiss yer wife and move yer *arse*! A messenger arrived a few moments ago. Could be from Tremayne."

O'Malley pulled Caroline flush against him and kissed the breath out of her. "I'll be back to check on ye, wife. Stay out of trouble."

She sighed and stared at him.

"Lass?"

She sighed again, but this time nodded.

"Let's go, Garahan," O'Malley barked. "What are ye waiting for?"

When they reached the bottom of the servants' staircase, the baron was waiting for them. He nodded to the men and smiled at O'Malley. "I trust you enjoyed your evening off."

Garahan rolled his eyes, and Flaherty shook his head.

"Aye. I made the most of me time away, yer lordship," O'Malley replied.

Summerfield's lips twitched, and he cleared his throat. "This just arrived from Tremayne. O'Ghill caught Anderson trying to abduct Melanie and Olivia when they were picking flowers in the vicarage garden this morning."

"Bleeding bugger," Garahan bit out.

"Where is he now?" Flaherty asked.

Summerfield replied, "Cooling his heels in the empty stall at the smithy."

"I hope Coleman hasn't changed the straw recently."

The baron smiled. "For someone of Anderson's ilk, being locked up in a barn in itself is an insult. Soiled straw just adds to it."

"Has Tremayne sent for the constable?"

"Aye. Apparently, Anderson hired three more sharpshooters, who arrived during the night. Masterson caught one of them— the man wasn't about to go off to the gaol without taking his partners in crime with him."

"So, they've rounded up all of Anderson's lackeys?" Garahan asked.

"Aye. The constable was asked to bring his wagon, as he'll have four prisoners this time."

"What do ye think will happen to Anderson this time?" O'Malley asked.

The baron shrugged. "I wish I could say for certain that he will spend more time away from Society, contemplating his actions. With the prince regent as a close friend, who knows? I've already informed Timmons. He will let the footmen and the tenant farmers know that the crisis has passed. Thank you, men. I'm ready for things to return to normal around here."

"Aye, yer lordship," O'Malley agreed.

"I'm going to give Phoebe the good news."

O'Malley waited until Summerfield was out of earshot before assigning shifts. "Garahan, if ye'll take the first shift on the rooftop, Flaherty can guard the exterior. I have another sennight guarding the interior, until the stitches are removed, and then I'll be able to resume me full duties."

Garahan and Flaherty shared a knowing look, and Garahan said, "Ye have another duty that's more important."

"Than me vow to the duke?"

"Aye." Flaherty grinned.

"In nine months' time me son, or daughter, will be needing a cousin to play with," Garahan told him. "Best see to it, O'Malley."

O'Malley let out a whoop and hugged his cousin. "Congratulations, Ryan. If ye're lucky, he or she will look like yer darling wife."

"And if *yer* luck holds," Garahan told him, "ye'll have a daughter or son with red hair and freckles."

As one, Garahan and O'Malley turned and stared at Flaherty, who held up his hands. "I'll not be getting snared in the parson's trap!"

Garahan laughed. "I wouldn't bet on it, boy-o. What do ye think, O'Malley?"

"Flaherty won't know what hit him until he's standing in front of Vicar Chessy saying his vows."

"Feck off!" Flaherty said.

Garahan put his arm around O'Malley's neck as they watched Flaherty yank the back door open and storm outside. "Dillon is such a sentimental bugger."

O'Malley snorted with laughter. "Who would know better than yerself?"

"Ye would," Garahan said. "Remember yer duty, Thomas. I don't want me son or daughter to grow up without a cousin they can boss around."

"Ye're such a soft touch, Garahan."

"That I am. I'll see ye at shift change."

O'Malley was smiling as he ascended the back staircase. He had just enough time to kiss his wife before he manned his shift on the second floor.

Life was good.

EPILOGUE

NINE MONTHS TO the day, O'Malley stared down at his newborn son tucked against Caroline's side. He could not believe his wife would ever agree to go through another birthing. He wasn't certain *he* could! It unmanned him to admit, but he'd had to bite the inside of his cheek to keep the tears at bay, watching his wife battle the pain while she labored to bring his son into the world.

At the tiny snuffling sound, he shifted his gaze to his newborn daughter cradled against his chest. The little bit of thing surprised the *shite* of him when she'd arrived right after her brother. "She has a halo of red-gold hair." He frowned, but only for a moment. "So does our son, which wasn't the plan."

"You're the one who mentioned six sets of twins, Thomas, and a daughter with red hair and gray eyes."

"But not twins first off, lass. That was supposed to be next year."

Caroline narrowed her eyes and stared at her husband. "Do not even suggest such a thing while I have yet to fully catch my breath after delivering our twins!"

He pressed his lips to his daughter's forehead and whispered, "Yer ma is partial to me. She cannot keep her hands off me." At the sound of Caroline's laugher, he lifted his gaze to meet hers. "It won't be all me doing if ye find yerself in this same position a year from now."

"I will have no trouble at all keeping my hands and my lips to myself, O'Malley. Just you wait and see."

TWELVE MONTHS LATER, Caroline delivered their second daughter, who had a halo of blonde hair. This time, she did not tempt fate by declaring that she could keep her hands to herself. They both knew it was a lie and would only add to the number of children they'd finally agreed upon…six.

O'Malley bragged to Garahan that whatever number of children his cousin had, he and Caroline would have one more.

At last count, Garahan had three daughters and two sons…

O'Malley had five daughters and one son.

About the Author

In case we have not met yet, here is a little bit about me:

I write Historical & Contemporary Romance featuring: Hard-headed Heroes & Feisty Heroines.

I fell in love at first sight, when I was seventeen, with the man who will hold my heart forever. DJ and I were married for forty-one wonderful years until my darling lost his battle with cancer. We have three grown children—one son-in-law, two grandsons, two rescue dogs, two rescue grand-cats, and one rescue grand-puppy.

My Hardheaded Heroes and Feisty Heroines rarely listen to me. In fact, I think they enjoy messing with my plans for them. BUT if there is one thing I've learned in dealing with my characters for the past twenty-nine years, it is to listen to them! My heroes always have a few of DJ's best qualities: his honesty, his integrity, his compassion for those in need, and his killer broad shoulders.

I have always used family names in my books and love adding bits and pieces of my ancestors and ancestry in them, too. I write about the things I love most: my family, my Irish and English ancestry, baking and gardening.

Happy reading!

Slàinte!

CH